E IS FOR EVIL

Book 5 of the Alphabet Anthologies

Edited by Rhonda Parrish

Poise and Pen Publishing

EDMONTON, ALBERTA

www.poiseandpen.com

Book Layout based on one © 2014 BookDesignTemplates.com
Edited by Rhonda Parrish
Cover design by Jonathan C. Parrish
Cover art licensed from DepositPhotos.com

E is for Evil / Rhonda Parrish.—1st ed.
ISBN 978-1-988233-33-8 (Physical)
ISBN 978-1-988233-34-5 (Electronic)

CONTENTS

Michael Fosburg

Dix tried to run.

Vin Barton aimed down the sights of the old Remington, breathed in a lungful of cold air, hissed it out through his teeth, and squeezed the trigger. The report rolled across the mountain, startling crows from the trees and Dix went down, legs folding beneath him, a scream bitten off as he hit the ground.

Barton pocketed the shell casing and ambled over.

Blood gushed from the kid's thigh like oil from a busted pipe as he squirmed and mewled into the dirt. He'd be going into shock soon, and would be meat not long after.

He'd been on Case's old crew, came down from Ontario to put some distance between him and some bad shit he didn't talk about. He started using what he was supposed to be selling. Went dark for days, hassled Barton's other guys, and generally made business more difficult. But he'd given the kid another ounce for Case's sake, sending him to canvass the trailer parks and cheap hotels off Route 45. Dix returned once again with no cash and no product, just some story

2 · MICHAEL FOSBURG

about being rolled by a couple of tweakers. He'd practically chomped for *another* ounce, that junkie gleam bright in his eyes.

So Barton gave it to him—along with a GPS tracker.

The terrified look on Dix's face when Barton kicked opened the door to the doublewide was worth the long drive up into the mountains. But Barton had stopped short when he saw Case was also there. His lieutenant's eyes were wounds. He made wet, slobbering sounds, wept and muttered and scratched—clawing at the floor like a dog trying to bury a bone. Die Hard played on a plasma TV against which some unidentifiable organic matter had spattered and dried. A miasma slunk through the trailer, a strange and low-down smell that stood his hackles on end. Cloying, like rotten meat with a coat of green fuzz. Like dead things left in the dark. A terminal cancer patient's stink—only worse.

A snowy field, freezing metal in his hands, the sky an unblinking white eye...

That's when Dix had bolted. He didn't get far.

A nimbus of dark blood now surrounded the kid, and Barton had the unpleasant sensation that they were poised at the lip of some deep well; that at any moment they would tumble down into the depths together, the pusher and the pushed, snapped up by the hungry dark under the Appalachian mountains.

And he felt, for the briefest moment, like eyes were watching him from the blood.

Dix was trying to speak. One shaky hand tried to rise and weakly gesture toward the trees. His color had drained away, leaving his lips pale as moonlight. His unblinking eyes stared up into the sky.

"Shut up," Barton said. He didn't like to admit it, but he felt rattled. Seeing Case like that had been a nasty shock, and that *smell*.

Dix insisted. He croaked a breathless syllable, lips rasping. He was dead but too dumb to realize it.

"*Damn* but you don't know how to die peaceful," Barton said, and brought his heel down on Dix's throat, feeling bones snap and crunch all the way up through his thigh. The kid's back arched. The body shuddered for a few moments before the life finally left it, a gurgling rattle fading while night sounds washed back over them.

Barton breathed in the cold air, reigning in his thoughts. He avoided introspection like something dead in the middle of the road. There was an emptiness at his core into which all the horror he'd seen, all the shit he'd done, drained into, and thus was gone from him. But sometimes his mind disobeyed and tried to dwell on the lives he had taken, all those living, breathing people gone to meat. But there was no remorse there; no spiritual fear of a reckoning. Their faces blurred into one face, their wounds into one wound. Into meat.

Case was still scrabbling at the floor of the trailer when Barton walked back in.

"Case," Barton said, snapping his fingers under his lieutenant's eyes. But Case continued his single-minded excavation of the floor, the tips of his fingers torn into red ruins.

That's when Barton began to feel it. The night had *bent* somehow. Maybe it was the smell of dead meat suppurating in the trailer, or the sight of a hard man reduced to little more than a rabid dog, but something turned in his mind as neatly as if a switch had been flicked, and he *knew*, with a certainty he felt in his flesh, that something was coming.

The glint of sun on snow as his stepbrothers closed in from all sides, faces cracked into grins, livid with the anticipation of violence.

Barton let the memory slide off. Just paranoia from a minor contact high from all this shit still in the air. He moved throughout the trailer with a familiarity that came with having lived in one all his life, checked the cabinets and dresser and under the bed, thinking that there was a cat or something that had died in here that they had forgotten about. But there was nothing. Case slobbered and moaned as explosions lit the TV.

That smell was beginning to drive him crazy. It was in his nose and down his throat. It clung to his clothes like burrs and it was all he could taste on his tongue.

He stopped cold, shoulders hunched as if he'd been struck across the back.

There it was again. That sack-shriveling feeling of being *watched*.

Eyes in the blood.

It was this trailer. It had to be. It had soaked up a dozen pounds of crank and the shit was in the walls like mold, breathing into him, snaking its tendrils beneath his skin. And he knew that wasn't possible, knew it with authority, but his mind was veering away from the knowledge because that fucking *smell* was coating his brain, settling into each wrinkle and fold and fogging his thoughts.

"What the *hell* is that, Case?" Barton asked. But Case didn't answer him, only went on digging wetly at the floor, the occasional moan punctuating the scratching.

Barton had lost count of how many people Case had killed. He'd looked on as his lieutenant had sawed a man in half—*lengthwise*; had watched him drown a junkie in his own shit-filled toilet. Had even seen him cut the throat of a woman who had claimed, weeping, to be pregnant. The level of violence to which Case was willing to rise was matched only by his skill in carrying that violence out, and he took to the work with the detached calm of a surgeon. Even with hands wrapped in blood and screams in his ears, there had always been serenity in Case's eyes.

But that man was gone. Barton glanced at the foil-lined bowl askew on the couch. Crank wasn't to blame for this. It was too easy an explanation, and Case could ride out a high like a champ.

The smell was coming from everywhere now. Barton gagged, mouth flooding with spit as bile touched his tongue, and stumbled outside for air.

Dix's body was gone.

Barton brought the Remington's stock to his shoulder so hard he banged a bruise into his flesh. This was the Mexicans' doing—they were fucking with him, sending a message. They must've dosed Case with some south-of-the-border shit—Peyote and LSD or something—and then took to the woods when they heard Barton's truck approach.

But his mind screamed through the scrim of black stink to think smart, to think *straight*—if anyone had wanted to screw with him, they would have simply killed Case and Dix and festooned the trailer with their guts.

But what happened to the body?

Barton advanced to where Dix had died, rifle swiveling in a wide arc. Long blood-smeared striations in the dirt. Barton followed the blood smeared to the lip of the woods.

Dragged away.

He stared into the dark for a long moment. Dix had weighed one-ninety, easily. What kind of animal could drag away so much weight so quickly, and without making a sound?

"Fuck this," he heard himself say. This situation was officially out of his control. He'd come back with more guys tomorrow, when there was light to see by. He'd sort out whatever was wrong with Case and they'd look for Dix's remains and Barton would put an end to whatever *this* had been by burning down that trailer.

"I'm outta here, Case," he said, walking into the trailer to retrieve his keys. "Get your head clear—"

But Case was gone.

The stench redoubled. It was like being downwind of a pile of corpses that had putrefied in the sun, of meat corrupted and debased—the stink of flesh before it became something else.

It followed Barton as he stumbled back to his truck, hijacking his nostrils and burning in his nasal passages. Cold sweat plastered the shirt to his body. He'd been in shootouts, and had taken a bullet to the shoulder when he was twenty-two. He'd been sliced open with switchblades and stabbed with the jagged necks of broken bottles.

He'd killed men slowly, intimately; close enough to read the final thoughts in their eyes. And while fear had always been there, Barton had dismissed it as an inconvenient side effect of the life he led. Fear tempered risk, but risk separated those who got ahead from those who stayed behind.

Barton always got ahead.

But here, with the cancer stink oozing into his nostrils, he acknowledged the fear. He *understood* it. And when he saw that the tires of his truck had been slashed to ribbons, and the tires on Case's car as well, he felt the fear take root and grow. It coiled around his guts and puckered his asshole and pulled his balls into his stomach, and soon he was tearing down the dirt road, a hundred thousand stars staring impassively down as he ran. Barton had never run from anything in his life; not from his wolfish stepbrothers, not from the Mexicans, not from the street itself. But all those things had rules— patterns you learned to read.

Here, the rules had been obscured with blood.

It took a moment for Barton to realize he was running, the dark woods flying by on either side, the stars a thousand pale eyes impassively watching his flight.

But he hadn't run in forever, and it showed—his breath burned and his legs seized with cramps. He slowed, gasping foul-smelling air into his lungs. Something thin and grey shivered at the edge of his sight. A glimpse of impossibly long limbs; the blanketing aroma of decayed meat.

His head snapped around, but there was nothing on the road in either direction.

Everything bleeds, he thought, trying to reign in the panic he felt stirring in his guts.

Everything's meat.

He forced a few deep breaths into his burning lungs and tried to think. This dirt road ran into State Road 6 in three miles. If he could make it there...

So he threw his body back into a run. *If he could make it there* looped endlessly through his mind, a fevered mantra, the words rearranging and coming back together in a background hiss. He maintained the run for the first mile, sometimes stumbling over sticks or dips in the road. By the second mile shin splints were shooting agony through his legs, and his nipples were chaffed raw from rubbing against his shirt. He couldn't keep up this pace. His lungs felt torn and he tasted iron. A hot stitch skewered his side.

Light footsteps close behind him. A wake of rancid air.

Barton brought the rifle around and fired blindly. But there was nothing on the road—just the shadows of trees thrown down by a million stars. The smell of diseased meat hung cloyingly, and for a mad moment Barton wanted nothing more than to shoot off his own goddamned nose to stop from smelling it. He was trying to shut down the fear, but the smell was *in* him now, and the smell was fear. He was starting to wonder if he'd ever smelled anything other than this.

He had a mile and a half left to run. But his legs were cramping so badly he was having a hard time *walking*. There was no way he was going to make it, and whatever was tailing him *knew* that, smelled the uncertainty and exhaustion on his sweat.

A frozen lake covered in sunlit snow. The old tree fort. His stepbrothers closing in from all sides, goading each other on while a cold white wind blew snow into Barton's eyes. They meant to kill him this time. Years of beatings had been preparing them for this moment. He could practically smell their malice on the crackling air. So he climbed, the skin of his clammy palms sticking to the icy wooden struts hammered into the tree, and the cigar box was where he'd left it, hidden in a plastic bag.

He would never be weak again. Would never be meat *again.*

Yet here he was.

If he could make it there
If he could make it there
If he could make it there

More movement behind him. Barton dug his boots into the dirt, muscles screaming with each stride, the Remington growing heavier with each jarring step. He overrode his body, overruled its suffering. And when he slowed he could hear something keeping pace on his heels, the rapid pattering of its footsteps, peeking in and out of the edge of his vision like a thin crescent moon scurrying from cloud to cloud. The smell—*its* smell—forced its graveworm way through the heady punch of the looming pines. When he threw a glance over his shoulder he thought he glimpsed a vague gray shape slipping into the trees along the road.

A cramp locked up his thigh. He stumbled to a halt. Sweat ran from him in rivulets. His arms felt weighed down with lead, and his rifle was almost unbearably heavy.

Should've brought the glock—

That's when Case exploded from the trees, his face livid, eyes scored and feral. His crew-cut hair had fallen out in patches, and Christ, the *sound* he made—it was a guttering, caterwauling *howl*, as though an animal screamed *through* him. Barton stared dumbly for half a second too long before lining up a shot, but it went wild as Case crashed into him, lips peeling away from his snapping teeth. Barton fell but managed to wedge the rifle between them, holding the heavier man at bay.

His teeth. They jutted from bloody gums, and *Jesus* they looked *sharp*. Case was struggling for Barton's neck, chomping and snarling, runnels of drool falling into Barton's eyes and mouth. Case's skin was stretched tight across his skull, and even in the dark Barton could tell that his color was all wrong, a sickly grayish hue.

Barton snapped his head forward and cracked into Case's nose, but the heavier man wasn't fazed, and Barton was blinded by the sudden gush of blood. He sputtered and gagged—the blood *stank*—and brought his knee up hard into Case's groin. The bigger man *whuffed* in pain and went rigid. Barton seized the moment and shoved Case off using the rifle as leverage, scrambling to his feet while Case staggered upright. His eyes never left Barton. They were luminous mirrors filled with starlight, lighter than he remembered. Barton took an involuntary step back. No, not just lighter—they'd gone as white as exposed bone in Case's ruined face.

It hit him then—Dix hadn't been running away from *him*. He'd been running away from *Case*.

He advanced on Barton, body coiling to strike, howling in a voice that seemed to contain *many* voices, and as Case leapt for him Barton brought up the Remington and shot off the top of his head. Chunks of brain and skull blew back, and for an instant Barton was a kid again, the snot frozen on his face, an empty gun clicking in his hand as the bodies steamed and bled into the snow.

Barton slumped against a tree. He wiped foul-smelling viscera from his face and flicked it away.

All this over an ounce of fucking crank.

Barton ditched the rifle after wiping away his prints and walked along State Road 6, smiling a little despite his exhaustion. Whatever had been hunting him had cried off after he put down Case, and he was finally out from under the pall of the mountain. He was starting to believe he'd imagined the whole thing. Best yet, that wretched, godawful stink was gone from the air. He was already shifting around his organization's command structure, mentally promoting Joe O'Day to Case's position. Joe was a real bastard, not as artful with his violence as Case had been, but he always posted, and hardly touched the stuff.

He'd need a competent second-in-command going forward. Something told him he'd be expanding his territory.

The lights of a semi crested the horizon, and soon Barton was climbing into the cab, shakily thanking the driver and telling him how he'd swerved off the road into the trees some ways back. No, he was alright—just a few cuts. An animal in the road—no, he didn't quite make out what it had been. But it had looked fucking weird.

The trucker nodded sagely.

"Plenty of weird shit up Appalachia way," he said, and wrinkled his nose. "*Christ,* you smell that? Like something crawled up a dead skunk's asshole and died there."

"Nope," Barton said, looking out the window. His reflection stared back with eyes gone white as exposed bone.

He had reached the top of the tree fort just as his stepbrothers began their climb. They would break his neck and shove him off the fort and call it an accident, or push him onto the ice and watch as he broke through and drowned. They didn't care how it happened, so long as it happened. It was law to them, written across their pale, ice-glazed eyes and codified into the bruises Barton wore beneath his clothing.

The cigar box was frozen shut. He pried it open.

The pistol was cold in Barton's hand. He'd bought it off a haggard old Algonquin who had needed the cash to travel south, saying how the hard winters and harder drugs were pushing people wendigo *or something, but Barton, too tangled up in his own dread, had not been listening at the time. Something drifted on the air—a rank animal stink that made him think of carcasses squirming with maggots. He put his back to the fort's far wall and pointed the pistol at the entrance, finger trembling on the trigger, waiting for the first head to poke up over the edge, already anticipating the way their leering faces would crumple and explode into pink mist.*

He did not wait long.

The snowy woods kept his secret well into the spring thaw. And by then, Barton had gone south as well.

A is for Appalachia

Lynn Hardaker

Please, Brother, let me explain.

You were always so serious. Typical of a first child. You were the favourite son. Always. Not that I can blame Father.

Mother was always distant, but I think that was her dreaming of a different kind of a life. Do you remember the tales she used to sing to us as she sewed and spun into the long nights, using only the light of the fire? So many wonderful tales as you and I would sharpen our knives and practice our carving skills on bits of sheep bone, drift wood, or occasionally a piece of oak.

Yes. It was the only time I felt close to her, listening to tales of hope and heroism and vindication and revenge. They would give me goose pimples and rouse me to tears. But they made you turn in upon yourself even more, like a collapsing shed. How different could two brothers possibly be? Not unlike Father and Uncle Bjørn. You and Father, delicate as falcons; Uncle Bjørn and I, strapping as bears.

We were close then, weren't we, Brother? At least, I like to think that we were.

Remember when Uncle Bjørn came to live with us? So soon after Father's death. So soon after the turnaround in our fortunes. Things had been bad for a long time. Father was catching fewer and fewer fish; staying away for longer and longer periods and leaving Mother to look after us and the homestead. She never complained. Well, not overtly, but I could tell she was not happy. She had always hoped for more and let it slip in small things she would say to me; seemingly innocent comments or simply the tone of her voice.

There was no sorrow in her voice when she told me that Father had been lost out in his fishing boat. And Father such a good seaman. No, there was no sorrow, just a strange brightness in her eyes.

But then things did change, as though overnight. Uncle Bjørn came into that goodly fortune. Bought the lands around our home and a handsome flock of sheep to raise on them. He left the humble place he'd been living in and moved into our home; made it larger, cleaner, grander: made it his.

You were too young, but I remember the look Mother would sometimes give him. I didn't know the word for it back then, but I do now: conspiratorial.

Do you remember that one tale Mother would sing to us? The one about the raven spirit and the oak tree? About sacrifice and gain?

I can still hear Mother's voice ring clear in my ear, even though it's been years since I last saw her. Years since she and Uncle Bjørn moved away.

And in those infernal years, I've tried to make a home in Uncle Bjørn's old place, small and dank though it is. Of course they gave you the good house, our old house, and most of the sheep when they finally made the move to Hedeby. You were, after all the elder son.

Sorry. I've always promised myself to try not to be petty. So much tongue-biting I've done, you've no idea, Brother.

Well, Mother was set up in town—a proper town—even though she knew that it would quite possibly mean not seeing either of us again because of the distance. And so it has proved.

How I'd love to hear her sing a tale to us, just once more. The tale of the raven spirit and the oak tree. Do you remember it? How one had simply to give an offering to the raven spirit, and if it were accepted, the raven spirit would reward them with riches. Imagine never having to work again. Never having to chase down sheep who were too stupid to stay away from the cliffs in snowstorms. Never having to wrestle the filthy coats off their backs.

Gods. I've never been good with the sheep. Neither is your good Astrid, as I've heard you complain so often. No good with sheep, but such a comely woman.

Yes, according to the tale, one simply had to find the nearest Oak tree and hang your sacrifice by the third branch from the ground. And wait. If your offering is accepted, good fortune will be granted. Simple as that.

Though it wasn't a simple decision for me to make. Believe me, Brother.

So, brother. You decide. Am I evil? Is what I did so wrong? Perhaps. But I won't take your silence for either condemnation or forgiveness. It's not for me to say, to put words into your mouth, to read into your silence. Your stillness.

There. All that's needed is for a gust of wind to set you into motion. The oak branch groans, but it won't let you fall.

I don't know whether I was surprised or not, when I first brought you here, drugged and heavy as a dead seal child, to find that there were the remains of a rope tied to the branch.

Shall I sing you a tale, Brother? While we sit in the evening's biting wind. While we wait for the raven spirit to come and assess my offering. I do have a passable singing voice. Or so Astrid tells me.

B is for Brothers

Stephanie A. Cain

Murphy O'Hare eased his 1998 Chevy Cavalier into the narrow alley behind his apartment building, driving slow enough to give the dealers and punks—and the occasional ogre—plenty of time to scatter before his headlights hit them. Good thing the rent was cheap. No matter how many times his packmate Elliott said he wouldn't mind a roommate, Murphy wasn't going to move. His apartment might be a tiny place in the dangerous near northside of Indianapolis, but he liked it. He even kind of liked some of the people who shared the building with him.

As much as he liked anyone, anyhow.

He shoved his hands in the pockets of his jean jacket and scuffed his boots across the pavement on his way to the back entry.

"W—who's there?" It was a young woman's voice; she was trying to sound tough but the tremor betrayed her.

Murphy sighed. "How many times I gotta tell you it isn't safe for you to hang out back here, Von?"

Yvonne Jackson was one of the neighbors he actually kind of liked. She was about twelve—a little too gangly to be pretty yet, but just give her a few years. Murphy liked her folks okay, too, as much as he saw them—her dad worked two jobs and her mom was a night-shift nurse.

She hitched one shoulder in a shrug. She was getting more like a punk teenager every day, but Murphy didn't really mind. He'd been a punk teenager himself. Sometimes he still forgot he wasn't. *Shit, I'm getting old without even realizing it. Turning into my mom.*

"All right, sit," he said, gesturing at the back steps. As he joined her, he realized her brown cheeks were streaked with moisture. She'd been crying.

Murphy swallowed the growl that rose in his throat and sat on the lowest step, letting her be taller than him. "What happened, Von? Someone hurt you?"

She hitched that shoulder again—just the one—and Murphy realized she was holding the other arm funny.

"Someone hurt you," he said grimly. "Let me see."

He'd been working closing shift, so he'd left the restaurant around eleven-thirty. That meant it was probably almost midnight. Yvonne's mom would be at the hospital already, and Murphy couldn't remember her dad's work schedule.

"Come on," he coaxed, as Yvonne pooched her lower lip into a frown, her eyebrows drawing together. "I can see your arm hurts. How can you go out for the volleyball team if your arm's hurt?"

"It isn't that bad," she mumbled. "Just a bruise."

She eased her sleeve up. A large bruise spread across her upper arm. Murphy thought it looked swollen. From the way her breath hissed in her throat, it hurt worse than she let on.

"What happened?"

She hitched her other arm and looked down. "I fell on the steps."

"Try again."

"I fell on the steps."

Murphy sighed. Why was he arguing with her? He wasn't her dad. Or her big brother. Not even a friend, really. Just a guy twice her age she talked to sometimes, because they were both into comic books and superhero movies.

"Your dad home?"

"He's sleeping."

Murphy shook his head and stood. "For this, we wake him up."

"Murphy!" She stared at him wide-eyed. He could tell this was a betrayal, but he wasn't going to help her hide an injury that looked like it could be serious.

"Who were you with when you fell?" he asked, motioning for her to get up.

"No one."

Mingled with the scent of her own fear, he could smell the person on her—a man. He couldn't believe her dad was the one who'd hurt her. Murphy didn't believe in the perfect family, but Isaac and Belinda Jackson were two decent people who were doing everything they could to give their kid a good life. That didn't include hitting her.

"It wasn't your dad, was it?" he asked, pitching his voice so she'd know he didn't really think it was.

"No!" Her voice rose sharply. "I *told* you I was alone!"

"And we both know you're lying," Murphy said flatly. "Come on." He gestured at her again and she rose sullenly to her feet. She glared at him, but when he pointed at the door, she let herself in and went up the steps ahead of him.

The apartment building was probably about a hundred years old, made of yellow brick. Judging by the soaked-in cigarette smell the hallway carpet had last been replaced in 1973, and the off-white walls had years of scuffs on them. But the building itself was secure, with an electronic passkey system and only last names on the buzzers.

As Murphy trudged up the steps behind Yvonne, he opened his mouth a little to get a better taste of that odd scent on her. He didn't remember smelling that person in the building before—a mixed blessing, since it meant it wasn't one of their neighbors who'd assaulted her, but it also made it harder for him to track the person down.

What the hell are you thinking, track the person down? he thought at himself. *You're not a cop. That's Elliott and Braxton. Let them deal with it.*

Except they wouldn't, and he knew it. Not the way it needed to be dealt with.

The legal system, as much as Murphy's packmates might love it, was seriously flawed. The guy who'd ignored the restraining order to mess up Murphy's mom had proven that to him fifteen years ago. It had been a hard lesson, but he'd learned it well. No way was he going to turn whoever hurt Yvonne over to the cops. It was time for werewolf justice.

When they reached the landing, Murphy realized he had a savage grin on his face. He bit his lips together and smoothed his expression before Yvonne unlocked her apartment door.

"Dad!" she called, and glared at Murphy again.

Murphy folded his arms across his chest and stayed several feet away from her. He didn't think Isaac would pin this on *him*, but there was no sense tempting fate.

"Dad!"

"Coming." Isaac's voice was a little grumpy, but mostly just tired. Murphy thought it was nicer than how he'd react if he'd been woken up unexpectedly.

Isaac Jackson was a tall, muscular black man. Murphy didn't consider it a threat to his masculinity to admit Isaac was also a seriously good-looking guy. He *did* consider it a threat to his continued well-being that Isaac was currently looking at him like he was trespassing.

"Murphy made me come wake you up," Yvonne said.

Isaac gave Murphy a penetrating look. Murphy held up his hands in a 'hear me out' gesture, and Isaac's gaze went to his daughter's face. His expression softened.

"Why did Murphy think you needed to wake me up, baby?"

Yvonne glared at Murphy. "I fell down. Hurt my arm."

Isaac's face hardened and then he rubbed a hand over it. He looked at the clock. "You just getting home from work?"

"Yep. I think she probably needs a doctor."

"Why didn't you tell Uncle Charlie this, baby?"

Yvonne stiffened. "It happened after he left."

Bingo. Murphy could hear the way Yvonne's heartrate picked up. Uncle Charlie was the one who hurt her. And Murphy had Uncle Charlie's scent.

Isaac got taller. Murphy wasn't sure how he managed it, but he was looming like a bridge troll when he stomped over to Murphy. "Did *you* hurt my baby girl?"

"Seriously? Would I have had her wake you up if I did?" Murphy shot back. Then he wanted to bite his tongue. When would he learn to keep his smartass comments to himself?

Never, probably.

He wouldn't hurt a kid, but then again, if he had a twelve-year-old daughter who liked hanging around a guy twice her age, he'd probably look sideways at the guy too. Even if all they ever did was trade comic books on the back steps of the apartment building.

"Daddy, no," Yvonne protested. "Murphy noticed my arm and kept pestering me to wake you up."

Isaac sighed. He didn't loom any less, but he tightened his lips and nodded. "Okay." He looked at Yvonne. "Why don't you get a comic book or something? We might have to wait a little at the ER." He watched as Yvonne went down the hall and then turned back to Murphy. "Thanks for having her wake me up. I'll take it from here."

"Who's Uncle Charlie?" Murphy made his voice sharp.

Isaac's mouth tightened a little. "My brother-in-law. Got laid off a while back—his job closed up, sent the work to Mexico. You know how it is. So Belinda thought it'd be good for him to spend some time with Yvonne."

Murphy nodded slowly. "Yvonne's scared of him."

Isaac sighed. "He's got a lot of bitterness about his job shutting down. But he's just a redneck blowhard. He and Bel were close when they were kids. He might not like me much, but people can't change if you don't give 'em a chance." He gave Murphy a sad smile.

Murphy didn't think people deserved a second chance if kids were involved, but he shrugged. Isaac had probably never seen what happened when some asshole made himself feel like a bigger man by hurting a woman. Lucky Isaac. "Sure. Well, I'll see you. I hope it isn't as bad as it looks."

He went up the hall to his own apartment, situated kitty-corner from the Jacksons. So now he knew he was looking for a white guy who probably resembled Belinda at least a little. With a little digging, Murphy thought he could find Belinda's maiden name, and then he'd have everything he needed. With a full name, Charlie's scent, and a little time he could sift through the million-and-a-half people in the metro Indy area.

He might hate being a werewolf, but there were times it came in handy.

Uncle Charlie Bialaski turned out to be the kind of guy who had a "Heritage Not Hate" Confederate flag in front of his house and a Make America Great Again ball cap on the dash of his pickup truck. And *that* was the guy Belinda Jackson wanted spending time with her smart, lonely, mixed-race daughter? Murphy peered into the bed of Bialaski's truck, shaking his head.

It had only taken him a day of searching through phone books to pinpoint the right Charlie Bialaski. It helped that Bialaski wasn't a common name. As soon as he had the addresses and a good idea of where to find them, Murphy had gone scenting.

Of course, there were other considerations now. Murphy was pretty sure a guy with a Confederate flag was also going to be a guy who exercised his Second Amendment rights pretty heavily. The silver bullet thing was true, but even if steel-jacketed hollowpoints wouldn't kill him, they'd still hurt like a bitch. Werewolves healed faster than people, but Murphy didn't fancy missing a week of work when he was already having to come up with excuses to miss work on full moon days—or nights, depending.

He needed a plan to get Bialaski out of his house, and preferably away from his neighborhood. The area was depressed, weeds growing through the chain-link fences surrounding back yards, and people were getting used to coyotes stealing pets now and then, even inside the 465 loop. But no coyote was going to take down a human, and Murphy didn't want to start a witch hunt for some neighbor's pit bull.

He liked most pit bulls more than he did most people, after all.

This was going to take some planning. Wolves were pack hunters. Murphy wasn't a pack kind of guy himself, but he knew his instincts had been altered by that bite. After a year of full moons spent hunting with his pack in Eagle Creek Park, he was getting used to the idea of having someone alongside him in a hunt. Bialaski might be different prey than usual, but he was still prey.

Murphy's lips were curling up in that nasty smile again. He shook himself and took a deep breath.

Cut it out, asshole, he told himself. *Just because you're a werewolf doesn't mean you have to be* that *guy. There are other ways to handle this.*

Like the cops. Yeah, right.

Murphy sighed and rubbed a hand over his face. His cheeks felt hot. What else was he supposed to do? Wait for Yvonne to tell her parents or stand up for herself—once the cast came off her spiral fracture, anyway? Talk to the dude and try to reason with him? Try to intimidate him? Murphy was tall, but he was scrawny as shit, and he knew it. He didn't look threatening, and he definitely didn't sound threatening.

This was a dumb idea. Just like every other idea he'd ever had. *High school dropout. Fast food burger slinger. Loser.*

"Shut up," he whispered.

"Hey, punk, what do you think you're doing to my truck?"

Shit. Murphy went still. He hadn't meant to confront Bialaski yet. He was usually better at blending into the background.

"I'm talking to you, asshole," Bialaski said. He had came around the side of the house, a can of Miller High Life in hand.

Murphy took a step back from the truck. "Sorry. Looking for a buddy's house. I thought this was it." *Loser. Coward,* chanted the voice in his head.

"Yeah, right. You better not be stealing gas." Bialaski was still approaching.

"I think I just took a wrong turn." Murphy cast around for some excuse and came up blank. He was rescued by the appearance of a thin woman with limp, dishwater blonde hair.

"Charlie? I think the burgers are about done." She flicked a glance at Murphy and then away, her expression too weary to be curious. She wore jeans and a long-sleeved shirt despite the heat. Murphy's fingers curled into fists.

Bialaski's look made her freeze. "Did I ask you to interrupt, Darlene? Take the burgers off the grill if they're done. You don't want to piss me off by ruining my supper."

Darlene didn't protest or even apologize. She just disappeared around the back of the house again. Murphy watched her go, deliberately unclenching his fists. His stomach was churning.

Bialaski turned back and scowled at him. "The hell are you doing still here? Get the hell outta here. You need to learn to keep your paws off someone else's truck."

Paws. Murphy couldn't quite restrain the smirk that twisted his lips.

"You laughing at me?" Bialaski chucked his beer can aside and stormed down the driveway towards him.

"Not at you, man," Murphy said, his fingernails digging into his palms. He choked on the words, and the rage he'd been pushing down surged into control. "I don't think guys who hurt little girls are funny."

That made Bialaski pause. His face twisted, going red. "Who the hell do you think you are?"

Shit. Shit.

"I'm the guy who's here to stop you from ever laying a finger on Yvonne again."

Bialaski stopped walking and looked Murphy up and down. Then he snorted. "You must be pretty desperate if you gotta go that young."

Murphy snarled. "She's just a little kid, asshole."

His skin prickled and shivered. He was close to losing control. His packmates kept telling him he'd learn to control the change, to suppress the way his temper affected it. Murphy figured they were lying to make him feel better.

Bialaski stepped closer and shoved him, two hands planted on Murphy's chest. "Who you calling an asshole, asshole?"

Murphy staggered back, the snarl escaping. He gulped down on the anger like he would a rabbit. *Can't lose it in the middle of the street.*

"You on something?" Bialaski sounded uncertain. Murphy could feel his upper lip drawing back from his teeth. This was stupid. You didn't snarl at your prey. You didn't warn your lunch that it was about to be lunch. Then again, most rabbits didn't fight back. He curled his hands into fists, locking gazes with Bialaski.

His eyes must have done the gold flash. Bialaski faltered. "Get the hell out of here before I hurt you."

"Bite me," Murphy said, his voice distorted by the rage choking him.

Bialaski's hand darted behind his back. He was reaching for a gun. Murphy had a sudden vision of his pack leader having to arrest him for brawling—or another packmate having to investigate his shooting.

Fuck. He couldn't let this turn into a gunfight. He leapt on Bialaski, feeling the man's nose give a satisfying crunch under his fist.

It was the only good punch he got in.

Bialaski shouted. Blood was gushing down his face, but he rolled away from Murphy and threw a knee in his stomach. Murphy launched himself at the guy again, but Bialaski was ready for it this time. He hooked a leg around Murphy's and threw him over backwards. At least he didn't go for his gun again. He had his blood up, and Murphy looked like a good punching bag.

Murphy lost track of the hits after four. If he let go and shifted, he could rip the guy's throat out. But if he let go and shifted, there would be a full-size gray wolf running the streets of east side Indianapolis. No telling how long it would take him to shift back, and in the meantime, his beater of a car would be parked just down the street from a murder scene.

Yeah, you're not stupid or anything, taunted the voice in the back of his head. *You loser. You dumb dropout. Quitter. Idiot.* The words hurt almost as much as Bialaski's steel-toe in his kidney, but he'd only be pissing blood for a week; the words would last forever.

Eventually it must have registered that Murphy wasn't fighting back anymore. Bialaski stopped kicking him and stumbled back away from him. Murphy coughed and gagged.

He wasn't going to lose it. He wasn't. He would stay in control.

"Get the hell away from my house," Bialaski said. He sounded breathless though Murphy hadn't put up much of a fight. "And keep your nose outta my family business."

Not the time to press the issue. If Bialaski was going to let him leave, Murphy would leave. He managed to roll to his hands and knees, then stood slowly, cringing visibly. He knew he looked pathetic. Maybe that would make Bialaski think he was beaten.

You are *beaten, dumbass. Too stupid to even know when to give up.*

"My... mistake..." Murphy rasped, and backed away. He wondered how many people were watching from behind their curtains.

He flicked a glance at Bialaski's house and saw Darlene in the window. The rage surged up again, but he bit down harder on it.

He was not a monster.

The last thing he heard before he shut his car door was Bialaski's laughter.

The pack had a doctor until a couple of months ago, but she'd been killed in a fight with a necromancer. Murphy would have to treat his injuries the way he did before being a werewolf; raw meat on the wound (for as long as he could hold out without eating it) and lots of whiskey.

He called in sick to work, even though he knew he was skating on thin ice, and ignored several calls from his pack leader, which, honestly, Braxton ought to be used to. Then he sulked on his couch, vigilant for Bialaski's scent in the apartment building.

When he thought he could get away with slinking around at dusk without scaring people, he went looking for Yvonne. She was probably sitting on the back steps. Murphy wasn't really too worried about most of the guys who hung around the parking lot. They were mostly into dope, maybe a little petty larceny, but they weren't the kind of guys who hurt kids. But a couple of times he'd seen red caps hanging around the area. Not in the parking lot, exactly, but close enough that it made him uneasy about Yvonne.

Maybe he ought to put a couple of lawn chairs on the landing at the end of their hall. Someone would probably walk off with them eventually, but that way he and Yvonne could talk comic books without him being creepy and inviting her to his apartment.

Some instinct made Murphy go out the front door and walk around to the back. He was glad he did, because as he came around the corner of the building, he saw Bialaski's big black pickup truck parked in the first spot.

Murphy stopped walking. He hadn't smelled Bialaski in the hallway, but the truck was empty. Had the asshole found him, or was he just there to see his sister? And if so, why hadn't he come inside?

He suddenly wished it was a little darker. Leaning against the building, Murphy tilted his head, trying to catch a scent on the wind. He got it just as he heard Bialaski's voice.

"—tell anyone about what happened?"

"No, I swear, Uncle Charlie." That was Yvonne, and she sounded earnest. She didn't sound scared. Murphy wasn't sure if that was a blessing or a curse. Charlie ought to scare her... but no twelve-year-old ought to be scared of her uncle.

"'Cause some punk showed up at my house the other day, harassing Darlene and calling me names. He said he was a friend of yours. You putting out for that skinny asshole, is that why he came over? Did you tell him where I live?"

"I didn't tell anyone," Yvonne repeated. She sounded resentful, and that didn't sit well with Bialaski.

"Don't you take that tone with me, you brat." Murphy scented a spike in Yvonne's fear. He tensed, wondering if he was going to have to stop Charlie from hurting her.

Right, like you could, loser.

"Sorry," Yvonne muttered. "But I didn't tell anyone anything, I swear. Dad asked what happened and I just said I fell."

Poor kid. Murphy wanted to butt in and tell Charlie she was telling the truth. It wasn't her fault her neighbor was a werewolf with a skewed sense of right and wrong. But it wouldn't help. Anyway, he had to give her a chance to stand up for herself.

That worked real well for Mom. Murphy pushed the thought away.

Bialaski snorted. "The people at the hospital ask you if your daddy hurt you? Not like his kind is much good at sticking around and taking care of a kid right."

"His kind?" Yvonne's voice wobbled. Murphy wasn't sure if that was tears or rage until he caught the piquant surge of adrenaline in her scent. "You better not let Mom hear you say stupid shit like that."

That *crack* of sound had to be Bialaski slapping her. "Shut your mouth, you little bitch! Your daddy teach you to talk like that?"

Murphy's fists tightened. How much anger had she been exposed to while she was spending time with her Uncle Charlie? How much ugliness had that racist asshole spewed at her? Sure, it was messed up that Charlie lost his job. But he should suck it up and do what other people did—get another job. Get a job doing whatever it took to pay the bills, because that's how life worked.

That's what Murphy had done, after all. And when one job wouldn't quite pay all the bills after his mom got sick, he got a second job. Maybe he wasn't as educated as some people, but that didn't mean he didn't work hard.

He'd lost track of what Charlie and Yvonne were talking about. By the time the blood pounding in his ears had quieted enough to hear them, Yvonne was saying, "Mom's going to come looking for me if I don't go upstairs soon." The sass in her voice was all posturing—Murphy could smell the quick spike of fear and adrenaline mixing in her scent. "Dad's fixing supper."

Murphy took a slow breath, wishing he could send her courage. *Tell him if he ever hits you again, you'll tell your mom. Belinda may be his sister, but she wouldn't stand for someone hurting her baby girl.*

Charlie's voice was low and ugly. "I'd better not see that punk again. And if you breathe one word of this to your momma, I'll break your other arm, you snotty little half-breed."

Murphy could hear Yvonne's sharp intake of breath. Her voice trembled as she said, "I'm going upstairs now."

He looked over at the truck. It was almost dark. Would Charlie notice if Murphy hid in the bed of the truck? He wasn't in top form, but he could change while Charlie drove. He was as scrawny as a wolf as he was as a man. Someone could easily take him for a Malamute if he were seen. The day had been hot; the windows were open. He wouldn't have trouble getting into the cab.

What you're contemplating is murder, said a voice in his head that sounded a lot like Braxton's.

Murphy took a slow breath. *What I'm contemplating is keeping the promise I made to myself fifteen years ago,* he said back. *What I'm contemplating is putting an end to one small evil that happened to cross my path.* The voice subsided.

Charlie growled, "Just remember what I said."

It was now or never. Murphy stole a glance around the corner of the building to make sure Charlie had his back to him and then he darted to the truck and rolled over the side into the bed. He flattened himself against the side of the truck nearest to Charlie and Yvonne and tried to quiet his breathing.

Murphy waited until they were crossing the Fall Creek bridge to surrender to the change. He let the anger flood through him, let his skin prickle and itch and tear open as the fur sprouted through it. His lips pulled back from his teeth in a silent scream at the agony of reshaped bones and muscles reknitting into new shapes. Then it was over and he panted, a skinny, scraggly wolf with an aching kidney.

Werewolves retained their human minds after the transformation, though the wolf instincts were strong and accessible. Murphy knew he needed to bide his time. There was a wooded park not too far from Charlie Bialaski's neighborhood. They would have to go past it. That's where he would strike.

Murphy let his mouth fall open in a lupine grin, tongue flopping out like a dog's. He only wished he could make Bialaski recognize him somehow. He wanted the man to be afraid when he died.

Then he shook himself. Wolves attacked silently when they were hunting. They didn't try to make their prey afraid. They didn't even want their prey to know they were coming. Murphy wasn't like Bialaski. He just wanted to put a stop to someone who was too evil to live. *Maybe that's what really separates the people from the monsters,* Murphy thought. *Whether you enjoy making someone afraid or not.*

He wasn't preying on someone weaker just because he could. He wouldn't have done this if Bialaski hadn't broken Yvonne's arm, if he hadn't seen Darlene, with her submissive posturing. He wasn't a monster. He didn't even think this counted as murder. This was justice.

Then they were approaching the stop sign by the park. Murphy took a deep breath and crouched. He lifted his head just enough to see the man's head bobbing to a song on the radio. Bialaski's pulse was visible, strong against his skin. He smelled like alcohol and cigarettes and satisfaction. He had broken his niece's arm and terrorized her into silence. He would go home and drink and hit Darlene and feel good about himself.

No one would miss him.

Murphy's muscles tensed. He would tear out the man's throat. The truck would swerve and Murphy would drag the man's body out into the park. They might find him, they might not, but he would be nowhere near Murphy's building.

It was now or never.

Bialaski never knew what hit him.

C is for Carotid

Andrew Bourelle

Bill usually briefed me before I went into a situation, but this time he just called and said, "Get over here, dude. Now!"

I took my time. I was still pissed about what happened and decided I'd let him sweat. I finished the game I was playing, got a snack, took a shower. Then I put my sweatpants back on, stepped into my flip-flops, and drove over to the address he'd given me.

The house was one of those tall two-story deals squished onto a postage stamp lot, sandwiched between houses that looked identical except for the paint job. One was a pastel blue, one a pastel green, another a pastel pink.

The door swung open as I came up the walk. "Dude," he said, out of breath, "where the fuck you been?"

"My sense of urgency equates to my pay," I said. "You want me to get here fast, then—"

"Yeah, yeah," he said. "Whatever. Just get in here."

He grabbed my arm and pulled me inside. His hand was shaking, and I took a good look at him. His skin was as pale as a wall freshly painted with Kilz. There was no color at all, except for two dark half-moons under his eyes and a hint of gray on his lips, like he'd used ashes for Chapstick.

"Damn, Bill. You look like you've been shot at and missed, and shit at and hit."

He ignored me and yanked me into the living room. A young couple stood there, stiff as statues, as pale as Bill and twice as haggard, if such a thing was possible.

"This is Ted and Rachel," Bill said.

Rachel probably would have been pretty if she got some sleep. She had sandy blond hair pulled back in a ponytail and intense green eyes that really stood out. Ted looked like a douchebag—in his thirties but styling his hair like a teenager. His fucking house was haunted and he still had time to rub mousse in his hair and blow it dry?

I hated him immediately.

I had a crush on his wife already.

There were pictures on the walls of the wife and husband with a little girl, pictures of her throughout childhood: an infant, a toddler, and elementary-age. I looked around, but there was no girl to be seen.

"You don't look like a ghost hunter," Rachel said, squinting at me as if trying to see what she was missing.

"Happy to leave if I'm not wanted." I shrugged indifferently, looking around at the Pier 1 décor.

"No, no," Bill said, putting an arm around my shoulder. His clammy skin rubbed against my neck, and I squirmed away. "He's the real deal. Trust me. We need him."

It was like this. Bill was a pretender. And he was a pro at it. He made people believe he was connected to the spirit world. He came in with supplies—faux holy water, crosses of various materials and sizes, a bunch of old-looking books—and talked real vague about the presence of evil. He charmed the people with his charisma, said a bunch of nonsense in what sounded like Latin, shouted for the evil to be gone, and then smiled and told people their houses had been purged.

They felt better. He left with a fat check.

But it was all bullshit. Their houses weren't haunted.

Except sometimes they were... and then he called me.

I'd come in, wearing sweat pants, my feet in flip-flops. Unshaven. My hair disheveled and greasy (even after I'd taken a shower). I was about a hundred pounds overweight, and I only ever exercised my hands—by playing video games or masturbating.

I didn't look like the real deal.

But I was.

Bill and I used to be partners. I'd go along on the bullshit jobs and play along. But I started to get real tired of the ruse. It just seemed like a pain in my ass, especially when I was the one with the real talent. So I started skipping the initial visits and told Bill to just call me if it seemed like there really was something amiss.

Of course, I insisted that I get paid on *all* the jobs, even the BS ones I didn't work on. The way I figured it, my powers gave him his credibility. If it wasn't for the rare jobs where I really had to clean out ghosts, then he wouldn't have the reputation that allowed him to pull his scams. I thought the 50-50 split was pretty goddamn reasonable. Especially since this shit takes its toll on me. It's not like I exorcise ghosts and send them to heaven or hell, or I just lift a curse and it disappears—*poof!* No, I sop up the evil like a sponge, but I have nowhere to wring it out. I hold it inside me, like a big vat of the worst possible shit in the universe, and I'm the storage container—or prison—that keeps it all from spilling out.

I found out he was doing jobs behind my back. *Oh, business is real slow right now*, he'd said. But then one day he'd called me to a real job, a haunted cell phone with text messages from beyond the grave, and it turned out that client got his name from another client he'd seen the previous week—even though he'd told me he hadn't gotten a call in a month. I didn't need a lot of money. Hell, I lived in my parents' basement. But it was the principle of it all, him lying—that really irked me.

I got rid of the phone's ghost (a dead girlfriend jealous that her boyfriend was seeing someone new) and then Bill and I got into a big fucking row right in front of the guy's house. It ended with him calling me a leech and telling me I needed to do something with my pathetic life, and with me crying and yelling at him that I wished he had just let me die all those years ago.

We hadn't talked since, but I knew he'd call me when he needed me. It was just a matter of time. I was the MVP of the team and he couldn't keep me on the bench for long no matter how mad he was.

"Okay," I said, clapping my hands together and looking around at Bill and the shell-shocked couple. "Let's get this show on the road. What are we dealing with?"

"A demon," Bill said, almost shouting it.

I started to roll my eyes and caught myself before Ted and Rachel saw me. In our adventures, we'd encountered haunted artifacts, etheric revenants sucking the life out of their hosts like parasites, wandering apparitions attempting to possess people, phantom animals, and your typical run-of-the mill ghosts.

But a demon?

Never.

I didn't even know if my powers would work on a demon.

Bill saw the skepticism on my face. "I'm telling you, it's a demon, definitely a demon." He leaned in closer to me. "And it's got the kid hostage."

If the house was haunted, I would have felt it as soon as I walked in. If there was a curse on the couple, I would have sensed that too. The fact that I felt nothing made me think Bill was overreacting. He once called me in for some pipes that banged around every time the hot water heater kicked on.

I yawned. "Okay, so where is it?"

He led me to a door, and swung it open. Stairs descended and disappeared in darkness. All was quiet below.

"Before I do this," I said, "I want to talk about my pay."

He looked at me incredulously.

"Man, we been friends a long time," he said. "That argument, that's behind us as far as I'm concerned. Our friendship is bigger than that. Let's get through this and then we'll talk about money. I'll treat you fair."

I opened my mouth to argue, but he cut me off before I spoke.

"Dude, there is a little girl down there and her parents are scared shitless. This isn't the time. More importantly," he said, and put his hand on my shoulder. "If I die down there, I just want you to know you're my best friend and I love you. I—"

"Shut up," I said, elbowing him and turning away.

But I was grinning. The asshole knew just which buttons to push.

I flipped the light switch, and when the light came on, Bill flinched like he expected a Michael Bay-sized explosion or something.

"Jeez, dude," I said, "if you're going to piss your pants, just stay here."

I started down and Bill followed. I knew he would: I'd shamed him into it.

"Kid's name is Missy," he whispered.

The basement, with thick carpet over the concrete floor, was set up like a kid's playroom. A professional-looking mural of lions and giraffes and zebras was painted on one wall. A bunch of toys scattered in a corner. An Easy-Bake oven pushed up against another wall. A bunch of crayon drawings were tacked nearby. All monsters. Drawn in harsh black and red lines, like she'd dug the crayon into the paper with all her strength.

Maybe this wasn't bullshit after all.

Then I noticed the little girl, seven, maybe eight, crouched in the corner. Next to her was a child's rocking chair with a simple doll, probably two feet tall with purple yarn for hair and a red triangle for a nose, sitting in it. White cloth skin. The doll was old but well taken care of. There was a thin line for its mouth made of black stitching, curving upward in a half circle—a big fucking clown smile. Its eyes were plastic, but I felt it staring at me.

The chair started to rock.

Chills ran through my body, and my eyes watered.

I almost turned to Bill to tell him he was right, this thing was bad fucking news, but I didn't want the thing, whatever it was, to know I was afraid.

I'd never quite sensed anything like it. When a house is haunted, I can usually see the ghosts, sort of like shadows that move around independently of any source. But even when I don't see them, there's this strange feeling that permeates the house. Even when it's an object that's haunted—a stopwatch inhabited by a spirit, a gun haunted by the person it killed—the feeling kind of drifts out from it. Like a fart that stinks up the whole room.

But this doll... whatever was in it was compact, drawn down inside and curled up, like a piece of matter so dense its weight was disproportionate to its size—a small moon that weighed more than the sun.

"Missy?" I said.

"Yeah," she said tentatively. She'd been crying, and now she wiped her nose with her shirtsleeve.

"When I say so, I want you to run upstairs."

She gulped so loudly I heard her from across the room.

"But what about Mr. Snugglemuffin?"

"Don't worry about Mr. Snugglemuffin," I said. "I'll take care of him."

She was in the corner, pulled into a ball, her knees drawn to her chest and her face nearly hidden.

"But Mr. Snugglemuffin says if I try to leave, he's gonna bite my legs off and chew them up and spit them out, and then he's going to make me eat them. He says legs taste like green Jell-O."

"Mr. Snugglemuffin is just trying to scare you. Legs don't taste like Jell-O. They taste like blueberry pancakes."

Bill punched me in the arm and mouthed the words, *What the fuck?*

I shrugged. I was never very good at the public relations part of this job.

"Once this starts," I said to Bill, "the shit's really going to hit the fan. Get that kid upstairs and get the family out of the house."

I turned back to the doll without waiting for a reply. It just sat there, grinning, the chair rocking slow and steady.

I took a deep breath.

It's hard to explain what it is I do. When I was a teenager, Bill and I were messing around with a set of lawn darts, and one came down on my head, sticking right through my skull and into my brain. He picked me up and carried me three blocks to my mom's house. He cried the whole way, begging me not to die. I watched it all, floating above him. I thought about floating away. There wasn't any tunnel or any light, but I knew, just sort of intuitively, that there was another world I could cross over into. The truth is Bill didn't do jack shit to save me. He probably should have just run and called for help. He might have even caused more damage by hauling me around with that piece of metal sticking out of my head. But his lame heroic attempt touched me. I floated back into my body mostly because I felt sorry for him, crying and sniveling and talking about how he couldn't live without his best friend.

Ever since the doctors took the Jart out of my head, I can do what I do.

I guess the easiest way to describe it is this: I concentrate.

"Okay, you fucking piece of Satanic dog shit!" I shouted, focusing on the evil coiled up inside the doll. "Your pussy ass is mine!"

The doll flew up into the air, shaking like it was having a seizure, its body contorting and shifting and changing shape. Its mouth opened, splitting the fabric with a puffy regurgitation of white stuffing. Then, from the hole, a second mouth emerged, reptilian and with teeth like kitchen knives. A fat tongue came slithering out, eyeballs growing out of it like tumors. A screech filled the air so loud my ears started ringing.

"Run, Missy!"

God bless the kid—she did it without hesitation.

One of the seams on the doll's arm split, and a black tentacle came shooting out, lassoing her leg. She shrieked. Bill ran and grabbed her, yanking on her arm, her body pulled taut between him and the tentacle.

"Hurry!" he yelled.

"Almost there," I said.

I was trying to get my mind around the thing. That's how it works. I have to encircle it with my thoughts, just sort of blanket it. Cover it up, tie it in a knot, and pull it into me.

But I'd never tried with anything half this gargantuan before.

Another tentacle burst out and wrapped around Bill's neck. Bill grabbed at the slimy rope with his free arm. Veins were bulging on his forehead. A high-pitched wheeze of air whistled in and out of this throat. He never let go of the girl though. You had to hand it to him: when hell broke loose, he gave it his all.

The doll's chest split open and out came some kind of limb, armor-plated like a crab claw. The end of the limb split in two and revealed a head, like a giant snake with the teeth of a saber-tooth tiger.

The thing rose up, about to impale Bill, hissing like the creature in *Alien*, ooze dripping from its jaws.

"Hurry!" Bill gargled through his constricted throat.

I was there. I had it. I could feel that I was right on the edge of controlling it. With one little push of my mind, I'd squish it up into a ball and pull it inside of me with the rest of the darkness.

"What's the hurry?" I yelled. "Let's talk about my fee."

I'd never seen such disbelief on a person's face.

I winked at Bill and gave him a smile. "Just kidding!"

Then I concentrated on the monster and...

Nothing happened.

The demon was pushing back, and all my efforts weren't doing a goddamn thing. You don't have too many honest-to-God epiphanies in real life, but I had one at this moment: the thing had just been fucking with me. I was never even close to controlling it.

The creature's shrieks turned into a thick, wet laugh that echoed off the walls.

The body of the doll started splitting all over the place, and the demon came pouring out, like the dough that spills out when you break open one of those Betty Crocker muffin-mix tubes. Only this dough was black and slimy and full of strange orifices: eyes and mouths and who knows what else. Tentacles came flying out, flapping in every direction, and the tumor-like body unspooled and flopped down to the floor, turning the rocking chair to splinters. The doll was in rags now. Strips of cloth floated in the air like pollen.

I was paralyzed. I smelled urine and was pretty sure it was mine.

The big bulbous body seemed to keep growing and growing, this grayish mass of gunk and scales and patches of slick black fur, with eyeballs probing on the end of antennae, and greasy flapping tongues coming out of a dozen different mouths. The globular body started to split open, like a giant vertical mouth—or the nastiest vulva ever—and out came a thicket of writhing tendrils. They all went straight for Missy, slithering around her legs and getting tangled in her hair. She let out an ear-splitting scream.

Bill kept his grip on her arm, but his face was as blue as a sports drink. He couldn't hold on for long.

And still I didn't move. All the ghosts we'd ever encountered had been corporeal beings, occupying this weird space in between worlds. They'd never taken physical form like this. There are things in this universe even I can't explain. Not only are there ghosts, but there are dark worlds that overlap with ours, and there are monsters in them. Somehow Mr. Snugglemuffin had stepped from its world into ours. Whatever this thing was, it was alive—and my powers were as useless as screen doors on a submarine.

I heard the pounding of footsteps behind me, and Ted came barreling down the stairs with a kitchen knife in one hand and a cheese grater—of all things—in the other.

Out of the creature's giant mouth, which was as big as a doorway, came a scaled appendage with a giant pincer. Ted went right for it and it went right for Ted. The pincer blades diverged on each side of his neck and closed as smoothly as scissors cutting paper. Ted's head popped up a good ten inches and then toppled to the floor. His body fell to its knees, spraying a fountain of blood all the way to the ceiling, and then slumped over.

The pincer moved toward Bill and closed over his outstretched arm.

I opened my mouth to shout "No!" but nothing came out.

Snip!

Bill's arm came off like a branch being trimmed on a bush. The tentacles yanked Missy toward the creature's big gaping mouth. Bill's stump was raised, as if he was reaching for Missy, and instead he was showering her in a spray of blood.

Holy fuck! I thought. *Bill, what should I do?*

And then it hit me. Not an epiphany exactly, not a realization of what I should do. More like I realized what Bill would do in my situation. He wouldn't give up. Out of his depth, unprepared, no chance of success—it didn't fucking matter to Bill. He would give it his all!

I started screaming and rushed forward. I grabbed the tentacle wrapped around Bill's throat and sunk my teeth into it. Goo burst out of it, like the gel in the middle of Tidal Wave bubblegum, filling my mouth with the taste of rotten animal and maple syrup. But I kept chewing. Screaming. Growling. Gnawing. The thing in my mouth felt like a really tough piece of asparagus. Finally I bit through. The side of the tentacle still attached to the creature retracted, zipping back like the cord on a vacuum cleaner.

I loosened the other end of the tentacle around Bill's throat and lowered him to the floor. He was unconscious.

I was in a rage now. I ran to Ted, my feet sliding on the blood- and slime-coated floor, and I pried the knife and the cheese grater from his hands, screaming the whole time.

The giant mouth of the creature had closed, with Missy in it, and all of the tentacles and arms and other weird appendages were directed toward me. I ran through them like a gauntlet, swinging the knife, swiping the grater, kicking at them. There was a small seam where the big mouth had been, and I started slashing and chopping. I hacked my way into this strange sort of cave made of living tissue. Imagine being inside a giant pumpkin, with all the guts hanging down around you—only these guts were moving, with eyes and mouths and claws. The pincer came at me and I ducked and rolled like I was Indiana fucking Jones. I sliced at its appendage and severed it in one stroke.

"That was for Bill, you dickhead demon!"

Missy was encased in a sort of clear cocoon. There were worms crawling all over her, shitting out this slimy stuff like KY jelly that solidified almost immediately, turning into hard candy. I started chopping at the shell, like I was chiseling rock.

Then a tentacle with fat suction cups wrapped around my waist. Another around my leg. I went to hack at them, but another grabbed my arm, this one lined with tiny sharp spikes that sunk into my flesh. A hundred wasps stung my arm at once, and I let go of the knife.

Missy was unconscious in the crystalized cocoon. She looked peaceful. Like she was sleeping.

I took a deep breath and thought about giving up.

But then I saw, hanging above us, some kind of strange organ the size of a beach ball that looked like a heart and a brain all in one, throbbing and pulsing, with a faint glow coming from inside shining through the membrane. It was just hanging there on a bunch of ropelike blood vessels.

"I'm not giving up, Bill!" I shouted.

I put the cheese grater in my mouth and jumped up and grabbed hold of the tendrils hanging down. The tentacles tried to pull me away, but there was no stopping me now. I threw my arm around the heart/brain, and started swiping at it with the grater. Slivers of tissue crawled out of the grater like tendrils of ground beef, orange blood pouring out like water through a screen. The whole creature shook. The tentacles and tendrils flapped around me, unable to control themselves.

Once I had grated a big enough hole in the side, I tossed the grater and jammed my arm in. Light shot out, green and purple and warm, like sunlight on a spring day. I thrust my arm all the way through and found my own hand on the other side. I pulled and yanked and finally ripped the whole organ from all the weird webbing keeping it in place. My chest heaving, my heart pounding, I stood over the heart/brain, now flaccid as a squished tomato. The rest of the creature's body shook around me like an earthquake.

When I pushed my way through the opening, with Missy under one arm, the two of us were covered head to toe in slime, like newborn babies soaked in afterbirth.

Rachel was there, waiting, and I handed off Missy to her.

The creature was collapsing in on itself, deflating like a hot air balloon at the end of its trip.

I'll admit it: I felt fucking fantastic. I felt like a new man. Life was going to be different now. I wasn't going to be such a fuckup anymore. I was going to move out of my parents' basement. I was going to be a better friend to Bill. I was...

I saw a shadow out of the corner of my eye. I turned, looked up, followed it—a dark shape hovering above us.

It was Bill.

I ran to his body, pale and cold on the floor. I looked back and forth from it to his ghost, floating up around the slime-splattered ceiling.

"No, Bill," I shouted. "I can't live without you."

I could tell he was going to cross over. Ted already had. And soon Bill would too.

I don't know anything about heaven and hell and all that. But I do know that good souls go one place, bad souls another. And I also know this: the souls that stick around are always evil. All the ghosts that I hold inside me, every one of them was bad right down to the core. Good souls always move on. And Bill—despite scamming people out of money and holding out on my share of the profits—was a good person. He meant well. He tried hard. He had run to save that girl without hesitation. And when we were kids and he threw the Jart into the air and it came down on my head, he carried me down the street, determined to save me, because he couldn't live without his best friend.

I couldn't either.

I concentrated and wrapped my thoughts around him like a blanket. He struggled, but he was no match for me. I enveloped him up, suffocating his soul like a child's head in a plastic bag, and I pulled him into me.

That was ten months ago.

These days, when Rachel and I make love (yeah, we're together now; I was just lucky that her husband got decapitated on the same day I saved her daughter's life) or when we take Missy to the park and watch her play on the swings and go down the slides, it's in those happy times that I think about Bill and feel bad about what I did to him.

I put him in the only place I could: the dark container inside me with all the evil I'd captured over the years. I know it isn't right that Bill's in there with them. But I can't let him out. It doesn't work that way. It's a one-way trip, like a vacuum cleaner. If I open the door to let him out, the others might come spilling out instead, wreaking havoc like they did before only this time in a big fucking gang. I have to live with the fact that Bill's trapped in there, like a cop imprisoned with all the felons he helped put away. God only knows what they're doing to him right now.

After that day with the lawn dart, for a long time, I wished I'd crossed over to whatever heaven might lay beyond. But these days, I want to live.

For one, I'm pretty happy. Now that the police investigation is over and the detectives pretty much just shook their heads and said they couldn't make heads or fucking tails of what happened, my life is better than I ever could have hoped for. I'm in love with a beautiful woman who has a sweet little girl who looks at me like I'm her hero. I only get sad when I think about Bill.

And another reason I want to live is I get scared when I think about my own death, whenever it comes. I'm not worried about all the things trapped inside me getting out. I'm pretty sure that when I die, that's when they'll move on to the dark place they should have gone to when they died. Hell maybe. Or something like it. Hopefully, Bill will get to go to a good place.

No, I don't worry about the ghosts or about Bill. What worries me is what's going to happen to me. After I did what I did to Bill, I don't think I'll get to move on to a good place. Despite all the good I've done—freeing people from what haunted them, going into the guts of a demon to save Missy after all hope was lost—I erased all that good with one selfish act. When I trapped Bill inside me, I damned myself.

That day in the basement, after I pulled Bill into me, a bigger shadow rose up, a black cloud that covered practically the whole room. Rachel was hugging Missy and crying, completely oblivious that there was a cloud of evil so thick it was like a canister of demonic tear gas had exploded. The demon, or whatever the hell it was, had been a physical being. It had been alive. But now it was dead, and I could see its ghost—the blackest of souls—floating above me just like Bill had.

I considered trying to pull it into me. But I was too scared. I didn't want that thing inside me. Relief washed over me when I saw it was dissipating—crossing over to hell or whatever dark place exists for the souls of evil.

But in the days and weeks and months that followed, that relief faded as I slowly realized something: when I die, I'm either going to be stuck here on earth, like all the shadowy souls I captured over the years, or I'm going to a place much, much worse.

And Mr. Snugglemuffin will be there waiting for me.

D is for Demon Doll

Suzanne Willis

My last clients were Fire-Dreamers, most ruthless of the Elementals. For while water is their natural enemy, they gobble air and earth and her creatures voraciously, too. The three had disguised themselves well and to the unwary they would have seemed like anyone else but the touch of their skin as I shook their hand was like hot coal, the sound of their footsteps the crackle of flaming wood. I would have been unwise to turn them down, even had I wanted to. A man I once loved took that foolish path. The Fire-Dreamer who asked Tom to bring him the ocean jewels of Riverlee – it was rumoured that whoever held those jewels controlled the seas themselves—was calm enough when Tom refused. Then the fire dreams it sent ate him from the inside out, until he leapt from the Gale Cliffs into the ocean as it crashed on the rocks far below. If they'd had any honour, the Riverlee mermaids would have saved him from those horrors, but what was one more casualty in their endless war?

I asked them to sit down, offered them brandy, which appealed to their flame-hearts. This battle between the Elementals has been going on for millennia. What did I care who had the upper hand, who ultimately won or lost? Taking a side inspired no loyalty, did you no favours. Only left behind the ones you loved feeling as though they had died in the fire with you.

In the years since I had talked less and less, listened more. Soon, I could almost *disappear* into the background, lose myself in the lives of others. I honed my talent and sold it where I could, until it became sought-after. It kept me busy and kept the memories at bay. My emptiness was filled with tracking down lost art, catching siren song in glass bottles and conniving with the Orran witches for their winter sacrifice, before the three Fire-Dreamers met me at the snug below my home and made their proposal over brandy, like civilised men.

They gave me only the first letter of her name. E. The direction of a compass, the fifth note, Euler's number irrational.

E. My target and my tools.

The monster they sought had hidden herself from them so well, with such cunning, that that first letter was all they knew of her. No matter to me, for I didn't need more than that. I worked in the shadows and the whisper of a clue was enough. So, into the night, armed with only a single letter and the instruction that this one – the most malicious, whose nefarious heart held the secret to the end of the Elemental wars – was to be delivered to them alive.

Elderberry wine: finding a direction on the map.

The first step to listening is knowing how to loosen the tongue. Uncover the desire to speak, to reveal, and know how to hold your own tongue so that the speaker forgets that you are there at all.

Although my clients were city folk, my prey was not. Old monsters rarely are. Instead, they live in forests and glens, in deserted sand dunes where warriors' blood was spilled by the axe and the spear. The places where shadows have the chance to grow long at dusk and where worlds come to spawn, and die.

I arrived at the inn on the edge of the moors, a gathering place for farmers and the tiny population of the town. In my case were half a dozen bottles of elderberry wine. Elder is the bridge between life and death, and I was sure this was no creature of light for whom I searched. Elderberry also has the rather interesting property of inducing vivid dreams which translates into producing a vividness of tale-telling in those who drink my wine. It was...useful in my line of work.

The owner of the inn – a jolly enough chap with ruddy cheeks— was happy to reduce the cost of my stay in exchange for the wine. "I never partake, myself," I explained.

After a supper of smoked goose breast, wild greens and speck, I settled by the fire, oh-so-still, my back to the bar as the bottles went pop, pop, pop. The inn was full and talk was gentle enough, to begin with – the harvest, a romance between the barman's daughter and the town blacksmith, the local cricket team's victory last season. But as the wine flowed, talk turned to darker things. I could have been taken for a statue or a dead woman as I listened to each and every word.

Sometimes, it is not what is said, but that which is left alone which is the most telling. That night, tongues elderberry sweet and bright, they spoke of tales and creatures to curl the toes, to shiver the spine. They spoke of red caps, blood-soaked and violent. Of wolves whose howls could chase away sanity. Of chimaera roaming the mountains, speaking poison words and calling forth storms from the past. But there was not a single mention of water creatures that haunt the ocean, the rivers, the lochs.

So my direction was set.

Eels: singing in E minor

Sinew and song, sleek ink-black sliding through the depths. Eels are the magic-makers, strange fish who spawn in the fresh water springs then make their way to the brackish sea. Their bodies twining together, then separating again in an endless dance, choreographed to their own song.

Eels always sing in a minor key for they know the sadness of the world, carried through her rivers and seas. I marvelled that, despite knowing the sadness, still they sang. The second night I set out for the Seven Pools, which bubbled into streams and rivulets and waterfalls, widening into a river that ran into the sea. I had a lamp to light my way, but the moon was bright enough and I followed the sounds of swimming and sighing until I reached the water's edge. Yew trees, gnarled and bent as an old ferryman, lined the banks. A silver mist hung over the water as the eels danced in the shallows. Waiting.

I ran my fingertips across the surface, icy with a late autumn chill. "Will you sing for me?" I asked.

A watery laugh bubbled upwards. "Why should we sing for you, Eavesdropper?"

I hadn't expected them to know me for this. Was I part of the sadness in which they swam? I wanted to reply "For if you don't I will send the Fire-Dreamers here". The words, though, stuck in my throat. It wasn't that it seemed too easy – I'm no hero – but that to threaten something so heinous was to align myself with them as more than just the hired help, as it were. Once I took that step, I wasn't sure that I could leave it behind.

"I have been charged with searching for a sinister creature and have only the first letter of its name as a guide. You are the keepers of the water stories. I—"

"We will sing for you," the eels murmured, gently nipping at my fingertips as though snapping at a dragonfly "and it may lead you to that which you seek. It may also lead you to what you want to avoid."

I thought they were just naturally melancholic. Their warning went unheeded.

E. The fifth note.

The eels sang in E minor, a song without words. I watched the mist as the music held me down, as their song danced to life, graceful, night-black, night-bound. It wove through the thin fog, shaped it into an amorphous, four-legged creature that faded as quickly as it appeared. The smell of salt and low tide lingered after it.

It wasn't enough. I listened closer. There was something else *under* the music, as delicate as a spider web... there! Underneath the eels' song, another still, wending its way through the chords in a melody none but an Eavesdropper could – or should – hear. It washed over me like tears, ululated like grief. It opened up a wound I thought long scarred and ignored. My traitorous ears would not shut it out. I had not felt this alone since Tom died. I had not let myself think of what it meant that he was no longer here. In that terrible alone, I found what I was looking for.

The creature had a twin.

In the same way a minor key has its relative major. For their song in E minor, an equal in G major, which did not speak of hope and happiness, necessarily, but of balance. Under the eels' music were all the notes unchosen and waiting. Without which there would be no song.

I became so still I barely breathed. The creature's twin was its opposite and unsung, bound to it in every way. The monster had hidden herself and him, too, so they were both protected in a way that I had never protected Tom. Despite the cold night, shame flamed my cheeks. After losing him, I had become the unsung notes, the song underneath that no-one hears. A shadow of life, listening to others without living my own. I should have listened to the eels' warning.

Thunder rumbled and rolled toward me, making me jump. It was like the clamour of the hooves of wild horses cracking open the sky. Immediate to that thought, the song of the eels shifted and changed its rhythm to match the fading thunder. In the lightning flash that followed, the snaky fish writhed and twisted, a new urgency curling through their movements. I tensed, waiting for the next thunder as the storm rolled across the night. It crashed again, the gallop of something untameable shaking my bones as it hunted the unnamed. The song sung that its freedom is in knowing its brother runs wild too, opposite but not oppositional. Each an anchor for the other.

"Is the monster equine?" I whispered.

The eels fell silent and in the space between the storm and the song, the mist fell like a shroud. There would be no more answers for me that night.

Eyebright: to find that which can't be expressed easily or rationally.

It didn't make any sense to me that I had encountered no difficulty to this point. The kind of people who hired me weren't necessarily pleasant, or without enemies. The Fire-Dreamers, if anything, epitomised this. I hadn't stopped thinking about Tom since the night before and I was almost *hoping* that something or someone would stand in my way. I ignored that thought—not only was it unprofessional, I'm not that lucky.

So, I took stock of what I knew. It was a water creature, with a twin of opposites, of all the things it was not. And I thought, though I couldn't be sure, that it was equine. A waterhorse, sinister of heart. I didn't even bother with my books, for if the answer could be found there, my clients wouldn't have bothered with me. I knew it wasn't a kelpie, or anything that resided in the ocean, for that was too uncontained for Fire-Dreamers. Streams and rivers were generally out, due to their sheer size. No, the creature's twin would need to know where to find it. It had to be a loch. I was close, but not so close that I didn't need help.

Eyebright, an old herb of gentle, healing reputation, was usually used to restore the sight. Mixed in the right quantities and steeped with rosewater infusion, fennel and vervain, the liquid was a curative. For some, a miracle. Mixed in different quantities—a drop of belladonna here, a dash of rue there—and it would dim the best eyesight, replace it with a different kind of seeing. The kind that would give the user a glimpse of the eldritch that hides itself in the cracks of this world.

On the third night I walked to the loch, where the water from the Seven Pools turned to salt, and sat with my back to the enormous tree that was split and charcoaled from a long-ago lightning strike. As I settled myself, I tried to push away the thought of how Tom would feel if he knew I was helping those who had taken him from me. *Don't you need to think about what evil really means, Leila?* He would ask. "Look what good it did you," I said softly. "Your ethics got you killed."

The only answer was the wisp of an old sea breeze rippling across the loch.

I tipped my head back, blinking away tears I told myself were caused by the cold night air, and pulled the dropper from the bottle. Three drops in the right eye, three in the left, squeezing them both shut. I waited for the stinging to subside, then opened my eyes onto an awful nothing. Panic churned my gut and I fought the urge to run. Forcing myself to breathe evenly, deeply, I leaned back against the split tree and listened, ignoring my blinded vision.

In the inn, miles away, someone had begun playing a scratchy violin, while a breeze blew across the banks and over the water. Something in the loch was swimming upward, upward from the depths, through green weed and over the ancient, drowned church that lay at its centre. Up, until it broke the surface, its breathing become louder as it reached the shore. Its feet found purchase in the mud, squelching as it climbed out. The ground rumbled as it shook itself dry, water spraying my face. The sound of its stillness traced an image in my mind's eye and then the Eyebright began its work, tracing the creature before me in delicate strokes.

A horse so thin each of its ribs was outlined against its dark, shining coat. Its size did not make it fragile, though. There was power and strength in those slender bones. She pawed the ground impatiently with her front leg, hoofs covered in long, black spurs and tendrils of what looked like maidens' hair. Her eyes were like midnight gravestones, silver, ancient. Secret keeper eyes. A wintry frost rolled off her and I shivered. She raised her nose, snorting and sniffing the air.

In my eyebright blindness, I could *hear* the beast's thoughts. Like the eels' music, a song without words. She was looking for her brother, as she did every night. A twin of opposites. And I recognised, then, what she was. The Each Uisge, most malevolent of waterhorses, who lived for capturing humans, offering them a ride on her back, then taking them down to the depths. She hungered for human flesh and there was fierceness, brutality in her. Her hunger seemed to eat away at *me*. Sniffing again, she turned her head toward me, baring her teeth, yellowed and sharp.

The Each Uisge turned and walked toward me, head lowered. *Gods, am I going to be eaten alive?* The thought paralysed me. But the cacophony of her brutality receded as she approached and reached out her nose towards me, almost tentatively. I stretched out my shaking hand, until there was just a hairs-breadth between us. Underneath the ferocity, the loneliness of centuries filled her. At the bottom of the lake, she dreamed of her brother, of running together across the moors and the seashore. And the children that she took upon her back, then into her watery larder? *I never take a soul alone,* she seemed to say. Only those in groups, in a fit of jealousy that would overcome her.

Her ears pricked and voices—real voices in the real world, not my eyebright one—called out behind me. The spell between us was broken and she disappeared from my sight. All I was left with was the thunder of her hooves, then a terrible scream and a great thud as she was pulled to the ground.

Each Uisge and Each Tened: twins of opposites.

Immobilised by blindness, I waited for my vision to return as the sounds of struggle and of whinnying ripped through me. Finally, the world around me blurred, then sharpened into focus. Firmly tethered to the fallen half of the split tree was the Each Uisge, panting heavily with exhaustion. Standing a safe distance away were my clients. The three men, sweat sheening their pale skin, were whispering to one another. The largest of them saw me watching and beckoned me over. Foggy-headed from the eyebright, I stood slowly, shaking with anger. It was less for the fact that they had followed me—I *always* work alone—and more for seeing the waterhorse so bound. Like bait in a trap. Oh! How could I have not seen this?

"Well done," he said, shaking my hand. Was it my imagination, or was his skin cooler than the last time we met? His two kinsman sank to the ground, looking terribly weary.

I took a deep breath. "Am I right in understanding this is not your ultimate quarry?"

He nodded. The heat emanating from him was akin to that from a dying furnace. Something wasn't right, but I couldn't put my finger on it.

"Did you know it has a twin?"

He looked surprised, then pleased. "Not until now! We suspected the monster we were looking for would lead us to one of the forerunners of the Fire-Dreamers, but we could never have believed that it would be...*this*."

So, the Each Tened, a horse of flaming fire whose purpose was to rid the world of evil-doers, was the grand prize they didn't know was at the end of their search. I could have cheerfully bitten off my tongue as I watched the Each Uisge struggle against her bonds. Not only was I sliding quickly into being unprofessional, I was getting soft into the bargain.

But I still couldn't understand *why* the Fire-Dreamers would want the Each Tened. I frowned as my client sat down on the ground, breathing shallowly. When he spoke again, it was barely a whisper.

"Leila, you know that fire does not burn forever without a source. It needs fuel to stoke it. By bringing the Each Tened to us, we will have a source that will burn inside us for decades. And we will be ridding the world of two of the old creatures, cutting off the myths of the past and leaving us in their place. And we will burn bright with belief and fear and, in time, be victorious against earth and air and water, forever."

My own knees felt weak. Who were these monsters with whom I had aligned myself?

My vision blurred again in a surge of eyebright and the Each Uisge turned to me. *I knew they would come one day. I hid us as best I could.*

"Will he come now?" I said softly.

The Each Uisge bowed her head. *Yes.*

My eyes focussed on the real world again and I looked down at the Fire-Dreamers. They seemed less solid, flickering in and out like moribund candle flames. Straightening, they flared and pointed to the horizon. A flash of flame raced down the mountains and across the flatlands towards us, fast like a forest fire ripping through scrub and consuming all around it. This fire, though, was contained, galloping on four enormous hooves, embers leaping from its mane and tail, smoke expelled from its nostrils. The Each Tened stopped on the shores of the loch, far enough from us to turn tail and run if it was spooked. Its lips curled back as it saw its sister was tethered, but didn't come any closer to us.

The Each Uisge didn't take her gravestone eyes from her brother as she rose to her feet. I can't imagine the control, the discipline that she exercised in not trying to run toward him. I recognised the longing in her as akin to my own longing for my Tom. Then I recognised what the Fire-Dreamers plans were—they were canny enough to know that the Each Tened would not be so foolish as to get within their reach. But his sister was tied with a long, long rope, so she could easily run to her brother, but still be under their control. They could then reel her back toward them, coax him into coming closer, closer. *That* is why she didn't run.

The air was still, the kind of stillness that wells up in the moments before disaster. The only sound was the crackle of the Each Tened's vermillion flames, their light sparking off the sharp silver blades the Fire-Dreamers held. I felt sick. If the Each Uisge would not go to her brother, then they would hurt her until he came to save her. They moved toward her and the Each Tened stamped and screamed.

"Stop!"

They all turned toward me. My heart was pounding. My clients had told me I was on the trail of a monster with a vicious heart. I didn't know if they had lied or really believed that. But good and evil, they are more intricately complex, so magnificently subtle in their incremental manifestations. In tracking down the Each Uisge, I had come to know my own heart better; to know that wickedness, like the Fire-Dreamers, flourishes when people like me stand aside and use excuses to not take a side, to not examine our own notions of morality. To do nothing.

That night, I chose my side and I could only hope that their quarry had hidden more than its name from them.

"You will only get one chance at reaching him," I said. "You should untie her, show her trust. And ask her if she will take you on her back to him. After all, you are creatures of fire, too..."

The waterhorse and firehorse pricked their ears, and the Fire-Dreamers shook their heads and continued to walk forward, knives outstretched.

"He won't come to you, no matter how many holes you put in her. That much I do know." It was risky, but I bent down and untied first the rope from the tree, then gently freed her neck. "You have followed me this far and I found her for you. Trust me just a little more," I implored.

The biggest one dropped his knife first. I rested my hand on the mane of the Each Uisge and she bent her forelegs, so they could climb upon her back. The screams began as the third one settled behind the others. They pulled at her mane and she reared, but their flesh stuck fast to her coat. She had hidden herself and her traits well, after all.

She galloped toward the Each Tened, who reared in return and watched as she sped past him, diving from the shore into the loch. The fear of the Fire-Dreamers made them burn white-hot. As she dived deeper, the light dimmed, until there was nothing but the blackness of the water and the sky above.

Ether: that which might be believed but isn't there, or can't be proved.

I don't know if redeemed is the right word. I'm not a religious woman and am uncomfortable with the idea of some sort of saving grace. I have a choice, though; I always had a choice. Grief had rendered me anchorless. It had made me stop caring and that was enough for evil to slip through the cracks of my life, worm its way up in a different guise.

My last clients, the Fire-Dreamers, would not have dreamt that an Eavesdropper could have spelled their end. They picked me, I think, because I moved through life listening, taking snatches of the lives of others without living my own. So their kin won't expect me to have chosen my side. They won't know me for the hunter I have become or that I am listening and waiting for them to come for me.

E is for Eavesdropper

Samantha Kymmell-Harvey

When she returned from the morning market, Mathilde found the note on her chopping board, fresh ink still glistening. His French was scrawled so quickly, it was barely legible:

> *Ma chère Mathilde, I need to know for certain. Please understand. I love you.*
>
> *-Julien*

Mathilde took the butcher's knife from the block and halved the cabbage, its leaves burying the note under a pile of crisp, green confetti. As a pot of water came to a boil on the hearth, she diced the white onions and julienned the carrots. Her work blurred by tears, she kept chopping, knife firmly in hand. Artists were carried on the wind like pollen. She knew it from the start. Julien was who he was.

With the rabbit suspended by its feet from the beam in the ceiling, Mathilde made two quick incisions at it ankles and shimmied its fur off like a coat. One quick slice severed the twine and Mathilde laid the creature onto the board, Julien's note pressed underneath.

Mathilde wiped her wet face on her apron, not caring that she was dirtying herself with bits of rabbit fur, then slit the rabbit's belly and peeled the skin back like butterfly wings.

"Will he come back?" said Mathilde, pulling the organs and entrails out. Haruspicy was dirty business, but she never let the carcass go to waste.

The thumping of her mother's cane on the cobblestones startled her. Mathilde glanced up from the board, her hands warm with blood.

"Go easy on the poor thing or you'll never read that correctly," said her maman.

"I know, Maman." Mathilde held the liver up to the light streaming in through the window. It was dark and slick with blood. It slipped from her fingers and flopped on top of the letter. Mathilde felt Maman's broad hand on her shoulder.

"That's quite a shame," her Maman said, shaking her head. "The organs never lie."

The dark blood swirled into pools, yellow bile floated in globs. A sob escaped her throat.

"There, there." Maman stroked her hair. "I'll finish up here." She peeled the wet letter from the board. It shred between her fingers. "You have paints to mix. Your artists won't want to wait."

Something small and dark caught Mathilde's eye in the mess of entrails. "Maman, look." Mathilde plucked the heart from where it sat. She grinned, half-laughing. "He will return." She took a tin from the shelf and poured a bit of gray sea salt in then dropped the heart inside.

"Mathilde, you only see what you want to see," said Maman. "The heart betrays."

"No, Maman," said Mathilde. She snapped the lid shut. "The heart binds."

Maman stopped stirring the broth. Her gaze turned dark and cold. "Mathilde, be careful who to whom you bind yourself."

"Bonjour! Vous êtes Mathilde Lanière, n'est-ce pas? Je cherche l'Hôtel Lanière," the dark haired man said, his untrained tongue butchering every word. Mathilde couldn't help but pity this handsome stranger shivering in the rain on her front stoop.

She smiled. An American had come. "Oui, c'est moi. Please come in, Monsieur."

"I'm George Campbell," he said, hanging his soggy tweed hat on the peg by the door.

Mathilde led him down the dark corridor to her study. "We have much to discuss, Monsieur Campbell."

"What's that? It smells delicious." George placed a hand over his stomach.

The stew had been bubbling since this morning, filling the hotel with its scent of garlic and rosemary. *All my artists arrive hungry*, thought Mathilde. "It's a rabbit stew. You can have some when we finish up."

She opened the door to her study and invited him inside. Paintings covered every inch of the walls. The landscapes, still lifes, and portraits shimmered with colors so vibrant, it seemed as though the artists had put real nature on canvas.

"This is amazing," he said, examining a seascape. "I've never seen paint like this. I swear I can smell sea salt on the wind and it looks as though the sea is moving."

Mathilde tried to avoid looking at the smaller landscape she had hung by her curio—the only spot in the room she couldn't see from her desk. The paint was still fresh. It smelled of Breton grass.

Mathilde retreated to her desk and shuffled her paperwork into order. "Those pigments come from plants and insects here in Brittany. You can't imitate them anywhere else." She spoke slowly, English not being natural to her any more than French was to him. "Any color my artists need, I make. I could do the same for you, if you like."

His eyes widened as he sat in the wing-back chair. "They say you make great artists. That every single one of your tenants has made it to the Salon." George leaned across the desk, clenching his fists. "I've been in Paris for two years ago, and I still haven't been accepted."

They all dream of the same thing, she thought. "That's because you went to Paris first, Monsieur Campbell. A grave mistake indeed! Here in Pont Aven, the natural beauty is magic for your art."

"Do you have any openings in your hotel, madame?"

"Mademoiselle, actually," she said. "And yes. A room just became available this morning. I can offer you two meals a day and hot water. My specialty paints can be included, for a bit of an extra cost. If you can't pay the rent, then you can pay me in art."

"Hence your collection?" George said.

"I take pride in the artists my humble hotel houses," she said. "They always manage to pay me back. What do you say, Monsieur Campbell?"

"I will take it, mademoiselle," he said, his sea-grey eyes joyful. He was too serious, like Julien.

She slid the contract and pen across the desk. He swiftly signed his name.

"Degemer mat." Mathilde dropped the brass key into his hand. "It means 'welcome' in my native language."

"That doesn't sound very French to me."

"You're in Brittany now, Monsieur Campbell. You've left France behind." She led him into the kitchen.

"Please, call me George."

"Sit, eat," Mathilde said, showing him to the table. "George."

She ladled the stew into a wooden bowl. As it cooled, she opened the small canister of gray sea salt and took the preserved rabbit heart out. He didn't seem to notice as she chopped it up and slipped it into the broth.

George sat hunched over his bowl, eating so quickly he slurped loudly. She hoped he didn't taste the rabbit heart she'd diced up finely and added with chunks of lardon.

"Cider?" she offered, holding out a mug, but he shook his head.

"Non, merci. I don't drink."

Another Protestant. Mathilde poured herself a second glass. "George, there is something I must ask of you, if you are interested in my unique paints."

"Yes?"

"My paints are tailored to the individual artists' needs. The way I am able to do that is by including a drop of blood in the mixture."

George set his spoon in the bowl. "You are asking for my blood?"

"Just a drop. It is necessary. These are special pigments, you see. They know what you need, they know what your artist's vision because you become a part of your paint."

"That sounds like magic," said George. "No, thank you. I'm a Christian man."

Mathilde pursed her lips. She'd only been rejected once before. Julien held out for as long as he could. `Give it time.` George would give in. They all did.

Mathilde liked to mix pigments in the morning, before the artists awoke. They always stayed up late, drinking, smoking, following their inspirations wherever they found them. When they finally arose by eleven or noon, they were anxious for more pigments, after a hearty breakfast first, of course. Julien was never up before noon. She'd set aside a pastry, baguette, and tea just for him.

But Julien would not be taking breakfast here today, she reminded herself.

Standing at the table, Mathilde crushed a few miligrams of dried beetles with her wide-bladed knife. They left a shimmering dust on the marble grinding slab. She added five drops of linseed oil and began to work the pigment with her palette knife. Instantly, the paint bloomed green, like an oxidized copper. It satisfied Mathilde, the way the paint folded underneath her palette knife like a pat of butter. When it reached a thick consistency, she rubbed it with the glass muller, bringing a smoothness to the paint.

To her left was a wooden stand of thin, glass tubes each with a few drops dark brown liquid. Mathilde picked up each tube and read its label. She came to Julien's tube. *Maybe I should pour it out*, she mused. *If he doesn't need me anymore.* She swirled the blood, chewing her lip. Holding the tube out the open window, she questioned. It felt heavy in her hand. She thought of the little painting in her office, the one with fresh paint still drying. *He might need me after all.* She put the tube back into the rack.

Instead, she chose another, Alain. He had requested green for his pastoral scene. She added a drop of his blood to the green. The red didn't affect the color except to make it more vibrant. Mathilde envisioned the possibilities of a green like this, how beautiful it would render the Breton landscape. For a moment, the scent of fresh cut grass emanated from the slab.

Julien loved this color, she mused. He said it was the color of Brittany.

How could he have left her? Mathilde fought back her tears as she took a knife and pricked her own finger. It stung as she squeezed a drop into the green for Alain. She blended it in, the red vanishing.

"Good morning," said George, crossing the threshold into the kitchen, his foldable easel under one arm, satchel slung over the other. Mathilde noticed his smooth olive tone skin, his high cheek bones catching the morning light just so.

"I did not expect anyone this early," said Mathilde as she wrapped a tea towel around her bleeding finger.

"Did you hurt yourself?" George said, concerned.

"I'm fine, the knife just slipped." Mathilde scraped the buttery pigment into a small jar.

"I do not like to waste my day," said George. "Is there any breakfast?"

Mathilde nodded to the basket of baguettes on the counter.

"Merci!" Baguette in hand, George left the house.

"Madame Lanière, I have wonderful news!" It was Alain. He stood in the doorway with arms folded. Dark, puffy circles threatened to swallow his eyes. His gaunt face, tanned and angular, showed the bones beneath. "I received word yesterday that I have been accepted to the Salon."

"Congratulations, Alain, that is wonderful news." Mathilde chewed the inside of her cheek. Another one leaving me.

"Madame, I need my requested pigment. Now. I don't have much time. I have to get back to work." He shifted his weight anxiously, as if he were dancing.

Mathilde gave him the freshly made pigment. Alain said nothing but hurried away, his footsteps creaking on the steps. Maman clicked her teeth.

"Monsieur Alain looks unwell," said Maman.

"All the artists are unwell, Maman," said Mathilde. "The desire for fame devours them from the inside out."

A wave of dizziness overcame Mathilde as she leaned over the grinding slab. Her hands shook, her forehead glistened with sweat. She sat, swallowing down the nausea.

"Ah! Ma Mathi!" said Maman as she entered the kitchen. "You are using too much magic. You must stop."

Mathilde rested her head on her mother's shoulder. "I miss him. Why do they all leave me, Maman?"

"Ma petite," said Maman. "I taught you better than this. You are risking too much. It will claim your life."

Not if I can draw on the life of others, thought Mathilde.

"Mathilde!" yelled Maman.

"J'arrive, Maman." She sat up in her bed. No more headache.

Mathilde hobbled to the sitting room from her office, disturbed by the noise. Her dizziness had worn away, though her legs still ached with weakness. She discovered her tenants, some with models working in the sitting room. Blotches of paint dotted the old oak-knotted floorboards.

"I have told them they are not to paint in here, but they refuse to listen."

"Is there something unsatisfactory about your studios?" Mathilde planted her hands on her hips.

"It's Alain," said Paul, the artist in number eight. "He's been screaming all afternoon."

Mathilde didn't wait for him to finish. She hurried up the steps to the fifth floor where she found Alain's door shut. All was silent.

"Alain?" She twisted the doorknob and it gave way.

Shreds of curtains blew in the wind, and a storm of paper bits swirled like snow. His mattress was splattered with paint. A weak groan startled her.

Alain was sprawled on the floor, gripping his arm. His paint had rolled under the easel, brush still wet with Brittany-green. At first, Mathilde thought he was bleeding. As she knelt down, she recognized the red shimmering pigment as her madder root blend. Alain was leaking paint. His forearm had become part of the sunset in his pastoral scene, the flock of sheep oozing white from his palm. He lifted his head. His transformation into his own art had begun.

"Mathilde, the paint you made me." He raised his arm, causing the setting sun to leak more scarlet onto the floorboards. "Look what it's done, make it stop!"

"Only you can make it stop, Alain. It's part of you. You're becoming your work." Mathilde spotted the switchblade he used to cut his canvases.

"I don't know how!" He reached for her, smearing green hills on her black wool dress.

She took the knife. "I'm sorry, but there's nothing I can do. You cannot leave. I won't have it."

"You're a monster," he whimpered. "I'm going to tell everyone what your paint actually does."

Warm energy pulsed through her body. She felt well-rested. "Alain, this is what obsession brings," said Mathilde. "You have no one to blame but yourself."

It only took minutes for the paint to consume Alain. His willowy figure stood amongst the sheep in the form of a shepherd. Mathilde picked up the canvas and took it with her.

At first, the other artists whispered about Alain. But after a week, they had accepted that he moved to Paris and would be showing his work at the Salon.

"No more spells. You can't risk our reputation," said Maman. "You haven't made amends for your magic yet, have you?"

Mathilde said nothing. Maman didn't understand. The loss was too fresh in her mind. *My artists don't appreciate me.* She crushed the paint with such force that the knife blade broke from its handle. Her pulse rushed, heartbeat thumping in her ears.

"Mathilde! You know the rules! What you take must be paid back," Her maman pointed her gnarled cane at her. "Go to the Aven. Do not delay."

Maman's grip was firm and strong on Mathilde's arm, her calloused palms rough. "Do not think I am blind to your pain, child. But the Aven gives and it takes." Her grey eyes were like sharp flint, her jaw cinched tightly. "And it will take you, too, if you are not careful."

Mathilde pushed her maman away and fled from the kitchen.

The path from the house down to the riverside was a familiar one. Her eyes blurred with tears as she ran down the dirt trail, the tall oaks shading her from the late afternoon sun. The sound of the Aven's ripples tripping over rocks guided her to its banks. She knelt down, the edge of her calico dress soaked with its cold waters.

"An dour a vuhez man," she greeted the Aven in Breton. *Behold the waters of life*. "I have used your magic in the ingredients to which you gave life, and for this, I am in your debt. But I too have had my resources taken and not atoned for. My heart is gone."

She leaned over the edge and caught sight of her face in the reflection. Green eyes swollen and purple, brow lined with melancholy, skin pale as fresh milk — this face had already changed in the week he had been gone. "No atonement until I have been repaid." Closing her eyes, Mathilde listened to the river. Its trickles thumped rhythmically over the rocks. *No response.* Twigs crackled behind her. Mathilde stood to see who had come. George stood before her, easel in hand, canvas tube slung over his shoulder. *The river sends me the only man to reject my paints? What does this mean?*

"Mademoiselle Mathilde," George said, tipping his straw hat to her. "I didn't expect to find you here."

"Sometimes the river calls to me," said Mathilde. "When I need a place of solace."

"The Aven is my muse. See?" He opened the tube and unrolled the canvas.

Though it was only a blue and gray-splotched streak, Mathilde saw the faithfulness with which he had rendered the Aven. It was honest, like him.

"Do you like it?"

Mathilde nodded. "I love art, but I was born with a different gift."

"The gift of patroness, no doubt," he said, setting up his easel and squeezing some of his oil paints onto the palette.

"Something like that." She watched him dot clumps of green onto the canvas. His rudimentary technique made the grass flat and lifeless. "What if I mix some paints for you?"

"I like these. I bought them in Spain."

She laughed. "I see you don't need me at all then."

With a grin, George swept up her hand in his. "I do need you, Mademoiselle Mathilde." He kissed her knuckles one by one.

His lips were soft. She blushed.

George dipped his brush into the paint, his blue eyes bright with inspiration. Mathilde knew the look well.

"You inspire me as much as the Aven," he said. "You ought to know that."

She smiled. "Merci. You are as sweet as you are kind."

As she walked up the hill back to the house, she could almost feel his gaze. *He'll never stay*, she thought. *They never do.*

Mathilde found three empty jars and a thimble with blood on the kitchen table. Beside it was a note from Yves, the artist in number five. She inspected the dried up pigments in the bottom of the jars: autumn hay, Anjou pear, and crocus orange. These were no doubt for the still life he planned on submitting to the Salon.

In her mortar, she ground up dried wildflowers and hay with gray salt, slowly adding the linseed oil. As she folded the mixture on the slab, it flashed a metallic gold. Mathilde inhaled, letting the sweet, grassy aroma soak in. Hay was Julien's favorite color.

She stood at her mortar and pestle grinding the salt when she heard the door click softly. Julien's heavy boots gave him away as he neared the kitchen. He lingered on the threshold, his tall figure filling up the doorway. Boots caked in mud, brown hair dusted with hay, plaid shirtsleeves rolled up revealing strong, tanned arms, Julien was a sight to behold.

"Am I just in time?" Julien said, crossing to her. He stood behind her and rested his head on her shoulder. "I want to make the paint."

The smell of fresh hay intoxicated Mathilde as she placed her arm on top of his. "I'll guide you," she said, moving his hand to the bowl of dried wildflowers. "Just a pinch."

He nipped at her earlobe as he sprinkled it in the mortar. Wrapping his arms around her waist, he pulled her against him. His hot breath prickled her neck...

"Mathilde?"

It was George, standing where Julien had so many weeks ago now. "Yes?"

His eyes darted from the herbs on the counter to the mortar. He neared slowly and carefully picked up the vial of blood.

"Please don't touch that," said Mathilde.

"What is this?"

She took it from him and emptied it into the paint mixture. "Blood."

"You're doing magic again?" His eyes grew dark, brows stern. "Why?"

"The artists enjoy these paints," she said. "They know exactly what you need. This is why they all have come here. Except for you."

He opened his mouth to respond, but his breath escaped wordlessly. Mathilde heard his footsteps across the stone floor, but she didn't look up. She didn't want to spill the paint.

Mathilde knocked on George's door and when he opened it his trousers and shirt were covered in his ordinary paint.

"Yes, Mademoiselle Mathilde?" He sighed. "I'm quite busy."

Canvases hung drying about the room on laundry lines, drop rags littered the floor.

"You seemed upset," said Mathilde. "I wanted to make sure that everything at my hotel was to your liking."

George leaned against the doorframe and crossed his arms over his chest. "Pierre received his Salon acceptance letter this afternoon."

"He hadn't told me yet," she said. *Another one, gone.*

"And yet I haven't heard back about my submission. It's been three months. How much longer will I have to wait?"

"These things take time," said Mathilde.

"I have to wonder, is it that I am not good enough or is it your magical paints?"

His words stung. She'd heard them before, from Julien. "George," she said, crossing the threshold. "You could try them."

He sat on his bed and held his head in his hands. "I try to be a good Christian," he said. "But your paints are magic. I cannot partake. Then again, praying for my own success over others' isn't very Christian either. Do you think God will forgive my sins?" His face contorted in contemplation.

Mathilde wrapped her arms around him and cradled his head against her bosom. "You are just as talented as they are, George. You will be famous, you will go to the Salon."

"Mathilde," he said, fingers playing with the laces at the back of her skirt. "I want to see the world like you do. I want to know how you inspire them. It is you who is the key to the Salon." He caressed her face and pressed his lips to hers.

A warmth rushed through her body, awakening her senses. It had been too long. She didn't realize how much she craved his touch. She leaned into him, inhaling the scent of linseed oil in his hair. He peeled off his shirt and drew her down on top of him. Mathilde ran her fingers over his bare chest, remarking on the freckling on his pale skin. His smooth hands traced her legs. It tickled and she giggled. Her lips traced his neck up to his earlobes. He moaned. She helped his hands through the layers of petticoats until she felt him. Mathilde arched to meet him and he filled her like the Aven.

It was two weeks later that Yves received his Salon acceptance letter.

"I can accept him leaving as long I have you," said Mathilde, head nuzzled on George's naked shoulder.

George sighed, disgusted. He sat up. "How could you say that? Do you know how painful for me it is to watch everyone leave to find their glory in Paris while I am stuck here?"

Mathilde clutched the sheet to her chest. "Stuck?" Her eyes narrowed.

It took George a moment to realize. "I'm sorry, that's not what I meant." He kissed her. "You know I love you, but I won't be here forever."

Mathilde pushed him away, pulled on her chemise, and laced her skirts. "I have paints to mix. I can't be your muse all day long, George."

"Wait, Mathi," said George, grasping for her sleeve, but the fabric slipped away.

Biting her lip to fight back tears, Mathilde shut the door behind her.

Mathilde was standing on the wooden chair in her office, new painting in hand from Yves when her maman barged in. The door slammed against the wall rattling the paintings.

"You still haven't made amends, have you?" said Maman. Her slap stung Mathilde's cheeks. "This hotel has three empty studios now. The Aven is no longer gifting us."

Mathilde hung Yves' still life beside Alain's pastoral scene. It still smelled of fresh hay. A small figure stood on the horizon line crouching behind the bowl of fruit, his crooked back distinct. Pierre's seascape hung above the bookcase. Her eyes tempted her to look at that smaller landscape she'd hung in the blind spot. The paint would have fully dried by now. She forced herself to look away. "Maman, we have been gifted. Look at this collection."

Maman took a step closer to the new canvas, squinting as she examined the fine details of the still life. Her eyesight wasn't what it used to be in her old age. "No paintings will make up for what you have cost us. You must go to the Aven, Mathilde. Just as the river is used to things coming and going, so must you be."

"Never."

There was a light knock on the door. It was George, standing in the doorway, his eyes red and swollen. He held a coffee cup. His finger was bandaged.

"I need blue," he said, handing Mathilde the coffee cup. "Like the Aven."

She looked down. His fresh blood coated the ceramic in red. Before she could answer, he was gone.

"You should go too," said Maman. "before it's too late."

Mathilde admired her collection of art, arms folded across her chest. She clutched the coffee cup and smiled. *I don't need you any more, Julien.*

"George," said Mathilde as she knocked on his door. "I have your paint ready."

"It's open," he said.

She found him at his easel. He anxiously reached for the jar of shimmering blue paint in her hand.

"Are you sure about this?" Mathilde said.

"If your magic comes from nature, and it is God who created the world, then is it not God who is the creator of your magic as well?"

The canvas hung on a clothesline he'd tacked up. It was his Aven scene. This time, Mathilde recognized her own thin figure clad in black. He'd painted a lace headpiece on her head, though. She laughed. "I see what your blue is for," she said. "Though you may need some extra brown to get rid of that horrible hat atop my head."

George dipped his brush into the new pigment. "You're the only woman in Brittany who doesn't wear the pardon."

"And I like it that way." She watched him apply the pigment. The Aven shimmered with each brush stroke. Little ripples had begun to trip over the river rocks.

"I see why your paint makes Salon winners," he said. "Look at the way it shines. Like the river might run off the canvas."

Mathilde marveled at the landscape. It wasn't just her pigments, but George's skill. She drank in every detail. "George, this is your masterpiece."

She kissed his neck and tried to slip her hand into his, but he held the paintbrush firmly.

"Not now," he said. "I'm working."

Mathilde's eyes narrowed. "Can I get you anything else then?" She punctuated each word with annoyance.

"I need more pigments," he said. "I left you more blood over there."

She grabbed the tea cup from the bureau. "As you wish."

Mathilde found George's acceptance letter on the front door mat. She squatted on the stoop, head in her hands. *He's going to leave you. They always do.* She folded the envelope and tucked it into her skirt pocket. Standing, she wiped all evidence of tears from her face.

Mathilde knocked on George's door. "George!" She opened it.

He stood at his easel, just as he had been every day for the past month. Shadows cast by the afternoon sun accentuated his gaunt figure. His dark, swollen eyes squinted in the light. He applied the Aven-colored paint in short, frantic swoops.

"I'm busy," he said without looking at her. "Is it important?"

Her fingers toyed with the envelope in her pocket. Glancing around the tiny room, fifteen jars of her magic paint had been emptied. His clothesline was crammed with landscapes, each more life-like than the last. She had allowed him to overindulge in her pigments. She'd allowed Alain the same luxury. And Julien.

"This came for you," said Mathilde, handing him the envelope.

George dropped his paintbrush, hands shaking. Eyes wide, a grin spread across his skeletal face. He dropped to his knees, eyes cast to the Heavens. "Praise be to God! I've finally been accepted!" He grabbed Mathilde's hands. "Pray with me, Mathilde. God is so good."

Mathilde knelt and bowed her head while George said a prayer in a tongue she didn't understand.

"Amen," he said. "Mathi, you are a truly the best patroness."

She leaned in to kiss him, but he returned to his easel instead.

"No time for that, I must finish this last piece of my collection."

"But you will come back? From Paris?"

He dipped his brush in the Breton green pigment. "All of the great artists are in Paris, Mathi. And now I'm a great artist, too."

Mathilde pressed her lips together. "I won't bother you anymore."

When Mathilde entered the kitchen, she found her maman waiting for her. On the chopping board were fresh rabbit entrails.

"Mathilde," said maman. "The organs never lie." She held up the heart. It was shriveled and gray.

"Oh, maman," said Mathilde. "haruspicy is a delicate matter."

"Blind child!" Maman stuck the knife in the board. "Spoiled child! I told you Julien would not return. It was in the organs. But no, you selfish child! You saw what you wanted to. I told you to go make amends for the magic we are working, to keep our artists in balance."

Mathilde's hands shook.

Maman held up the liver, black and shriveled. "You have poisoned them and poisoned yourself." She took the rack of vials from the cabinet. "You trap them here, like a spider in its web," said Maman. "No more, Mathi." She smashed the rack of vials on the stone floor, flecking blood everywhere.

"Stop!" Mathilde's heart raced, her breath shortened. "No!"

Maman grabbed Mathilde by her hair and forced her to the chopping board. "Your blood started this," said Maman. "And your blood will end it."

"Maman, no! You don't understand," said Mathilde through tears. She struggled and pushed, but Maman held her hair even tighter. Mathilde screamed as her Maman grabbed her wrist and forced her hand onto the chopping board.

And with the knife, Maman slashed Mathilde's right palm and then the left. Mathilde howled. Her ears rang, her vision blurred. The floor was cold and hard against her body. She rocked, clasping her hands, palms hot and stinging.

"You will never mix paints again," said Maman. "And I am sending you away."

The knobby wooden handle of the knife hung at the edge of the counter. Mathilde inhaled sharply, grinding her teeth as she sucked in the pain. She gripped the knife.

"You can't send me away, Maman," she said. The knife was sharp. It slid through Maman's ribs smooth as oil paints. "I won't be abandoned again."

Mathilde limped up the steps to George's room and pushed the door open. She'd wrapped her palms in linen, though crimson stains were seeping through. She clutched them to her chest. George stood at his easel, palette in hand, yet he didn't move.

"George?" said Mathilde. He didn't react. She reached for his shoulder, but connected with nothing but wet paint. His shoulder was blue sky, white clouds floating the length of his arm.

Her stomach twisted. "George, how long have you been like this?"

He dropped his palette. "Mathilde, can you please get that for me? I have to finish this." His voice was soft yet frantic.

His body was much further gone than Alain's. Or Yves'.

"It's time to stop," she said.

"No, not when I'm so close to fame. I've worked too hard for this."

Mathilde tried to touch him, but her fingers went numb. Pulling away, she saw paint where her fingers once were. `It's begun.`

George hobbled away from her and limped down the stairs leaving puddles of green and blue as he went. Mathilde grabbed the canvas and hurried after him. He hobbled to her office, smearing the white walls gray.

"Help me." He teetered to the desk. "You have to make this stop, Mathilde."

"I can't," she said, showing him her hands now part of the rolling green hills.

"You've been collecting us all along," he said.

His back gave way, bending like the Aven. Mathilde caught him on the canvas, letting his colors seep into it. Her hands seeped in too, forever binding to the painting. She lay beside him on the cold, stone floor beneath the small painting in the blind spot by the curio. Julien looked down on her, a satisfied smile spreading across his withered face.

"You don't understand the loneliness," said Mathilde.

The figures in the paintings moved with excitement. Above her, each of her artists sneered at her. Their lips moved, but the dried paints muffled their voices.

"You never loved me, did you?" George said, his blue eyes crystalline with tears. "God forgive me."

"I did. I still do," said Mathilde. "And now we will always be together." Mathilde pressed her lips to his forehead. Trees tattooed George's neck. Leaves enclosed his jaw before twisting around hers. Mathilde felt the Aven flowing through her as she took George's branch-hand in her own and closed her eyes. Her body stiffened into the oak trunk. His body entwined with hers, crimson leaves resting on her gnarled shoulders. She breathed her last.

F is for Fame

Hal J. Friesen

Professor Victoria Manassa looked into the time conservatory, her face close to the window. The Hand of Fatima on the wall behind, meant to ward off the evil eye, was a ghostly kaleidoscope of colours reflecting in the glass next to her own image. Peering past it, she surveyed the evolution of the krillids. There was only a month left until the rabbi's committee came through—a month until Manassa had to justify her purpose.

Dry climate adaptations, variations of cacti and other low-stomata plants, filled the environment of the time conservatory. The three-story ellipsoid patterned with a curved grid of glass panels was still a marvel to Manassa, where time could be accelerated to speed up evolutionary studies.

The cat-sized krillids with their thick clay-coloured armor plating plodded in a guarded fashion, staying clear of the nearby plants, and waiting for one thick limb to settle before moving the next. Their bodies had increased in size and their limbs shortened so their centre of gravity hung lower to the ground. They'd carved channels and caves into the rock. Reflections of dark yellow eyes shone deep within.

"Clarice," Manassa said, "remove the air from the conservatory."

Clarice, sitting at the computer terminal with her short legs dangling Fluvog shoes, sucked in a breath. Her bun had all but come undone, and one hand kept the flood of brown hair from enveloping her face. Her loose jeans and unicorn T-shirt had random scuff marks from the equipment.

She shot a longing glance at the krillids, then reluctantly typed a few commands.

A moment later the krillids dug into the rock with their extruding claws and flattened their bodies against the ground. Their chests swelled, stretching the gaps between the plating to reveal glistening porous tissue labouring to maintain the pressure differential between inside and out. Somewhere beneath lay the harder barrier, the other side of the creature's biological airlock.

One of the krillids uncurled an arm, wrenched a cactus from the earth, and stuffed the end into its mouth.

"Impressive. Very impressive." For the first time since they'd begun, Manassa felt they might meet the committee's deadline.

Clarice typed away, flipping between programs as she made notes to accompany her changes. Manassa felt heat in her chest from the way she'd guided her student to this end. She'd come a long way.

Manassa sidled up to the desk and half-sat against it, returning to the spectacle of the krillids rapidly recovering and continuing their business in a vacuum environment. Even as the plants bloated and in some cases burst, the krillids now reacted calmly to the changes, methodically transferring the vegetation into their bladdered bodies that could handle the gradients.

The krillids' progress astonished Manassa. Even in the accelerated reference frame she would have expected far more generational iterations to achieve the adaptations the krillids now displayed. It was as if the hand of God had reached down and given approval.

Manassa frowned. God didn't do that. No, this was too easy. She walked closer to the window and leaned with her palms pressed against the glass. As she did so, the krillid on the rock closest to the window jerked its head toward her. God, these creatures were sensitive—

Manassa lifted her hands from the glass. She remained motionless, staring hard into the krillid's yellow eyes. There was no way he could see her through the one-way transparent glass, but he kept his head up seeming to watch her as the krillids around scampered for the remaining vegetation.

She clenched her fists then hammered both on the glass. The sound ricocheted off the cramped walls of the lab. Clarice jumped and several krillids turned to look at Manassa.

She knew very well that sound didn't propagate in a vacuum. Tightness pulled at the base of her skull.

"Clarice," she droned. "There is a vacuum inside the conservatory, is there not?"

Clarice's voice croaked. "Yes, Professor."

"Then why can they hear me?" With her back to the glass, Manassa stared at Clarice's hunched form. The pride she'd felt earlier at guiding Clarice's hand twisted into a knot. She'd felt the same when excuses had piled up for her inability to go into space.

"They must have developed some advanced adaptations to sense impending environmental changes." Clarice's voice held a slight tremor. She kept her gaze on the monitor.

"Advanced adaptations that defy physics," Manassa said through thin lips. "Sound can't propagate in a vacuum."

"Th—that's a good point, Professor. I don't know how they're doing it."

"Show me the readings on the vacuum gauges." Manassa strode to the desk in a few steps and loomed over Clarice.

Clarice brought up a display showing fractions of millitorr for pressure. A pretty good vacuum for the size of the chamber.

It didn't make sense.

"Show me the irradiation spectrum."

Clarice tabbed to another window showing a spectrum ranging from the infrared all the way to high-energy gamma rays, several giga-electron-volts. It was a broad, flat spectrum.

Too flat to be real.

Manassa leaned closer, scanning the details and layout of the display. The knot twisted so much her insides vibrated. Without warning, she brushed Clarice's hands aside and typed in the hotkeys to show the programming tree and sources for all the instrument inputs.

"What do you need, I can—"

"Quiet," Manassa snapped.

The wiring tree of the program showed a pre-determined plot for the irradiation. The readings for the vacuum pressure were a random noise generator around a fixed, constant low reading. None of them connected to real diagnostics—they were all fake.

"Move," Manassa snarled, and Clarice scrambled out of her chair. Manassa slammed into the seat, and closed Clarice's dummy program. She opened the real diagnostics.

The actual values for the radiation and vacuum were much, much gentler.

"Clarice," Manassa whispered through clenched teeth, "what do you think you're doing?"

"I—I didn't want to be too harsh on them. When I tried your parameters, so many more of them died. Inky, Patches and Germaine... I couldn't watch it again. Th—they're doing well, and they're getting closer. They just need more time to evolve."

Manassa banged both fists on the desk, causing the Hand of Fatima to fall and smash. Shards of coloured porcelain scattered the floor.

"You're going easy on them!?" Manassa shouted. "After all I've taught you, you think going easy on them is the key?!"

"You didn't see the bodies—"

"Not only do you disobey me," Manassa said, standing and stalking toward a cowering Clarice, "but you lie about it. You waste your time creating this facade to make the krillids look like they're doing better than they are."

"I'm sorry." Clarice's lips trembled and she had her back against the window, as though protecting the krillids. "If you can wait a little longer, I can ramp them up to your requested exposure levels."

"No more waiting!" Manassa shouted. "In only a month's time we have to present results—present the evolved krillids—to the rabbi's committee." Her hands shook. "They're expecting to see creatures capable of withstanding the rigours of space. Creatures that can travel the cosmos and soak in all of Creation without the need for additional protection. If we've succeeded, the rabbi's committee will approve continued research. Or they'll squash our efforts."

"But we're still getting that coil warning. Pushing the system harder seems like a bad idea."

"I've told you it's nothing to worry about."

"But they keep dying—"

"You've disregarded my experience and seniority, and it's wasted more time than you can imagine. We're not going to have anything for the rabbi, and then the krillids' deaths really will be for nothing. You will have trivialized their entire existence. Your compassion will have robbed their lives of meaning, Clarice."

"Once I get a group adapted to the high-energy gamma, the natural disasters get them. If I get them adapted to the natural disasters, the radiation gets them. I've been going through... so many..." She shook her head, then ran her fingers through her hair. "Candy, Wilfred, Plainsworth... are all gone now, along with their families."

Manassa rubbed her temples. "They're experiments," she muttered. "You shouldn't get attached to them."

Clarice opened her mouth, but Manassa cut her off. "I've gone too easy on you." Manassa shook her head, her lip curling. "You're such a disappointment. I expected better."

Clarice's face whitened. The lines of her features stretched long with shadowed wrinkles and her brow curved in an arc of what Manassa took as self-deprecation and fear.

Good.

"W—what can I do to make things better?" Clarice said.

Manassa sighed. How could she better articulate the importance of the next month? With her own frail body not permitting her to ever go into space, the only thing she had left was to bring that possibility to others, in a more profound way than anyone ever had. She hadn't realized until now how much her own sense of personal worth entwined with the fate of the krillids. She had nothing left—her body and soul withered, and if the krillids failed, the few remaining reasons for her existence would vanish.

But she could say none of this to Clarice. She had difficulty admitting as much to herself.

Instead she said, "Clarice, do you know how to grow hot peppers?"

"No…"

"You can water them dutifully, make sure they get plenty of sunlight, and treat them to all the kindness in the world." Manassa clasped her hands to prevent them from shaking. "And do you know how those peppers will taste?"

Clarice shrugged.

"Bland. If you want to make a really hot pepper, what you have to do is stress the plant. Tip it over. Starve it. Keep it on the verge of death; make it struggle for existence. Then you'll get the spiciest peppers of all.

"We're trying to make hot peppers out of those krillids. We can't show them any mercy. God didn't create the wonders of the world out of compassion alone."

In fact, Manassa didn't think God had created much of anything worthwhile out of compassion.

"We're going to give the krillids the full treatment. Tonight, right now. And I'm going to watch you do it. You're not leaving until it's done. And if you ever try to deceive me again, you won't be my student, and I'll make sure you aren't anyone else's, either."

Manassa grabbed the smashed hand of Fatima off the floor. The fingers had broken off and left jagged edges so it now looked like a fist. She hung it back on the wall.

As a child, Manassa had dreamt of nothing but going into space. It represented all the glory and beauty of God, and all wondrous possibility. Her faith centered around getting closer to God by being in the cosmos. By entering that realm, she thought she could understand God better. Understand the entirety of Creation.

She had devoted herself utterly to this task, relying on God's grace to see her through to the end. When asked what she wanted to be when she grew up, she had a simple and clear answer: astronaut. When the inevitable follow-up question came about a backup plan, she would smile and revel that her faith glowed that much stronger than the questioner's.

After all, it had been made pretty clear to her that God served those who served Him, and blessed all His followers. Manassa reasoned she could make her dreams come true through stronger devotion to Him, especially since her goal was so intertwined with serving and knowing Him.

She tried to grow closer to God through more intense prayer, and repeating maxims passed to her by rabbis. Only when she was diagnosed with Stargardt disease and rheumatoid arthritis did she experience her first crisis of faith.

She remained in denial for many years, suffering through the gradual loss of vision and mobility without treatment, thinking it would go away if only she displayed more faith. She studied harder and went to synagogue every day until she opened her Torah one morning and could not read the words. Her eyes refused to focus, and a black spot had appeared just right of centre.

She had prayed dutifully to God her entire life, asking for compassion and grace in her goal, and been rewarded with resounding denial.

Around that time she began to hear the laughter surrounding her goal of reaching the stars. She spoke of her dream and would see the mockery beneath the surface. No one would send someone with her physical ailments, not when there were a plethora of other able-bodied women perfectly suited for the job. She applied to every program she could. They all rejected her.

The compassion and grace she'd sought and relied upon throughout her journey had brought her nothing. She had invested everything in her faith, and was now falling abysmally short. She had no idea what to do with herself. The religious platitudes began to feel frighteningly hollow, especially as the only comfort anyone still around her could offer.

She panicked. She needed to understand how and why this could happen—what could have made everything go so wrong. And because everything she believed had been fed to her by some external authority, this time, she turned inward for answers.

The only thing that made any sense to her, that fit with all the evidence she'd amassed in her ambitious mind, was that compassion had sown the seeds for her failure early on. If she had been presented from the outset with how ruthlessly and pitilessly the world would treat her, she would have been better able to prepare herself. She could have taken necessary steps to put in backup plans, to play other angles, to politically maneuver herself toward success. By having false notions of the world's kindness as a result of her mentors' compassion, Manassa had been set up for disappointment and failure.

Since then, she devoted her life to making sure those under her influence would have the knowledge and strength to make it in the world. Eventually she moved into the field of guided evolution, where she could steer God's hand and make creatures that could enjoy the entire universe, all of the dreams she'd had snatched from her.

For Manassa, Clarice's betrayal confirmed no one could be trusted to understand her faith, or to understand God as well as she did. She began sleeping in her office so she could check up on the krillids every few hours, even in the middle of the night.

A week later, on a Saturday at 3 am, she saw the krillids carving symbols into the rock. The ones who had survived the full rigours of the environmental stresses were emaciated and weak, but still managed to eke out an existence.

Out of curiosity, Manassa turned on an earthquake, and watched their work shatter out of their hands. Then when the rumbling stopped, they started carving anew.

"Relentless." She smiled. "Slow and careful, but relentless."

Manassa wondered if she were going too easy on them, building attachment like Clarice. Maybe the krillids shouldn't have time for such niceties as symbolic carvings. She programmed a few more disasters into the loop for good measure, then rose to go to her office and take a nap.

Manassa stopped when she caught sight of a large movement of krillids. They'd gathered on the rock outcrop jutting toward the window and pointed their thick, clawed hands at her. Their cold, yellow eyes seemed empty and unmoving. Manassa moved to the opposite wall of the lab, and their fingers followed.

She could feel their rough palms scratching up her back, creeping up her neck...

"H—how are they doing that?" Manassa whispered, her voice high. "I have to increase the dosage." Her throat tightened the more she looked at the mob of krillids.

Her hands shaking at the keyboard, she punched in a higher radiation dosage, bypassing safeguards. She clicked several times to start the time accelerator.

As the cloud from the time barrier swirled into view, it left behind a retina burn of the krillids' staring eyes.

Manassa didn't know why she'd been scared. She knew she carried out God's work. Was there doubt in her mind about its importance? She sipped coffee with quaking fingers, telling herself the krillids were experiments. They'd thank her for all she'd done for them when this ended.

"How are they doing?" Manassa asked.

It was the following Tuesday. Clarice leaned back in her chair and stared at Manassa with dead eyes, her red Fluvogs propped on the desk. She held the keyboard in her lap. Behind her, the time conservatory swirled clouds around its periphery. The Fist of Fatima hung above the computer, knuckles sharp and jagged.

She turned to the monitor and typed commands.

The swirl unclouded, revealing darkness inside the conservatory. Glowing orbs punctured the dark, hanging on metal-framed enclosures that housed the rock and shifted with the rumbling earth.

"Where did they get metal?" Manassa asked. She approached the glass and steadied herself against it.

Clarice blinked, then scrambled out of her seat and rushed beside Manassa. "My God," she said. "They've started taking apart the conservatory."

She flipped a switch and blinding light filled the space, revealing a layered garden, built almost high enough to hide the hole they'd started carving into the exterior walls, past the insulation and into the multiple metal layers girding the outside, nearly to the cloud wall.

Manassa paced to one side, and saw the krillids had also begun digging their way out the front, toward them.

"Why didn't the sensors pick this up?" she asked.

Clarice glared. "I've had to override just about everything to torture them as you requested."

Manassa nodded, squeezing and releasing her hands. "All right. We can fix this. We just have to—"

She stopped as the krillids emerged from their shelters, each carrying a globe. They came onto the rocky promontory, and began passing their globes around, sometimes struggling to work around the thick plating covering their limbs.

"What..." Clarice murmured.

The krillids gathered around several in the centre who held all the glowing orbs, positioned in a strange shape. Those not holding the orbs raised their arms and pointed.

Manassa stepped back and sent the chair scampering across the floor. As she did so, she realized they weren't pointing at her. She followed the line of their gazes and turned to the monitor, above which hung Fatima's Fist.

The fist they were trying to outline with their globes.

"They're sentient," Clarice said, her gaze darting back and forth. "Look at the carvings, the societal structure, and now ceremony. My God, they're sentient."

Manassa opened her mouth, but said nothing.

"That's the only way they survived everything we threw at them." Clarice stepped forward and caressed the glass. "They grew intelligent enough to adapt faster than the slow crawl of evolution."

Manassa cupped her chin and tried to keep her hands from shaking. She had to piece together the scene in front of her logically, to assess everything from an academic perspective, rather than see the myriad threats to everything she tried to accomplish. "Sentient krillids," she murmured, then added in a louder voice, "Did we erode the coatings on the viewing windows?"

"Must have," Clarice said. "It doesn't matter now. We have to free them."

Manassa felt as though the ground beneath her trembled with the quakes she'd given the krillids. This wasn't how it was supposed to go. The krillids were *her* creations, *her* development, *her* work. They couldn't run off into the world to do as they pleased—that would ruin the purpose of their existence. Of *her* existence.

She raised her hands as though they might ward off everything that was happening. She fought for familiar ground within her mind, searching for some argument to regain control.

"No, there's... no way," she said, fumbling. "We have no idea how they'll interact with humanity. Not to mention, they... still have to be trained for asteroid mining."

Clarice stared at her, mouth agape. "Are you serious? We can't subject them to continued torture now that we know they are intellectualizing their existence."

Manassa didn't want to think about that. What right did the krillids have to redirect things?

"Just think of how earth-shattering the development of sentient krillids will be if it's accompanied by a race of sentients symbiotically perfect to work with humanity for asteroid mining." The words sounded smooth, as though they poured from someone else's mouth. "We'll not only be famous, we'll be saviours."

Clarice jammed her finger against the window. "This isn't about fame. Those creatures have suffered long enough, and they need to be let out. If we don't let them out soon, they're going to find their way out. God would abhor the way we've been treating them in the name of science."

"If we just pass the krillids along now," Manassa continued, standing taller, "they risk a much higher chance of rejection from humanity. People will feel threatened. If we give them a reason to be symbiotic, we can live in harmony from the outset."

The words sounded good to her, but Manassa realized she might need more to convince Clarice—maybe a hint of sincerity.

Manassa clasped the Star of David hanging on a necklace close to her heart. "God would be proud of what we've created," she whispered. "He couldn't make us strong enough to explore His universe, Clarice. We've been limited to this narrow slice of Creation, with walls to progress because of humanity's frailty. Here we have created a hardened race capable of enjoying all of Creation's beauty. They just need to be shown how."

Clarice's eyebrows raised for a moment, then her gaze narrowed once more. "All while suffering through relentless tragedy, I'm sure."

"Not relentless. We have a purpose, and when that is achieved, they will pass beyond tragedy to triumph."

Clarice snorted.

"The thing I fear most," Manassa quoted, avoiding the krillids' stares, "is not to be worthy of my sufferings."

"That's enough," Clarice said. "This is over. We'll see what the krillids want to do, on their terms." She strode to the terminal, hopped into the chair, and began typing.

Manassa saw in Clarice's keystrokes the trivialization of everything she stood for. God would not want her to stand by and watch her own life be destroyed. What was Clarice's purpose in this life, anyway? Nobody had as grand a vision as Manassa did.

She curled her fists and tightened every muscle in her body. She felt like when she'd first discovered the ways her faith had led her toward failure and physical infirmity. The habits and patterns of the past seemed increasingly invalid. The lines of right and wrong were malleable—things she could, she realized, control and justify. With each hiss of hydraulics releasing, Manassa felt a thread of her old beliefs snapping free, ready to tie to something new within her control.

"No!" she shouted, surging toward Clarice. She pushed Clarice's hands off the keyboard. Clarice batted her arms away.

"You little—"

Heat rushed to Manassa's cheeks. The next moment, she shoved Clarice's rolling chair away from the terminal.

Clarice's foot caught the edge of the desk to stop herself from rolling too far. "What are you doing? Get away from me!"

"I can't let you do this." Manassa leaned against the desk, supporting herself with one hand.

"I can't let you torture them anymore," Clarice said, her hands white on the armrests. "They're my responsibility."

"Not anymore." Manassa stiffened her jaw. "Get out."

Clarice rushed Manassa, shoving her aside to reach the keyboard. She typed frantically as Manassa fell. Manassa arose seeing nothing but red. When her vision cleared, she heard the shrieking of equalizing air past metal.

"No!" she shouted. She grabbed the keyboard and raised it over her head to strike, but Clarice shoved it out of her hand and it clattered to the floor. Manassa fell against the terminal, and tried to yank it from the desk, but bolts held it down.

Manassa grabbed for the only other thing in reach—Fatima's Fist. She caught her balance, the porcelain fist behind her back, and reached for Clarice with her left hand. They clasped palms, then Manassa saw an opening.

Equipment released with a *pop-pop-pop*. Manassa thrust Fatima's Fist hard toward Clarice's ribs. Clarice darted away and it grazed her side.

Clarice shuffled back, eyes wide.

This, Manassa thought. This was what she was missing. Instant command—powerful, and so much more efficient than negotiating over compromises. Relief washed through her. Things would be all right.

Something burned in Manassa's eyes. She touched her temple and felt a trickle of blood running down. If this was all it took, she realized, why had she waited so long? Why had she been such a coward, so unwilling to follow through?

"You," Manassa said, struggling to catch her breath, "will never set foot in this lab again."

Clarice mouth worked. "You... you assaulted me."

"I was defending myself," Manassa snarled. *You were going to destroy me,* she thought. "No one will take your side. God is on my side. And He will not let you ruin this." Manassa held up Fatima's Fist.

Clarice opened her mouth to speak, but Manassa cut her off. "Get out. Now."

Clarice stumbled past Manassa and shoved open the lab door but turned before crossing the threshold. "You can't keep torturing them," she said, the steel returning to her eyes.

"I'm not torturing them. I'm preparing them for this world."

The door slammed behind Clarice, but Manassa continued to grip Fatima's Fist so hard it dug into her palm and drew blood.

She hung Fatima's Fist back up on the wall, dotted with flecks of blood. She let her gaze rest on it for a moment, feeling for the first time in a while that things were finally under control.

After Manassa reactivated the controls, she replaced the electronic access panel on the lab door with a deadbolt. With the rabbi's visit less than a week away, she didn't trust anyone—not campus security, not facilities, and definitely not weak-willed students trying to usurp her.

No one understood the importance of the work. No one realized the potential of all that could be learned. And no one realized the gift she was offering the krillids, of the ability to explore the entire universe without the hindrance of a frail body.

Manassa set up maximum irradiation in areas of the conservatory where the krillids were trying to get construction materials and claw their way out. The krillids responded by making ritualistic pilgrimages to these areas, sacrificing some of their own in order to secure resources. They would cheer each time a half-dead but triumphant krillid returned to camp wielding rods of aluminum. The pilgrim would die as a martyr.

Manassa had started to smile involuntarily at their tenacity, while wishing she could turn the radiation up even higher.

The krillids had taken to coming out in groups and making a glowing outline of the Fist of Fatima. It was just another way they deviated from their true purpose, and though it pained Manassa every time she saw it, she could not look away. She was terrified they'd emerge without her noticing. She studied them, ready to torch the entire experiment if they reached the barrier.

A day later, they got too close. She had to do something, and realized she couldn't bring herself to actually destroy them.

She could perhaps let them out and confront them alone. But there was a chance the krillids saw Manassa in the same distorted, negative light Clarice did. She needed to talk to them, make them understand their destiny and how she was helping them toward it. She'd made inroads to understanding their written language, but not well enough to communicate and avoid a bloody battle.

Maybe she was trying to fight God's will too much by avoiding conflict. Violence was, after all, a universal language, and she'd only harnessed a fraction of her potential when she'd shown Clarice. It was fast and efficient, and so easy. But the krillids were too great in number, and too strong for her to take on alone, even with weapons.

She needed to meet them with someone on her side, someone who wouldn't talk to the media, who was sworn or contractually bound to secrecy.

The pressure of the upcoming visit filled and rose all the way up Manassa's body to the back of her throat. The pressure to justify everything she believed in, everything she did, everything she was.

She pulled out her phone and called. The krillids in the chamber threw glow globes into the air to celebrate the successful acquisition of another chunk of metal.

"Hello?"

"Clarice, it's me," Manassa said, croaking through the knot in her throat.

A sharp inhale. "Why are you calling me?"

"I want to let the krillids out," Manassa said, "and I think you should be the one to do it."

A long silence, while the krillids paraded with the body of yet another dead comrade.

"All right," Clarice said at last.

Manassa bunched her fists. She knew Clarice's compassion for the creatures would win out over any of their past grievances.

She arranged everything for the following morning.

The pressure equalization of the time conservatory with the staging area took all of a long, sleepless night, during which the krillids reacted more startled and disturbed than during any of the hardships they'd endured throughout their long, accelerated evolution. Manassa reasoned this should have been easier on them, but maybe they had adapted to struggle to such an extent that when their environment grew friendly, they grew more wary, ready for an even greater fall.

As they should be. She'd prepared them well.

She and Clarice now waited in the airlock, each wearing white biocontainment suits. Their comms crackled with forced slow breaths in between countdowns from the computer. The suit reeked of bleach and heated plastic.

Clarice stood to the side, her head turned to avoid Manassa's view.

Manassa's fingers thrummed against her sides. Though instruments monitored and maintained the environment both in and out of her suit, she still shivered.

The airlock hissed as the last of the air equalized on either side. Then the door crawled open, revealing a pack of clay-armored krillids standing on all fours in neat lines.

Though Manassa knew the yellow eyes were now full of intelligence, they looked like the same animalistic ones who'd stared at her before they'd grown sentient.

Clarice lifted a placard upon which she'd inscribed the krillid symbol for welcome. The krillids drew back into a circle and put their heads together, a habit formed from the need to communicate in a vacuum.

Manassa held up the symbol for friend. Again, the krillids chittered in general discussion. The two species stared at one another for several minutes, then the krillids came forward.

The scout of first contact made stunted approaches toward Manassa and Clarice, while the rest of the pack shuffled a short distance behind. Moments later the scout crept centimetres from Clarice's foot. It leaned in, and pushed its head onto Clarice's ankle.

It spoke for a few moments. Clarice gaped.

"*Waifa*," she said, the word for friend. The krillid jerked its head back and turned to the others. They all charged.

The one nearest Clarice scooped beneath her and propped her up on its back as others clustered around to create a bed, a chittering chorus of *Waifa* in reply. Clarice leaned back giggling.

In a moment the krillids had carted Clarice off into the time conservatory, and surrounded Manassa. They laid glow globes at her feet in the outline of the Fist of Fatima, then dug their claws into the floor.

"They're celebrating!" Clarice shouted, laughing within the time conservatory.

Manassa tested a few of the words she had translations for, and the krillids tittered in excitement. Unlike Clarice, the krillids never touched Manassa, instead laying numerous things at her feet, which she picked up tentatively. When she smiled, bowed and said thank you, they rapped their claws on the floor. She took this as a form of excitement.

Clarice came back to the airlock beaming. "They're so gentle!" she said. She bent down to one who clutched her suit leg.

The krillids seemed... all right. Manassa exhaled and opened the external door to the whoops of the krillids. She closed her eyes and prayed she could get them ready in time.

The krillids stayed in the staging area outside the airlock, chattering to Clarice, who brought props to provide structure to her lessons. Manassa continued to have things brought to her feet, which she segregated in her office. In a few days she had filled the space. She was astonished by how generous the krillids were when they'd been deprived of so much.

At 10 in the morning—the morning before the rabbi's visit in the afternoon—Manassa came into the lab carrying her lab book in quaking hands, muttering about all the angles she could take to elucidate the krillids' value. *Her* value.

Krillids formed a ring around Clarice. Her face glowed. "I can understand them!" she cried.

"What are they saying?"

"That they've watched you for a long time." Clarice furrowed her brow as she listened to one of the larger krillids with a marbled carapace. "I guess the glass coating disappeared pretty early after we overrode the safeguards."

Manassa frowned, kicking the latest rocky gift laid at her feet. What did that mean?

"Their ancestors passed down legends of your greatness," Clarice continued. She shook her head. "I can't believe this is happening."

"You can't believe they would look up to me?" Manassa snapped. She was wound tighter than a bowstring, everything around her feeling like an attack. Violence... the thing she had once abhorred, now seemed an attractive way out of this mess, a much clearer way to articulate herself.

"No... I can't believe this whole experience," Clarice said. "They're saying how much they learned just observing us once every few generations when we'd appear through the mist."

"What did they learn?" Manassa asked, treading around crowds of krillids amassing near her shins. She wanted to tell them they needed to behave, to obey, to fulfill their destiny.

"I can't understand that part," Clarice said. "But they've spent a long time getting ready for you."

"They had better be ready." Manassa stared hard at one following her every move.

Claws wrapped around her ankles. She looked around—it seemed all of the krillids had turned their attention to her. Her anger and determination were stronger than their gaze now. She curled her lip.

"Let go," she snapped, kicking off the claws.

The krillids fell off for a moment, but claws clamped back on, harder than before. The krillids edged closer, a throng of glowing yellow eyes that bobbed inward.

Before Manassa could react, the krillids knocked her on her back. She cried out, raised off the ground by a platform of krillid armour.

"Don't worry," Clarice said, "they did the same thing to me. They just want to give you a tour."

This is no time for a tour, Manassa thought. But if it kept them happy enough to show well for the rabbi, maybe that was worthwhile. So she remained still.

Manassa's eyes widened as the krillids carried her through the airlock, past the barrier and into the conservatory.

For the first time, she appreciated the magnificence of the society they'd built in meagre conditions. They had intricate tunnels carved into the rock, structures they'd erected to withstand the quakes, and protective berths shielded from radiation. It was all astonishingly advanced.

All because of Manassa's steady guiding hand. Maybe they knew this, and were thanking her. Manassa felt confident in her superiority over them. She was their master.

A moment later and her suit vanished. She smelt and tasted copper. Her heart pounded, but she repeated inwardly there was nothing to fear from them—she had given them everything they had, and they knew it. They must know it.

They brought Manassa before a caged area which contained ornate carvings and a statue behind a triangle grid of bars. Manassa frowned, a sliver of recognition in her temple.

When they began to push her in, the fear and menace of all those haunting yellow eyes came rushing back, twisting her insides. She pushed away from the entrance with her foot, but the krillids pressed on, piling up beneath her until she tipped in. She scrambled for grip, then tried to reach into her pockets. She realized all her belongings, including her phone, had been removed.

She fell to the ground, choking on a mouthful of acrid sand. Her heart hammered. The gate slammed shut behind her, ringing. The krillids whooped.

"Hey!" She turned to see the krillids scuttling off the colony, capillaries collecting into an artery heading out of the conservatory.

Manassa screamed for fairness, for mercy. She shouted until she drowned out the wailing airlock siren.

A few minutes later, the airlock door shut.

Days passed. Manassa quickly discovered the cage was a shrine to the Fist of Fatima, with frescoes of it all over.

It was also a shrine to *her*. The ornate statue was carved in her likeness.

Her statue carried, in its right hand, a Fist of Fatima burrowing into a wide crack in the ground. Inside the crack the krillids had carved countless writings. In the left hand, the statue let a sculpted water drop dangle from its hand into the mouth of a waiting krillid.

The krillids had, after all, known Manassa's importance in their lives.

She grew delirious with hunger and thirst that lasted days. The paste they gave her only sated her for the minutes it took her to devour it. She imagined choking them, snapping their necks and pouring the blood into the bowl she drank from. Each time her visions grew more vivid and she felt stronger, more powerful, above the cage she'd been put in.

At some point past the disappearance of her time awareness, the krillids came into the lab on the other side of the viewing window, from which Manassa had watched them evolve. They typed with surprising deftness, but too slowly for her to see what they intended. She fell in and out of consciousness with her face pressed between the bars.

Then the swirling cloud of the time barrier appeared.

First they burned her, heating the sand beneath her until every touch scalded. They stopped before her insides cooked.

The second visit they tried to drown her, filling the cage with water so high Manassa could only breathe through a few millimetres at the top, millimetres robbed when the earthquakes began.

The third visit they stopped giving her paste and left her to starve.

When the vomiting started, Manassa feared she'd gotten radiation poisoning, but it passed, and a new cycle of torture began.

When they entered, she screamed at them that they were meant to go to the stars. That they were denying their purpose. That she'd made them who they were. Her voice sounded years older, not her own anymore.

Her fractured mind struggled to find meaning between the periods of intense suffering. She wondered if the Fist of Fatima had expelled God's gaze from her, both evil and good.

She couldn't think of what they were doing with the time conservatory. They weren't accelerating time for her, because then she would have had more reprieve between the tortures.

Her thoughts ran no deeper than this before the next round of torture began.

One day, the torture took the form of anticipation. Manassa huddled shivering and starving at the back of the cage, her mind only capable of wondering what new tragedy awaited her.

A procession of krillids came into the chamber, their armour carved with the same symbols Manassa recognized from the shrines. Between them, wearing clothes embroidered with those same symbols, came Clarice. Her small stature had hidden her amongst them.

The krillids parted, and Clarice approached the cage. The bright red Fluvog shoes seemed to Manassa to be stained by the blood of the krillids she'd imagined killing. They glowed in the weak light of the shrine. Manassa smiled.

Clarice lifted her bowed head, then her face fell. "My God, Professor. I'm sorry."

Manassa said nothing for a few moments. Her eyes flicked between Clarice and the krillids, wondering what new torture lay in store. "Tell them they need to go to space," she whispered hoarsely.

"I've been negotiating my way in here, Professor. The whole committee has," Clarice said, frowning and ignoring Manassa's request. "The krillids wouldn't let anyone near you. They said it's their religious right, part of their rituals. I think they've reversed the time chamber so time is slowed for you, so you will last longer. They... they think you're their God, Professor."

Manassa's head felt light. Her vision swam. God? All the pains of her body, her rusted joints, her burns, the water in her lungs... for God. The broken links in her mind started snapping together, and she twitched unconsciously.

Clarice chittered to one of the krillids, then one of them opened the cage.

"They've argued heatedly with what they learned from you: that cruelty needs to be unleashed and focused in order to allow compassion to breathe. We've been negotiating for so long to try and make them see otherwise. We couldn't barge in here and attack them—I'm sorry, I couldn't justify any more killing. We had to work to a diplomatic solution. But I'm finally here to get you out. I've talked them into enacting cruelty on... symbols instead of you."

Manassa imagined life outside the conservatory. Free of flood, earthquake, flame, pain, suffering. Free from the krillids.

"Committee?" she asked.

"Huh? The rabbi's committee? This is no longer research, Professor. The krillids are a society now, to live amongst us. You don't have to see them ever again if you don't want to, though. Come on." Clarice bent down to Manassa's level and extended her arms.

Manassa gazed down at her hands. The scars on her body were marks of her importance. Her purpose. Her state of being, finally realized for its grandeur and significance in the universe.

"Leave me." They were the first words that felt strong coming out of her parched throat.

"What? Professor, I can't leave you here." Clarice's face was laced with compassion, the same compassion that would again rob Manassa of her purpose if she let it.

Not this time. Manassa hobbled to the statue of herself and caressed the Fist of Fatima pounding into the cracked earth. "Go. My place is here. They need me. I'm not leaving."

"But Professor..." Clarice's voice faded as the krillids picked up on her defeat, and dragged her out. Manassa was barely aware of this as she pictured the next service the krillids would hold in her honour. The next time for worship. She would taste her own blood then, the sweet gift of faith she'd given to the krillids. The value they recognized in her.

Manassa fell to her knees, then onto her back. Tears in her eyes made the stalactite reflections seem like windows to the stars.

G is for God

C.S. MacCath

If Katus watched the sun set, a red stain slipping over the rocky lunar plain of the dome, if he stood transfixed like a tourist by its white companion shining in the distance, he might ignore the way people were staring. An artificial breeze lifted the perfume of the flower garden below. He leaned over the parapet and breathed it in. *A small, pure memory for a mind unworthy of it.* Somewhere in the outskirts of the Capèmont binary system, the Sun Thief was besieging the most formidable military in known space with all the patience of an indestructible sociopath. Here in the capitol habitat, Katus was bearing the infamy of his siege and all that preceded it, nearly a millennium of piracy. Shoulders squared, he turned to face the foot bridge, and a crowd of frightened civilians recoiled like prey from a raptor's talons.

All except a pale young woman in the vest of a judge's page, who was biting a full bottom lip, head tilted in his direction, a faint admission of sexual interest. Another time he might have charmed her with a flash of white teeth behind a tight beard, an inquisitive lift of the brow over gray eyes, a subtle toss of blond hair. Instead, he proffered a rueful smile, head tilting in return. Her interest soured to disgust, gaze dropping to the blue sun emblazoned across the breast of his dress uniform. He nodded, smile fading. *I might have ordered you chained to my bed for that look, might have told these people to do it.* Guilt gripped his gut like a poison. *And they would have.*

A stout woman of late middle years hurried toward him from the direction of Capèmont Seat. Stripped of the Gronsavet archemos, she was still a miner's daughter who had sworn to fight for her people and looked the part. Yesterday's blouse stained with coffee. Slacks that might have come from a company store on her home planet. Boots because pumps fall off in a low-g mine. Strong hands reached for his own. "They should have assigned you a security detail."

"Archem Sidet." Katus took them into his own, glad of her touch. "It's all right. The Menèllan Gallery is well-guarded, so I spent the day there." *Marveling at the canvases of the masters. Wondering what you really want of me here.* "You should have sent a page. When was the last time you slept?"

"I'm not on the payroll anymore. Call me Imion." She freed a hand to wave in dismissal. "They're ready to meet with you now." Imion Sidet led him back toward Capèmont Seat, tucking his hand under an elbow as if to make sure he did not go astray. "Thank you for doing this. I can't imagine what it must have cost you."

"Far less than I deserve," Katus said, throat constricting around the words.

They crossed the foot bridge and skirted the fountain, splashing and filled with colorful fish. The path continued through a stand of black trees bearing glossy, indigo blossoms. Cultivated natural beauty was a conceit of Capèmont culture; every planet, moon, and habitat was a thoughtful integration of landscape and technology. Even the guards on duty outside the Seat's renowned alexandrite doors were enhanced in ways that preserved their humanity.

Strong, fast, and smart, like every one of their fellow soldiers, which is why the Sun Thief claimed to be content with Gronsavet while his spies probed the rest of the system for weaknesses. Katus uttered an introspective grunt and tightened his grip on Imion's arm. *Is this what she wants, for me to play the heroic traitor who prevents the fall of Capèmont by convincing the Council of Archemi not to give him her planet?*

She stopped and patted his hand. "Are you sure about this, young man?"

"I'm older than I look," he replied, abstracted, turning the question over in his mind. *Surely not. She has nothing to gain from wish fulfillment, and neither do I.*

Imion eyed him sidelong. "Is it true what they say about frozen clones and cognitive transceivers? Could you jump to a new body if this one died? Have you done it before?"

"Yes," Katus murmured, stepping in front of the woman to scrutinize her face; the faint color shift at her jaw where the beige of cosmetic foundation met the ivory of skin, the bleed of lipstick into the lines around her mouth. "Are you a self-aware simulant?"

"She forgives you, you know." The Imion simulant brushed a fall of indigo petals from her blouse with a flick of the wrist. "*'Cleanse the way between you, that the water of humanity might remain unpolluted.'* Writ of the Elements, Verse 17."

"That scripture is about atonement, not forgiveness." *Now I'm arguing theology with a simulant. Nobody deserves that. Not even me.* The face of a similar construct came to mind; that of the pale, young page who had viewed him with such disgust a few minutes ago. Katus gritted his teeth, tugged the uniform jacket from his body and tossed it against a tree in sudden frustration. Crimson twilight settled over his white silk shirt like a cloak. "In any case, how could she? How could anyone? The Sun Thief kidnapped Capèmont's children, stripped the system down to its bones, siphoned its suns until they were black dwarves depleted of even their diamonds…"

The simulant interrupted, rebuking him with the exasperated tone of a prison warden impatient with her charge. "Do you think about yourself in the third person, too? It's unbecoming a man about to die. Have some dignity. Take responsibility for your crimes."

"It isn't that. I just...don't know who I am anymore." Katus turned into the breeze, blinked away tears. After a moment, he bent down, gathered a handful of petal-strewn mulch, and brought it back to her. "If you were human, I would ask you to touch this, smell it, and tell me if it makes you feel anything." Pensive, he let the mulch slip through his fingers. "There's a portrait of a woman in the gallery modeled after an actual portrait lost in the fall of the capitol, painted with oils so thick they were still drying after a hundred years. It's...I don't have the words, but all I want to do right now is stare up at that woman's lovely face." He flattened one hand, palm down, below the other. "But underneath all that; the paintings, the sunsets, the gardens, the touch of your hand is an ocean of regret and remorse so vast I will *never* be able to fathom it." The Sun Thief smirked and shook his head. "Justice Odern was a cruel poet. She gave a chemical conscience to a sociopath and sent him off to die among the memories of his victims."

The Imion simulant knelt and brushed her fingers over the ground, brow furrowing. "You don't have to keep taking those injections; only the first was mandatory. You don't even have to keep running this simulation." She rose and went to retrieve his jacket. "You're only obliged to stay alive and aboard the Bahlonet until it passes through the event horizon."

Katus laughed, a rough, wild sound like the cry of a gull. "Yes, because cognitive transceivers *might* be a myth, but the judge couldn't take that chance with a man who uses stars to power ships, so she sentenced me to die in a place even light can't escape. You'll brief her about my mindware soon enough though, won't you?" He snatched the jacket from her hands and slipped it on. "Cleverly done, that; waiting until the empathy drug took effect, distracting me with a simulation full of hostile constructs, and slipping me probative questions I wouldn't answer during the trial. Too bad I'm not in a position to hire an interrogator. What's really going on here?"

By way of answer, Imion gestured for him to continue down the path. Twilight faded to darkness across the dome, and a row of street lamps brightened the way before them. They approached the faceted doors of the Seat, glittering darkly in the lamplight. On the left, a square-jawed woman regarded Katus with a perfect lack of emotion radiating keen revulsion. On the right, a shorter man softened before the former archem's simulant with a deferential nod. White-gloved hands opened the heavy doors in unison, and Katus followed Imion inside.

Capèmont Seat was a showy architectural display of system wealth; mosaic floor tiles made of precious stones, onyx pillars, opalescent moonstone walls, high windows set in gilded casings. Once an extension of the Menèllan Natural History Museum, the entry hall was a command and control center now as it had been a decade ago during the fall. At the end of that bloody invasion, the Sun Thief had murdered the archems here with his own hands and fed their butchered bodies to his wolves in a public N-cast. *All except the original Imion Sidet, who went home to defend her beloved Gronsavet after the Council of Archems gave it to me. Ironic that, and miraculous.* The remembered stench of offal made Katus gag, and the tide of that terrible ocean rose like a tsunami over a mind already battered in the service of two masters. Falling hard upon his knees, he crumpled forward onto the floor and began to sob.

At length, the tide receded. Katus clambered unsteadily to his feet, stifling a volatile emotion he could not identify, probing the edges of his emotional acuity. *Two hours until the next injection. Three until I don't want them anymore. How long until my body is ripped apart by gravity tides, and I no longer have to worry about my mind?*

The Imion simulant handed him a handkerchief and waited while he mopped his face and blew his nose. "The original Imion Sidet sends her apologies. She wanted this simulation to be a gift of mercy, a chance for you to visit Menèllan City as it was before the fall, but I've been ordered to repurpose it."

"Repurpose it? For what reason?" Katus pocketed the handkerchief and swept his gaze across the entry hall of the Seat, still wrestling with a profound inner tumult. An ambient transmission array of his own Sul Fleet dominated the space. Behind it, a tall, balding construct in the stripes of a Capèmont general watched the ships with a blank expression. He was alone, but the simulation had been designed to include others, including the archems. The seven remaining Capèmont seals hung above an equal number of provisional N-com stations. Photographs and votive offerings decorated a corner shrine bearing the knife, candle, cup, and stone of the Holy Triumvirate. A smell of burnt coffee hung in the air, and a table along the far wall was cluttered with picked-over sandwich and pastry trays.

The general saw them and lifted his hand in a beckoning gesture. Imion nodded in reply and asked for patience with a raised index finger. She turned to regard Katus with a dispassionate gaze. "After consulting with the doctor who prescribed your medication, Justice Odern ordered me to create a scenario that would place you at odds with your own people for the sake of a greater good. If you responded well to it, and you did, I was ordered to ask for your help."

"My help?" If they had been voices, the clamor of emotions that followed this pronouncement would have deafened him. "Are you manipulating me?"

"You misunderstand. It's…"

"Shut up." Eyes lowered, teeth clenched, Katus backed away from her. He found and counted a spiral of azure floor tiles between them, affixing an emotion to each one as if the borders of those small, physical objects had mental equivalents. After a moment, his breathing slowed, deepened. Rubbing his face with both hands, he puffed out a sigh and said, "This drug only enables me to feel. It doesn't teach me how. So I'm at risk of becoming overwhelmed and going numb to compensate, which isn't much different from what happens to children who develop the sociopathy I was born with. Push me too far, and you won't get anything but a Sun Thief who doesn't give a damn no matter what you inject him with." Katus reached out, took Imion by the shoulders and stared down into her wide, gray eyes. "And I *want* to grieve. It's the only atonement left to me now. Please don't take it away."

Imion reached up and laid a hand on his cheek, an expression of human warmth so tailored to Katus' emotional needs that he wanted to slap her hand away. "It's your Second, Anku Disamalo. She's taken command of the Sul Fleet in your absence and attacked the Herungan system in reprisal for your trial and sentencing. We can't stop her without you."

Where the gilded window casings met the moonstone walls, there were flecks of gilt missing, Katus saw. Beneath the gold was only wood, plain and vulnerable to rot. He lifted Imion's hand from his face with a thumb and forefinger as if he might be removing a parasite and went to examine the window casing more closely. *Did Anku threaten Herungan before or after the empathy drug was forced upon me? And was the original Imion's claim of forgiveness genuine, or was her gift an emotional goad?*

Katus raised his voice and called back to the Imion simulant. "Have you consulted my legal team about any of this?" They had been his own people, hand-selected.

"They've been missing since the end of your trial. We have reason to believe they fled from your Second," Imion said. "You've been appointed a counselor and have the right to speak with him if you want."

"No thanks," Katus replied, and snorted, shaking his head. There *was* rot in the window casing, a softness in the wood beneath the gold. Unusual for the controlled climate of a lunar habitat, but there it was, a memory of the thing as it had been before the fall. He stared out the window at the lamplit night and crossed his arms. "I'm not acquainted with the original Imion Sidet and don't know what to make of her forgiveness or her gift, but it's been my experience that forgiveness is a pabulum for perpetual victims who don't have the stomach to demand atonement. The gift is too perfect a backdrop for my self-excoriation, so I don't much credit the claim that you repurposed it." A construct in formal dress hurried down the path outside, coattails flapping around his legs, a brightly-wrapped box tucked under his arm. Katus wondered if the box was empty. "So the moral ground in this situation is certainly uneven, but none of it is high, and your necessity doesn't offer any greater absolution than my hunger for power does. Still, if you can prove to me that Anku is on the offensive, I'll help you stop her. I'd rather not heap any more deaths upon this chemical conscience of mine."

Imion went to examine the fleet in the ambitrans array, making no pretense at a suitable response to these accusations. Katus rolled the tension out of his shoulders and joined her there. The Capèmont general stepped aside to give him a better view. At some undetected signal, the showy seat of government connected to the bridge of a Herungan heavy cruiser called the Dankammen in a shared N-cast. A half-moon bank of heads-up displays were the only light in the darkened space, leaving it still bright enough to make out faces, uniforms, and paths to the aft lift. On a central platform above, a tall, wiry man Imion identified as Captain Nevenigt monitored his own display and conversed sotto voce with his subordinates. They responded in the same tone, presumably communicating via military implants.

Captain Nevenigt addressed the Imion simulant and the Capèmont general in a raised voice. "Good. You've come. Let me know if he gives you something."

The general drew Katus' attention back to the ambitrans, pinching at the array with his fingers and thumb to zoom all the way out. Blue-white Herungan shone fat and energy-rich at the center of a vast, empty space. Near the outskirts of the system, three small habitats and an interstellar EME Gate huddled far away from the seething inferno and solar radiation of a star even the Sun Thief held in awe. "Your Second is concentrating her forces on the gate, near Ersona, here." He pointed at the rightmost quadrant of the array and fanned his fingers to zoom in again. "It's the closest planetary habitat to the gate and populated primarily by workers in the transportation sector, who operate and maintain it."

The Sul Fleet was settling into an orb formation around the gate. Half its heavy cruisers faced inward, gunning down the Herungan ships unlucky enough to be caught inside it. The other half fired outward from the formation, defending the ground the fleet had gained. Smaller, swifter Herungan strikers and Sul eclipses clashed around the heavy cruisers on both sides of the conflict. Blooms of fire erupted in the spacescape.

"The skirmish at the gate is just a distraction." Katus' face and hands prickled with sudden anxiety, a sensation he could not recall having ever felt before. He pinched the ambitrans as the construct had done and refocused it upon Ersona. "This is what Anku wants."

"Then why isn't the Sul Fleet there?" The Capèmont general peered at the planet. He was not richly programmed as the Imion simulant was; a key difference between the two kinds of artificial intelligences. Restricted cognitive ability. Limited human affect. He didn't even smell like a man.

Katus wondered who was driving him. That was often how it worked. Probably a young Herungan officer somewhere. He shook the prickly sensation from his hands, wiped them on his trousers, and explained. "If she takes the EME Gate, she'll have to defend it against Herungan forces and whatever help they summon from outside the system. But if she takes Ersona, Herungan will be forced to stand down and deal with a hostage crisis. Given her current foothold at the gate, that buys her time to plan further ingress into the system." A rising dread prodded him forward, around the construct, toward the Dankammen's captain. "You there! Listen to me."

Captain Nevenigt tilted his head, brow lifting, but did not turn away from his display.

Katus approached the platform, stopping a few paces away and backing up a step when the N-cast blurred, indicating a non-shared zone. "Tell Ersona to secure its life support, power, and transportation hubs at once. Anku has people on the ground there, and she's hoping to take hostages."

The captain cast a disbelieving glance over Katus' shoulder, waiting for some corroboration from the construct and simulant.

Katus raised a hand and snapped his fingers in front of Captain Nevenigt's face, heart beating as if a beast hammered within, demanding acknowledgment. He pointed at the man's badge of rank, voice low and threatening out of old habit. "You are a waste of that uniform if you don't do as I say, right now. I know my Second. She'll use the hostages she takes to keep possession of the gate and capture the other Herungan habitats. Move!"

Nevenigt moved, but with the same spare purpose he had demonstrated before. In the far curve of the half-moon bridge, a stocky young officer followed suit, and it soon became clear that he was online with the Ersona habitat.

Imion slid forward to stand at Katus' elbow and ventured, "Is there some other way to stop the Sul Fleet? Your Second doesn't seem like the sort who gives up easily."

"She won't move in-system if she can't hold the gate." Katus followed the ongoing battle from the ambitrans, now hanging in the aft left corner of the bridge near the lift. Anku's orb formation was a bristling knot of havoc, sending eclipses out like whips to harass the Herungan heavy cruisers, forcing the strikers into defensive positions around them. The Dankammen itself shook with weapons fire, so much that he began to wonder if the N-cast might abruptly end.

An hour passed. The weapons fire decreased. The Sul Fleet's eclipses returned to their various mother ships, and the battle fell to a standstill.

With visible relief for such a reserved man, Captain Nevenigt bent forward to lean on the platform railing and folded his hands. "The constabulary at Ersona just arrested four people inside the central power station and two more outside a sector life support hub." His mouth pinched in a faint expression of distaste, as if the words that followed were regurgitated from his stomach along with a mouthful of bile. "Thank you, Sun Thief. We have it from here. You may go."

The shared N-cast disconnected, and for a moment Katus could see the great, empty hold of the Bahlonet before it transformed again into Menèllan City and Capèmont Seat around him. He took a breath, closed his eyes, and felt...less, on the whole. It was seductive, that diminishment. He wanted to follow it all the way back to the man who had built the Sul Fleet and commanded it for centuries. Instead, he pulled the injector from his pocket, held it to his neck, and pressed the trigger. The instrument hissed. "Every twenty-five hours for the rest of my life," he reminded the Imion simulant. "Two doses left. Do I have enough?"

"You do, but there's a supply aboard the ship as well." Imion took a breath and bit her lip, watching him with the air of a woman who wanted to broach a difficult subject.

Katus could not bring himself to give a damn what this simulant tool of the enemy was thinking or feeling, and he was medicated to give a damn now. "I'm going to pray." He gestured at the altar and then at the picked over food trays. "Are those real?"

"No," she replied in a too-bright tone, "but I can bring you something to eat. Any requests?"

Katus went to the altar and floated his fingers over the candle flame. It was hot, and the wax smelled of spice. "Whatever food you can find, black coffee, and a bedroll. Anku isn't out of options yet, and I want to be here if Nevenigt needs me."

His concern was clearly the opening Imion needed. "If he does, is...is there some way to disable the Sul Fleet altogether? She was hesitant, not out of fear but in the way an effective manipulator spoke when something of note was at stake. Katus himself had employed the same technique so often that her efforts sounded hollow and clumsy to his ears. "I only ask because it would save so many lives."

"Of course." A sardonic grin slid across his face and disappeared. He leaned down and touched the holy objects in turn, a best-effort invocation from a man who had never prayed before. "So you *are* self-aware," Katus remarked in a mocking tone. "How do you feel about being sent here to die with me?"

"I didn't know you were a religious man." Imion evaded the question and came to stand beside him at the altar.

"I was alive when the Writ of the Elements was a collection of theological verse passed among a handful of heretics. So I'm not religious in the way you imagine. I just find myself in need of reliable symbols right now." Katus settled cross-legged onto the prayer cushion provided. "And you didn't answer my question."

Imion crossed her arms. "You didn't answer mine either."

"No, I didn't. Now go away and do as I asked." Katus bowed his head, closed his eyes, and listened while her footsteps receded. Behind him, the Capèmont general waited inside the ambitrans like a docked shuttle whose pilot had gone to bed.

The empathy drug coursed through his body again, and with it came another tsunami of guilt. He leaned forward to rest his forehead on the varnished edge of the altar and permitted the tide to carry him all the way back. He could almost smell the rain-drenched earth of his childhood home, feel the slippery organs of animals he had defiled as a boy, hear the grieving of his plain, kind brother for one missing pet after another. Tanko's almost-pretty wife had been so easily wooed, bedded, and abandoned to bear a son of uncertain paternity to a husband who knew and loved her even so, who had forgiven Katus just as Imion Sidet claimed to have done. *Tanko knew what I was long before my parents did, spent his whole life begging me to accept a corrective implant, and his forgiveness meant nothing to me. Now it's too late to atone; to him, or Isaro, or even to Togi, who was certainly my nephew and might have been my son.*

He sat this way a long time, tears streaming down his face onto the plain prayer cushion, mourning the dead whose names or faces came to mind along with the faceless multitude crushed beneath the tread of his ambition. When the inner tumult quieted of its own accord, he rose and massaged the table indentation in his forehead. Imion had come and left him a plate of baked polenta stuffed with tomatoes and cheese. A thermos pot of coffee and a mug waited beside it on the floor next to a military-issued cold weather bedroll. Katus ate mechanically but saved the coffee for later, shook out the bedroll, and fell into the sleep of a soldier who knows he will have to wake soon, forgetting for a while that soon he would sleep and never wake again.

Some hours later, he woke of his own accord, propped himself against the wall, and drank a mug of lukewarm coffee. The Imion simulant was absent, and the Capèmont general was pacing through the ambitrans in a pattern, looking up. Katus followed the line of his gaze. Anku's orb was dispersing amidst a clutter of battle debris. He waited for the gate to open, for the fleet to begin departing the system, but it did not. His brow furrowed. *Where is she going?*

Then, with terrible clarity, he knew.

Imion bolted into the chamber, shouting as she ran toward him. "You said she wouldn't…"

"I wouldn't, and I trained her, but she's not a sociopath." Katus shot to his feet and stumbled into the ambitrans array. "Reconnect us to the Dankammen. She has explosives on the gate, and she's about to attack Ersona."

Captain Nevenigt and his bridge crew were watching a recorded N-cast when they reconnected. It was Anku Disamalo herself; head shaved, eyes pale as the light of a distant star, skin painted in dark colors. Her Sul Fleet armor shone like a carapace, and her lips were tilted upward in a black victory smile. "She who can destroy a thing, controls it. Katus taught me that."

From infancy, after I slaughtered your mother and raised you to be my Second. Katus covered his open mouth and exhaled into his palm. *Curse me for a fucking fool.*

Her posture was elegant as a cat's, perfect nails painted black and resting on the control panel in front of her, jeweled rings glittering in the bridge light of the Sutagat, the Sul Fleet's capitol ship. "You will release our lord Katus Boudiko to us, or we will blow the gate, take Ersona, and force its people to rebuild while we raid the rest of the system. Her smile widened, showing canines. "We'd be stuck here together for a time. Wouldn't that be nice? Don't think too long about it."

The recording abruptly ended. Captain Nevenigt stepped down from his platform and fixed Katus with a penetrating stare. The low buzz of sotto voce conversation on the bridge quieted. Heads turned toward the men. "We're not giving you up, Sun Thief. Herungan is small; it's why you were tried here. We've evacuated every child by mandatory order and encouraged non-essential people to leave the system. Those of us who stayed behind are prepared to die if it means ensuring your descent into that black hole."

"Give us your fleet codes." Imion finally said the words aloud, squeezing his forearm as if to implore him not to view the demand as another manipulation.

"What a coup that would be for you; to execute the Sun Thief and hobble his fleet in the same blow." Katus shook free of her grip and scowled. "No. Anku will have changed them by now, anyway."

"You have private codes." Imion proffered the speculation with such smug assurance that empathy drug or not, Katus had a sudden and vicious desire to cut out her tongue.

"And you've been trying to get them out of me since I was convicted; empathy drugs, emotional exploitation, and now this." He remembered mouths full of blood, empty of tongues, and imagined what hers would look like. "I said 'no.' I'm aware that you have no love for my people, but I do now. Ironic, isn't it?" His mouth twitched in a smirk. An officer on the bridge stifled a yawn and wiped her eyes with the backs of her thumbs. She was weary after the battle. They all were. Katus sighed, shoulders slumping, and relented. "Go away and give me an hour to think. I'll find a better way to stop my Second."

Nevenigt turned on his heel and climbed the platform, plainly disappointed, jaw clenching around an unspoken response. The shared N-cast disconnected. Katus returned to the altar in Capèmont Seat, leaving Imion where she stood. The candle was burning down, but the flame was still lit, the glass still hot. He dropped cross-legged to the prayer cushion again and closed his eyes.

This time it was Anku he remembered along with all of the children like her; the infants, the toddlers with trusting hands, the older children with soulful eyes who were already too adult to be shaped into willing crew and were instead trained for other tasks. The plain boys and girls were enslaved, but the pretty ones were given to those among his Elites with a sexual interest in children. These were groomed for obscenities that left them brittle and paradoxically devoted to the people who were raping them.

Katus began to shake and buried his face in his hands, but there were no tears this time. *Anku isn't like me. She has the conscience I was born without, and that means she can be saved.* Fingers threading behind his neck, elbows resting on the altar, he cast both heart and mind into supplication. *Holy Triumvirate, hear this, the only prayer I have ever made. Help me save Anku. She can save the fleet, and that would save everyone.*

He rose, tucked the tail of his shirt into his trousers and poured a mug of cold coffee from the thermos by the bedroll. The Capèmont general was gone, perhaps because he was no longer needed, but the Imion simulant waited in the ambitrans array. He gulped the coffee down, wrinkling his nose at the unpleasant temperature, and joined her there.

Nevenigt was not on the bridge when they reconnected to the Dankammen, but the officer at his station assured them that he would return soon. Katus and Imion waited together in silence until the lift doors hissed open and a muted light shone into the darkened space.

The captain emerged and strode over to them expectantly. "Well?"

Katus frowned, bracing for protest, and said, "I need to talk to her."

"Under no circumstances." Imion raised a hand to stop the captain from answering and spoke to him directly, any pretense of pleasantry gone from her voice. "He has a cognitive transceiver. There's no telling what Anku Disamalo might be able to do if we allow them to communicate."

Katus thrust a hand into his trouser pocket. "Either you allow me to speak with my Second, or she becomes your problem in…" he pulled the injector out and held the display up for Imion to read, "…less than fifty hours?"

The Imion simulant, confounded by this ultimatum, opened and closed her mouth like a gasping fish before abruptly pacing away to where his dirty dishes and bedroll lay on the Dankammen's deck in the shared N-cast. Eyes unfocused, mouth hanging open, she looked nothing at all like a human being for nearly a minute and returned muzzy, blinking, vexed. "The sentient AI core of the Bahlonet, of which I am a part, is preparing to transmit out via N-grid to avoid being trapped by the black hole's gravity field. Both it and I will be gone in three hours. You'll be dead in six. Please, just give us the codes."

Six hours to count the suns he had depleted, the planets he had left a frozen ruin, the unique species of flora and fauna forever lost to the universe. "Well, it seems I have little time to argue," Katus observed quietly. "So you'll do as I ask right now, or I'll return to the altar in the simulation provided me and spend my last few hours in prayer. I'm no longer inclined to be patient with your sanctimonious abuse of my guilt."

"Sanctimonious abuse?" Captain Nevenigt's grave demeanor cracked, and a thin stream of hatred trickled through. He advanced upon Katus until he might have smelled coffee on the man's breath had they both been on the same ship. "You know, I am gratified beyond words that your flesh and blood and bone are about to be spaghettified in a place where they can't defile the holy elements any longer. I only wish we could find and send your clones in after you." Gaze shifting to Imion, face set in a neutral expression that masked the misgiving in his eyes, he said, "Tell the Bahlonet to let Justice Odern know that I've approved a conversation between the Sun Thief and his Second. If he escapes, on my head be it."

Nevenigt returned to the platform, giving orders sotto voce en route. Two of his officers responded; communications and security, Katus surmised. The Imion simulant retreated again to communicate with the Bahlonet, and the Capèmont Seat simulation replaced the Dankammen in the shared N-cast.

No sense in giving Anku any more intelligence than she already has, right? Chary fuckers. Katus went to the window and appraised his reflection in the glass. The edges of his clipped beard were softening with new growth. He stroked a thumb and forefinger down his cheeks and refocused on the artificial world outside. The red sun was rising over Menèllan City, illuminating the rooftops of diplomatic seats, museums, and other buildings. It was lovely, poetic even, just like the justice of an empathy drug for a sociopath and the forgiveness of a deposed and victimized archem. It was also nothing but a memory of soft, rotting wood hidden beneath a gilded facade.

Nevenigt's image appeared in one of the N-com stations. He walked through it like a ghost toward the detritus of Katus' recent inhabitation and joined Imion there. "Here she comes," he said in a tone of foreboding. "Holy Triumvirate help us."

Seconds later, Anku Disamalo appeared in the ambitrans array.

She pivoted in a circle, a faint sneer on her face, examining the positions of ships in the Herungan and Sul Fleets. Her gaze finally settled on Katus, and she hastened to him with the same brisk, not-quite-eager step she always used in his presence. "My lord," she began in a voice disciplined not to betray her emotions, "where are you?"

Katus gasped and beckoned her out of the ambitrans. Every adult in the Sul Fleet knew that Anku loved her lord and captain, but never before had he felt the urgency of that love, that fragility, that fierceness leaning toward him like some bright but lethal flower seeking sunlight. It was intoxicating. "I'm on a Herungan ship called the Bahlonet, bound for a black hole. I've been sentenced to die in a singularity so my consciousness can't escape to one of my clones."

Anku's eyes narrowed, and her arms crossed. One black nail tapped an armored elbow, making a subtle clicking sound. "Kill yourself now, while you still can. It's the fastest way to get you out."

"I'm not given access to anything that might kill me, and besides, the Bahlonet is piloted by a sentient AI who would endeavor to block my outgoing transmission." Katus smiled, and there was warmth in it, all the warmth he could manage. "I've missed you."

Anku's eyes widened, and the tapping stopped. "What have they done to you? Never mind." She held up an index finger clustered with rings and spoke to someone not a part of the shared N-cast. "Call up a map of every black hole in known space. Ignore the supermassives. Concentrate on the Herungan neighborhood. Send eclipses to investigate each one, right now." She tilted her head in Katus' direction, finger still in the air. "What can you tell me about the ship? The size of the black hole? Anything else?"

"That I plan to die here." He lifted both hands in a gesture of forbearance at her explosive 'What?' and leaned against an onyx pillar, crossing his legs. "After my conviction, I received a mandatory dose of a common empathy drug, and it has changed me enough that I take it voluntarily now."

"That's torture. They've tortured you, and now you are not yourself." Anku's mask slipped; a rapid blinking of the eyes, an indrawn breath between parted lips. "We're on our way," she asserted, regaining control. "An eclipse can break a standard AI transmission block, but yours will be tougher than most. We might have to take the ship, so brace yourself for weapons fire. The Bahlonet, you said?"

At the best of times, she was a dark flame moving over the fleet, cleansing everything in her path. This was the worst of times. It would be difficult to redirect that fire, perhaps impossible. Katus rose, noted the fine tears limning her lower eyelids, and resisted the urge to comfort her. Instead, his voice dropped again into the low, firm cadence of command. "Anku Disamalo, I order you to withdraw from Ersona, release the Herungan EME Gate, and leave the system. I order you to, and do this next, take all of the children away from the Elites. Don't give them any more. Do whatever you must to make that happen."

"My lord would not say these things to me!" Anku's temper flared, a sure sign of her anxiety. Sun Thief and Second strode toward each other, coming face-to-face in the ambitrans array, the ships of two fleets shifting about them. Morning sunlight gleamed into the windows of the Seat, casting a ruddy glow upon the moonstone walls.

Katus remembered blood on the floor and the stench of offal. "Your lord lived nine hundred and seventy-two years by jumping from clone to clone, tank-grown and never awakened. Your lord grew his fleet on the backs of billions and plundered their cultures. The only reason your lord hasn't taken you to bed is because he knew you'd make a more obedient Second if your love for him went unrequited."

"You can have me now." Anku's whisper was replete with longing, so full it poured out of the syllables like new wine, not ready to drink.

Katus wanted to vomit. He remembered Isaro, who had pleaded for him this way and Tanko, who had covered her heartache with love for the rest of his days. "You feel this way because I wanted you to."

I don't care."

"I do." He choked the words out and gazed down at her. Rays of red light shone through the carapace of her armor, blurring it. "Anku, I love you in ways I do not and will never understand, and I am sorry that you were raised with only the self-serving affection of a sociopath for nourishment. But this thing I've done to you, I've also done to the entire fleet. Some, especially the Elites, are like me and should be dismissed. Others are like you; possessed of a conscience and the time to make better choices with it. Become the sort of person who can help them make those choices." He paused, weighing the wisdom of what he wanted to say next, and finally regarded her sidelong from beneath a lock of hair. "And fall in love with a plain, good man, if you can find one."

Anku staggered back as if the words had struck her and glanced about, seeing what he could not, the Sutagat bridge and its crew. There were tears on her painted cheeks now, emotion overtaking her steely discipline for a moment. "I can't imagine a better life than the one you gave me."

"I know, and I'm sorry for that too." Katus might have gathered her cold hands into his own, they were always cold, might have felt the precious stones in her rings cut into the flesh of his palms. Instead, he watched his Second become the Sul Fleet captain by degrees, over a matter of seconds, as she let him go.

"I love you too, whatever the reason. I always will." Back straight, Anku flicked the tears from her face and was fierce again before she turned away from him. The last words Katus heard before the Sutagat disconnected were her orders to remove the bombs from the gate.

Captain Nevenigt joined him at the edge of the ambitrans, and together they watched the Herungan and Sul Fleets begin to disperse. "I think you could have escaped with Anku's help," he finally said.

Katus nodded.

Nevenigt lifted a brow in his direction. "Then why are you still here?"

"Because I can't atone to the dead. Because I don't want for her to carry my debt. Because I hope she'll learn to be fierce for something better." Katus withdrew and slumped against the onyx pillar again, fingers curling around the injector in his pocket.

"Thank you, Katus." Nevenigt emphasized the name as if to assert his humanity.

The Sun Thief waved a hand in dismissal. "Some of the crew is bound to defect, so make certain there aren't any stragglers."

"I will," the captain replied, turning away as the Dankammen disconnected.

The alexandrite doors swung wide, admitting a trill of bird song. The Imion simulant gestured toward them. "I'll be leaving soon, but you have a few hours left. My original programmed an excellent restaurant for the sake of your final meal. Will you go and enjoy it?"

"I don't think so." A small, dun creature flew into the Seat, sweeping its wings beneath a fresco Katus had never noticed before. It was Capèmont; red and white suns, planets, moons, and habitats, all in the brightest possible colors. "I'm not hungry anymore."

"Then may the Holy Triumvirate take pity upon your soul." Imion touched his arm again, but Katus shook her hand away as he had before. She nodded as he had yesterday in response to the page's disgust and left him there, boots thumping on the tiles until she was gone.

Katus went back to the altar, where the candle was altogether wet in its glass container, a bright flame burning the dregs of fuel away into smoke. He knelt on the prayer cushion, touched each of the holy objects again, and surrendered to all the tides descending upon him.

H is for Hindsight

Michael B. Tager

In the shadow of a shallow cave high on the cliff face, obscured by devil trees, Bevin watched the knight harangue his fellows amidst the dust. Nothing grew on the sandy ground that the group stood on. Lizards scuttled after insects. Goats and scrub plants dotted the sheer walls of the box canyon.

Bevin wondered when they would go underground.

Besides the knight, there was a tall, green-skinned elf and a short, stubby goblin, both carrying bows. Beyond them, a large woman stared down the canyon's narrow pass, two nasty-looking battle-axes resting on her shoulders. To the side, another woman in a skin-tight black velvet tunic with a long, intricately carved staff and an old, one-eyed man in red bickered quietly between themselves.

Bevin toyed with the fishing rod at his belt, his eyes following the sorceress' staff, gemstones flickering in the steady sunlight.

"Dibs on the staff," Kelly said, lying flat on her belly beside him, dirty fingers drumming the rocky ground. She'd taken off her heavy leather cloak and spread it on the ground for the three of them to share. She stretched, her back reaching to the sky. Since she'd gotten her moon's blood, she'd grown long and coltish. Bevin, as he always did, looked away when she was in dishabille. They'd been friends for their entire life; it felt like watching his sister undress.

Vayle on the other hand, took every opportunity to stare at her long legs and bare midriff. He did so, looking over Bevin's head. "That's not fair," he said. "I had my eye on that. Look at the gold inlays." Vayle was the eldest, dark and sullen. His cleft chin and twisted smile garnered the village girls' attention. "What about you, Bev?"

Bevin kept his voice low. Some months ago, a different party had caught wind of them and attacked. It had been such a waste. "Let's not get ahead of ourselves. We'll see if they even go inside."

At their nod, he suppressed a sigh of thanks. He was small and homely, uncoordinated and often ill. A clubfoot kept him from honest work and watery eyes disallowed advanced schooling. If his father weren't the constable, he would have been given to the priests, likely as not. But for whatever reason, his friends listened to him.

Bevin could use a staff like the sorceress held but there was always a reason to not invest in a cripple. For a moment, he imagined how he would look to the townspeople with that staff. Why, they *all* might listen to him then.

Vayle interrupted his woolgathering. "They'll go inside. They always do."

The knight finished his speech and the others resumed their bickering, loitering and guarding. Bevin's long breath stirred a miniature dust storm that dissipated into stillness.

"What about the knight's armor?" Vayle asked. "It would fetch quite a purse."

"Who would we sell it to? And how would we get it home, if we could even find it?" Bevin shook his head at his friends' shortsightedness. "Don't get greedy."

Vayle shook his head and mumbled, "This isn't as much fun as it used to be."

"It was never fun. We're here to loot bodies."

Now the six of them huddled. Bevin wished that he could hear. Was the knight in his shining suit of burnished steel extolling the treasures inside the cave? Was he asking them to pray for their safe return? Would he change his mind if he knew how many groups had disappeared into that cave, never to be heard from again? What would the knight say, if he knew Bevin would loot his body, strip his clothes and rummage through his pockets?

Soon enough, the companions disappeared into the cave's mouth, the goblin bringing up the rear. Bevin thought again of the staff and his fingers flexed in desire. He was surprised at how much wanted it.

Vayle stood first, brushing himself of dust. "I thought they might turn back."

"I could see the pompous knight's pompous eyes. Wasn't ever gonna happen." Kelli shook her cloak free of dust. When it was clean, she bent and twisted, her muscles popping and drawing a long look from Vayle. Straightening, she unfurled the long, coiled rope stored on the ledge. The rope burned Bevin's palms when he slid down.

The cave appeared innocuous: stalactites, piles of dirt, rock walls. It was only inside, around a nearly hidden curve, that it became something else. Roughly hewn steps lead into blackness and crude wall sconces appeared irregularly. Fresh tracks in a thin layer of dust led down into the deep. In the past two years he'd never seen dust build to appreciable levels. They came with the seasons.

They loitered at the entrance until very distantly, they heard muffled screams. It never took long. Vayle and Kelli hung their heads, their shoulders sloped. Bevin wanted to acknowledge their discomfort but instead, he grunted, and said, "That's it, I guess."

On Bevin's belt was a torch, made of iron and filled with pitch. He lit it, then descended, his friends following. The staircase was long and straight and steep; after a hundred steps, the wall to their left began to fall away and his clubfoot throbbed. After another hundred, the rock wall on the right morphed to ancient brick and mortar. Beneath them, rock steps turned to stone, intricate spirals inlaid; his muscles ached with every limp. Walking was rarely easy for him, but steps, especially this many, were slow torture.

The temperature rose, even as wind fluttered their hair and brought a deep chill. "I hate this," Vayle muttered. "The old kings built too well. It smells of old evil."

"You're not wrong." Bevin remembered his teachings well: there were hundreds of ancient castles under the earth, connected by passages and portals, haunted by demons and ghosts forbidden from entering the upper world. Circles of protection and magic spells laid down by the kings of the old world kept the dungeons alive, but also sealed them away. Only those of the modern world could enter and exit at will though why anyone would was beyond Bevin.

Bevin remembered the first group he'd sent to the cave: a priest, two burly barbarians, a barmaid and a wizard. They had seemed kindly, giving Bevin a silver coin when they met him in the streets of their once-rude town, to guide them to the inn. But when he protested later upon hearing of their planned expedition, the barmaid had said, "Shush, little boy. There's nothing to be afraid of. We've done this before."

He had followed them, Vayle and Kelli in tow, approaching them at the end of the canyon while the party of strangers loitered before the cave mouth. It had been night and the adventurers hadn't waited for them to speak, but, assuming they were foes, attacked. Before Bevin, Vayle and Kelli had turned tail and ran, the adventuring wizard - short, fat and young, with billowing grey robes - had called down lightning.

The next day, Bevin and his friends returned and descended into the cave. Instead of living adventurers, they'd found a dismembered corpse, a gore-covered sword and a small bag of gold. The gold had provided for all of their families for an entire winter.

Bevin's family never mentioned his expeditions. He heard from Kelli and Vayle that their parents tried to talk them out of coming. *It's too dangerous. Stay here, in the village, there's work here*. It was true;

the location of their home was fortuitous, commerce plentiful. But still, there was something about the scavenging, the adventure-by-proxy that drove Bevin. What drove his friends, he didn't know.

As if she were inside his head, Kelly asked, "You ever wonder why they keep on coming? Do they know something we don't?" Nervously, she giggled.

"They hear about all the treasure down here," Vayle said as they neared the final step, "and they want it. But don't they ever wonder how it got there?'"

At the bottom of the staircase, he spared a glance for the row of cairns shrouded in darkness at the wall before stepping off. He stood in an ancient courtyard to a once-mighty castle that had once, perhaps, seen the sun. It was vast, an open circle that stretched hundreds of meters, ending in pitch-blackness. Legend in the village said that the unnamed castle was the oldest of all the underground castles.

He imagined what they looked like. Enormous, towers and crenellations that had once tickled the sky, now wedged against the earth's bones. Hallways and stairways would lead nowhere; new paths would have formed through the debris. A maze, an underground warren with few egresses.

He kicked the ground with his weak foot. Etched into the hard white stone, hundreds of runes bled into one another with flourishes. The village priest would be impressed they'd recognized the runes of protection. Vayle especially had never paid any mind. But they'd known what they were the moment they entered the cave. Some were as tall as he was, some as tiny as his fingernail. Still potent, Bevin and his friends were safe so long as they stayed within the circle of protection. Easy enough to do. Every meter was inscribed with runes. Up until the dark.

He paced along the circle's edge, his friends following. They searched the ground; often adventurers were ambushed the moment they crossed the circle. Some fell back, others seemingly crawled back before death claimed them.

"There." Vayle pointed just past the circle to the facedown goblin. Working together, they detached makeshift fishing rods from their belts, hooked the little bowman and dragged him closer. They were long used to the dead. Despite his evisceration, they rummaged his pockets: a pouch filled with silver, rings, a treasure map.

"Another map leading right here," Bevin said, dismissing the weather-worn parchment. It had the shaky handwriting of a revenant, scratchy and indistinct. "How do these get out into the world, do you think? I've got ten at home."

"Who knows?" Kelli shrugged and hefted the bow that had been around the goblin's shoulder. "This is yew and iron, worth something anyway."

After arranging the goblin peaceably, they continued, satisfied; even if they found nothing else, the silver and bow would more than suffice. Later, they'd haul the body to the row of cairns and bury the poor soul. Bevin wondered if, were the situation reversed, someone would do the same for him.

Nearly finished the circuit, ready to leave, they heard the scream. Vayle's hand jumped to the long knife at his belt. Bevin said, "What are you going to do? Throw it?"

They stood there, twitching, waiting for something to happen. Finally, Kelli pointed, "Look. One's alive."

The sorceress emerged from the darkness, a faint glow illuminating her, as she half-hopped, half-ran, dragging her left leg, jamming her staff into the ground and hopping along with its support. Her right hand ended in a stump, she bled heavily from the forehead, and her eyebrows were lost to scorch marks. When she saw them standing there, her eyes widened. Her lips moved, "Help me."

Bevin pointed, "Behind you."

The sorceress stopped running, her good hand gripping the staff. Balls of blue flame burst from its obsidian top, illuminating the space around her and silently engulfing the revenants in swirls of fire that vanished with the darkness's return. When the flames died, her sides heaved while behind her, barely distinguishable, twinkled dozens of eyes.

"What do we do?" Vayle asked.

"Nothing." Bevin's hand rested on his own long knife. "She makes it or not."

"Do something," Vayle said to Kelli, his hands wringing.

She nodded and, still holding the goblin's bow, nocked an arrow. Somehow, the sorceress saw her and dropped to the ground while Kelli, her hands a blur, launched arrow after arrow into the blackness from which guttural animal sounds emanated.

"Come on," Vayle shouted and hurried to the edge of the circle.

The sorceress ran, her eyes streaming. Now that she was closer Bevin noticed her beauty, high cheekbones and deep bosom. She gasped and he refocused: but her gait was hobbled, her left ankle jutting in the wrong direction.

Before the sorceress reached the circle's edge, the monsters came into the light. They were bone-white cadavers, leeched of muscle and fat with teeth filed to jagged points. They wore no clothing or armor, just tattered leathery skins. Arrows protruded from one's eye, another's shoulder. Bevin wondered if they felt pain.

The sorceress, so close to safety, reached, teeth gritted, as hands emerged from the darkness to grasp her by the forearm, yanking her back. She was inches away, then less. Vayle cursed, crossed the circle's threshold, grasped her by the waist and threw her into the light.

A second later, a dark, misshapen hand grabbed Vayle's throat and pulled him into the dark. A revenant held him close, jagged teeth glinting. Kelli launched her last two arrows. The revenant ignored the arrows embedded in its chest and lumbered into the darkness, along with a struggling, weeping Vayle. Soon, Vayle's screams sounded. When they ended in a throaty sigh, Bevin pushed away his rising panic and grief until he could feel nothing and Kelli vomited. Bevin knew he'd feel the same later. Much later.

The sorceress stood before them, catching her breath, blood dripping off her cheek. "We'll get you out of here," Kelli said, her eyes scanning for signs of Vayle.

She grabbed Kelli's hands while behind her, pale-skinned monsters milled behind the circle of protection. They were bare inches away, separated by the invisible wall of magic that had stood for centuries. "It was terrible," she said. "It was like they knew we were coming. There were hundreds of them."

"You're safe now," Bevin said. The rubies encrusted along the curves and carvings of the staff twinkled. His hand moved, as if on its own accord, yanking the staff from her grasp. She fought back and in the brief moment it took to wrest it from her, Bevin turned and stumbled, only a few steps, but enough for him to feel a faint tingling as he passed through the circle of protection.

He stood motionless for a moment, perhaps two—long enough to feel the temperature drop, for his heart to rapid-fire—before a cold, strong hand touched the nape of his neck and pulled with inexorable strength. He clutched the staff to his chest, his stomach churning, bile rising, even as his body was wrenched ever further from the safety of the runes.

He fell heavily onto the cold dirt floor. "No," he said, "please." Legs milled around him as the revenants seemed to lose focus, their hands ever-grasping near him, at him, never quite touching him. His hands sought firm purchase so he could rise. One touched something wet and when he pulled it near, Vayle's unseeing eyes stared into his, his neck a stump.

He retched. The woman's staff still held in his shaking grasp, he rose.

"Bevin, run, hurry, please," Kelli called from her place of safety, the sorceress crumbled into a pile at her feet.

The monsters didn't swarm him. He breathed, took a step to the light, his feet thumping into something hard. The object rolled. He looked down.

Vayle's disembodied head moved almost lackadaisically and Bevin wanted to laugh as it passed the circle of protection. He took another step toward the light, dodging a monster's paw. He was closer. He moved again, and again, side-stepping one creature, ducking another. Five steps from safety. Four. Three. Tears built in his eyes, ready to burst. Kelli reached for him. Two more steps.

As one, the monsters stopped milling and turned to face him. One might have smiled, another might have chortled, but he couldn't be sure. He felt one grab the staff, felt the creature's inexorable strength as it began to tug. Vayle pulled and the staff came free. The cadavers circled him now, blocking his way. One, its eyes dark red and reached out to Bevin, dark long fingernails grasping. Bevin cradled the staff to his chest.

"Bevin, what are you doing? Run to us. Break through. Do something!"

He nodded, calm.

The cold hand that grabbed him seemed gentle until it began twisting.

Shush, he tried to tell Kelli, *there's nothing to be afraid of. We've done this before.* But his mouth was full of blood and distant pain. His eyes wanted to close, but he kept them open, staring as Kelli put her shoulder under the sorceress' arm, dropping the bow and bag of silver coin onto the ground.

When the pain receded, Kelli had already ascended the stairs leading to sunlight.

I is for Idolator

Jonathan C. Parrish

I love rules. There is something about them that compels me. It isn't even the actual rules, it's the following of them that makes them so particularly engaging. Having a good set of clear rules is just straight up *jammy*. It's my job, it's my passion, it's what I live for.

My name's Sam, and I am in charge of the Department of Miscellany. I have a window in my office which is nice. I can look through it. In fact, I take quite a bit of pleasure in looking through it— maybe because I just got it. I didn't have a window before the policy change but they had to move me afterwards to increase my space. Not much, there's only so much space to work with, but enough that I got this new spiffy window. *Jammy!*

Why did I need a bigger space? I know you want to know and since I mentioned it you know I'll tell you at some point, at least in some fashion, so let's do that.

The Oversight Committee decided the old irony-based system was too limiting and no longer an effective model so punishment protocols needed a general overhaul, to create a more self-directed system where the punishees could self-actualize their personal environments.

Personally, I suspect they got tired of coming up with new ideas, and the old ones started seeming stale after a hundred thousand turns or so. Not that they'd ever discuss it with me, not that I cared. *Policy* is nowhere near as interesting to me as *standard operating procedure.*

So now, instead of new entrees being assessed by performance review against a standard table they are brought in for an entrance interview, including a personality and memory evaluation. After a period of self-reflection, the interview cycle is iterated until the largest transgression is self-determined by the entree, at which point sorting to the appropriate Department occurs for awareness reorientation.

This is where my job begins, when the rules start getting applied. Everyone gets sorted, there are no exceptions. My Department was— and is—for everyone who doesn't fit anywhere else.

In the old system there wasn't really enough to do but someone had to be in charge of them, the misfits, and the application of rules was straightforward: *Experiential vignettes should clearly outline alternative non-transgression outcomes* in order to *enhance personal regret and contrition.* I had a lot of fun with these; I had a number of highly responsive units in my charge.

My favourite was Leo_1F48, who had redirected a train to reduce a casualty count and I had a lot of fun showing them all the alternatives where no casualties occurred. Good times. Anger and remorse harvests were off the scales and I always met quota. Leo_1F48 was reclassified with the policy changes, now under the jurisdiction of the Department of Dispatch. Last general meeting I asked about them, Leo_1F48 is currently getting repeatedly hit by trains and doing a lot of weeping. I'm sure someone thinks that's not lame.

I digress, so let's get back to my units. My Department is for units that fail to categorize themselves. The new procedures state that *all units must self-determine experiences in accordance with reflective practice* so my Department is tricky. *In the absence of successful reflection, no experiences can be forthcoming.* It's right there, in the rules. During my initial review of the new operating procedures I started getting worried about my job. It seemed there wasn't going to be enough to do: in fact, following procedure to the letter it seemed there was going to be nothing to do. I raised my concerns with my representative on Oversight, they told me there was going to be a period of adjustment and then they could re-assess. In their words, *Department clustering in response to under-utilization* was one possible outcome.

Then, my allocations started arriving. Shipment after shipment of them. Turns out, I had been unreasonable in my predictions of under-utilization. Oversight, despite their extensive consultation period, had not recognized the possibility that a significant number of the units *would not recognize any issue or error*. They actually constructed a new pipeline to bring my Departmental shipments in, and a new facility was requisitioned. That is what got me my new office. And my new window.

I thought I'd have nothing to do, but this is now my favourite posting. The new rules are straightforward: *Units must be recorded and placed into holding until next assessment.* The paperwork is clean and precise. I even ordered a new pen and ink to check off the box indicating "Unit arrived intact" and "Determination unspecified". I like my new pen a lot.

I also really enjoy looking out my window; I moved my desk so I can look out it while I fill out the paperwork with my new pen. The units might not be having a mandated experience, but they are not comfortable and the discomfort metrics are staggering. I have been informed that no further space requisitions will be entertained until the next review in another three hundred thousand turns. I might not be able to see very far out my window then, which will be sad.

We are allowed one personal embellishment as long as it *evokes a sentiment consistent with both the Department in which it is housed and the mission statement of the Oversight Committee* so I hung a sign outside my office door for the units to read.

It has one word on it, in big, bold letters. It says "Jammy!"

I smiled when I hung it, I like my new sign a lot.

J is for Jammy

Amanda C. Davis

Nadia had spent most of her life ignoring boys. She had school to worry about, anyway, and her family, and her books, and the occasional obsession with horses or painting or learning the guitar. But the way John strode down the hallway, the way he ran his fingers through his too-long hair... Well. She noticed.

"Hot stuff, isn't he?" whispered her sister Bernia.

"Mmm," said Nadia. She kept her voice low, just a rumble in her throat that wouldn't reach any further than Bernia.

"I can tell how you want him."

Nadia's skin reddened so fast that it stung.

"Want me to talk to him for you?" A sly offer, all mischief.

"No," muttered Nadia.

"Ah well," said Bernia airily, as if she didn't care after all. "Maybe he'll magically decide to take the first step."

John loped past, cool and smart, handsome hair in his handsome eyes. Nadia caught sight of him and stuck her hands in her locker, painfully aware of him, wanting not to be seen, wanting to be seen so badly it ached.

Just as he reached them, Bernia coughed loudly.

John swiveled as Nadia's face grew even hotter. At catching her eye, he went faintly red himself. "Are you okay?" he said. "Man, that—that sounded like you were dying."

"I'm fine," said Nadia, in a rush. "Just a little...." She tried, and failed, to make the same sound as Bernia. "Just under the weather."

"Too bad," said John. He shifted on his feet. Not quite looking at her. Not quite leaving.

Someone came past and punched him on the arm. "Friday?"

"Yeah," said John, over his shoulder as they passed. He turned those eyes to Nadia, wearing shyness like a cloud. "The thing at Hadley's barn. Friday night. Are you going to be there?"

Nadia's words dried up and vanished. Bernia gave her a hard nudge.

"Sure," said Nadia.

Relief washed over John's face, leaving it smooth and happy. "Cool." He gave her an awkward smile, like he wasn't used to them, and slouched off again into the crowd.

Bernia nudged Nadia again: knowingly, tauntingly, happily.

Nadia smiled.

"Nadia has a date," announced Bernia at dinner.

Their mother and Aunt Kee perked with interest, simultaneously. "A boy?" said Aunt Kee.

Nadia pushed around dinner with her fork. "It's just a party." She ventured a glance at their mother, who looked surprisingly calm. "We haven't even talked."

"There's nothing wrong with talking to boys," said Aunt Kee.

"No, there's not," said their mother, putting her words together cautiously. "You two are growing up. And Nadia, I know you'll be careful."

"Hey!" said Bernia.

Their mother raised her eyebrows. Aunt Kee snickered.

"We'll both be careful," said Bernia magnanimously. "Right, Nadia?" She rested against Nadia's shoulder. "What are sisters for?"

This time both women laughed together: a throaty laugh from their mother and a thin, sinister chuckle from Aunt Kee. "Trouble, mostly," said their mother, looking fondly at Aunt Kee. "But you'll be safer with your sister around."

"Have fun," said Aunt Kee, in a wicked way.

"Oh," said Bernia, sounding very much like Aunt Kee, "we will."

Hadley's barn was lit floor to ceiling with Christmas lights, but otherwise it was a pretty weak party: they had a cell phone playing music through a dollar store speaker and a table full of off-brand soda and chips. Still, it was a better party than Nadia had ever been to. She and Bernia got a soda and stood by the wall sipping it nervously and scanning the sparse crowd for John.

"There he is," whispered Bernia, her words like a crackle of electricity down Nadia's back.

He was with three or four other boys, all of them slouching and t-shirted with their hair in their eyes, but he was the only one who made Nadia's heart leap. John spotted her and peeled off from his group, after a few words and a dap or two. Nadia froze.

He approached with his hands in his pockets, nodded his head out the door. "Want to take a walk?"

Her laugh shook. Her nerves danced.

Outside it was summer-warm and autumn-dark. "There's a lake," said John, using the light on his phone to find the path. "Here." He put away his phone and held out his hand. His fingers were cool and curled around hers like a pocket.

They stopped under a solar light bulb duct-taped to a post halfway around the bank. The lake glistened where the algae and scum didn't cover the water. John faced her and took her other hand.

He's going to kiss me, thought Nadia, with a jolt in her chest. John is going to kiss me.

He leaned in, past her lips, so his soft young stubble brushed her cheek.

"Let's go skinny dipping."

Nadia jerked back. "What?"

He clung to her hands. "Come on. It'd be fun. I'll do it too."

She pulled on her hands, but he held them too tightly. Full-grown hands on a mostly-grown boy. "I don't want to," she said firmly, keeping the quaver from her voice. "Can we just hold hands a while?"

He screwed up his face. His voice went soothing. "Sure." One hand slid up her arm, down her back, around her waist.

She pulled back again. He hung on for just a moment, a breath's length that meant everything, before reluctantly letting go.

"Sorry," he said. "Sorry. I didn't mean to—we don't have to do anything you don't want to. Let's go back. It's too dark out here anyway." He extended a hand.

Relief pushed up through Nadia's chest and emerged in a breathless laugh. "Okay." She took his hand and held it. That cool and comforting pocket. Just as she'd wanted, just as she'd dreamed....

"Enough," hissed Bernia.

"No," said Nadia, "wait—"

From the pouch of skin in her side, Bernia slithered free, around Nadia's shoulder and down her arm. She clamped her suction-mouth, its funnel-tongue and its thousand teeth, to the vein at John's wrist. He let go of Nadia, spitting a garbled curse. Bernia's venom surged from his wrist to his heart and he fell like rags to the ground.

Bernia detached, squirming back to Nadia, gleeful. "So much for *that* hot stuff."

Nadia let out a cry of rage and grabbed her sister in both hands.

Bernia twisted, winding around Nadia's arms, hissing furiously. It was like fighting a fire hose. Nadia grappled and clawed until she got lucky and pulled Bernia off her. She hurled her sister to the ground.

Bernia rolled, muttering darkly.

"He said sorry!" Nadia shouted down at her, through stinging tears.

"He scared you," said Bernia.

"He said sorry." It was all mixed up now, sweet hand-holding and being held too tight. She wiped her cheeks, one after the other. "I liked him."

"Nobody hurts my sister."

Nadia closed her eyes. She felt dull, with only her own senses, and confused, with only her own memory. She picked Bernia up and tucked her under her shirt. Soon her hands stopped shaking. Bernia was right: John was hurtful, or would have soon been hurtful, and she could not trust herself to see the world clearly on her own.

Bernia squirmed gently, settling into place, and latched into Nadia again with a sting. "Don't tell Mom. I want to keep going to parties."

"Yeah," whispered Nadia.

"There will always be other boys." Bernia nudged her. Warm and familiar and more intimate than anyone would ever be. Could ever be. "Let's go talk to Ryan."

They left John by the lake, and went back into the party together.

K is for Kin

Lilah Wild

Sunny yellow. Bright orange. Mint green. Cozy little houses stood in a manicured row, their porches laden with handicrafts. Every door was open in welcome.

Sky blue. Brick red. Soft purple. Couples on a small-town vacation, local families out for the day, all strolling the winding brick paths of the Village Shoppes, water ice and soft pretzels in hand. Everywhere, fripperies: stained-glass lamps and fringy silk scarves, handpainted marionettes and specialty olive oils, embroidered dog collars and glittering candles, a shop dedicated just to Christmas. And fudge. There was always at least one place that sold fudge.

Hot pink.

Confections was nestled between Ye Olde Ice Cream Co. and Wheelhouse Pottery. Its window was graced with a silver satin torso dressed in the siren call of a red lace negligee. The tinkle of tiny windchimes greeted all who entered and presented a world of blush and cream, silks and fishnets, smooth jazz and good lighting. The walls were lined in tissue-thin nightgowns and sheer robes, while shimmering cinchers and bustiers hung from circular racks along the shaggy purple floor. Further back, the nuts and bolts of bodysuits, hosiery, and replacement garters waited in calligraphed white drawers. Here and there, a gilded cherub nocked an arrow down at the customers. Ava had thought they were goofy, way too much, you'd *never* get away with anything that twee in the city, but Opal had always been a needler, and even steely Ava only had so much patience.

Three folding metal thrones sat clustered behind the register, for three sisters.

Ava, the oldest, presided over Confections in smart blouses, tailored pants, and a pair of cateye glasses that hung from her neck on a beaded chain. She was the kind one, or the one who at least *seemed* kind.

Opal, the middle child and merchandise buyer, clad herself in only the most luxurious velvet tracksuits, and rhinestones sparkled from her hands and smartphone. Opal told it like it was. Loudly and frequently.

Baby Casey wore jeans and a ragged flannel, managed all of the stock, and sat slightly behind her sisters, usually silent, all wide and somewhat unsettling eyes.

Long, sharp fingernails on all three of them.

Before them, on the left side of the counter, a purple pillar candle burned. It gave off a sweet fragrance, not the expected drama of rose, but the lighter touch of passionflower. Passionflower—how on-point it sounded when a customer asked what it was, how well it fit for the shop, not like Opal's tacky cherubs, no, this had class. Oh, it's passionflower. Yes, isn't it *lovely*. And the implication was left to linger, the flower of passion, surely that conferred some powers of romance, or at least really hot sex.

But it didn't. It was true that the little starburst of a flower had an entry in the herbals of old enchantment, but not for love. Its properties encouraged friendship. If this had been the genuine aim, a pink candle would be greeting the shoppers. But purple meant domination.

Overpowering. For the purposes of Confections, faux camaraderie did just fine.

The chimes sang.

A tall brunette stepped into the store, and went right for the nighties. Her face was pale, and long curls fell down her back, which was slightly hunched, her posture apologizing for her height. A sensible little purse matched sensible little flats, couture. Money. Ava swooped in.

"Welcome to Confections. Is there anything I can help you with?"

"Oh, I'm just in town for the day." A shy little smile.

"Oh! Are you here on vacation?"

"I came with my husband on a business trip."

"Ah. We have plenty here to spice things up. Although, looking at you…" Ava put on her glasses, ran her eyes down and up the woman's figure. The stomach was always the first place to target. "I've got just the thing."

She led the brunette to another rack, and pulled out a lacy white bra. "This will instantly make you look like you lost ten pounds."

The brunette's mouth dropped open ever so slightly, a flash of hurt in her eyes—*I didn't know I needed to lose ten pounds*—before she eagerly took the hanger. Ava suppressed a delighted shudder, seized the moment and quickly followed up with three more bras, ensconcing the woman in the dressing room. That was an easy one—no need to push harder with suggestions about age-appropriate lingerie, or how men got bored so easily, the things you had to do keep them satisfied. More than once, Ava had found herself behind the heavy velvet curtains, playing soothing therapist to a customer sobbing away on the hassock, knowing full well that Opal was leaning back in her chair to eavesdrop, salivating over every gory detail. But now she walked around the shop, gathering more suggestions in her arms while Opal paged through a wholesale catalog and kept her beak out of it. Out-of-town customers were great—they were more likely to go for impulse purchases. That, with the juicy pocket of insecurity she'd just sniffed out, maybe there was some marital trouble after all...Ava wondered how big the imminent sale would be.

Five bras and a frilly robe later, the brunette was on her way, a cheerful pink bag emblazoned with CONFECTIONS in her hand.

"Check out these pasties," said Opal, from the counter. She held up the catalog, opened to a page where rows of round breasts modeled red satin hearts, holographic stars, sparkling tassels. Opal's finger was pointed at a cleavage that sported two orange balls of fluff, each one festooned with a pair of googly eyes.

Ava grimaced and shook her head. Casey glanced at the page, popped a piece of gum in her mouth, and smirked.

"Could you imagine?" said Opal. "Some stripper coming out on stage—oh, excuse me, *burlesque artist*—someone so desperate, she's gotta jiggle Muppets to turn any heads. *Ugh.*"

Exotic dancers did come into Confections from time to time, but found their business coldly dismissed. The cherubs were saccharine, but they were on-brand. Lucite heels, micro-bikinis, savvy women who were not easily pushed around...no.

The little bells announced the next customer, who came right up through the racks to the counter, getting right to the point. Her bulging tote bag was bright with floral watercolors, as were her stilettos. Not loaded, but she cared about looking nice. She was short and plump, with bobbed blonde hair framing a complexion of dark gold and a radiant coral smile.

"Hi! I need to get some shapewear, my daughter's quinceañera is next weekend."

Ava smiled, all benevolence. Another easy customer, who was already worried about her figure, already primed. After the stomach, the thighs were next. "Right this way. We have girdles in a variety of skin tones, something for everyone." She plucked a pair of tan high-waisted powermesh shorts from a drawer, but the blonde shook her head.

"I don't need anything that extreme, more like just a slip, something to smooth everything out under a sheath dress." *I'm happy just the way I am, thank you.*

Ava surveyed her customer, sent a crease of doubt through her features as she swept her eyes over the woman's midsection, planted the seed. "Of course. But just try these, I insist." She removed her glasses, and leaned in, conspiratorially. "I wear them myself."

And she did. Right at that moment, in fact. Ava would not sell a constrictive garment to another person that she would not wear herself. In this, she was honest, and the intimacy turned real, for just a few seconds.

"I can find you a slip, but I'm sure you want to look your best for your daughter. Mother of the princess, you'll be in a lot of pictures that day."

The blonde squared her shoulders. "No, really, I—"

"And you know how people are, on the internet," said Opal, looking up from her catalog, pointing a rhinestoned claw at the shorts. "You'll get that girdle, if you don't want nasty comments. Think of your kid." Opal could be an enormous thorn in Ava's side, but she could be counted on, when needed.

This one, Ava could tell, actually bought that line from the soap company about beauty coming in all shapes and sizes, chirping empowerment while hawking cellulite cream. The blonde's mouth tightened as Ava watched her try to stand her ground, try to summon some response against all the warmth, caring, *concern* that Ava was bearing down on her. A loving family photo, so easily turned into a cruel meme—a happy day was turning dark fast beneath a small cloud of paranoia.

Casey blew a bubble, and gawked. Three against one.

The blonde's shoulders crumpled as she took the shorts. Ava led her towards the dressing room, the velvet darkness hiding her twitches of pleasure.

The soundtrack lapsed into vintage female-fronted pop, and the candle danced. *Thank you,* Ava mouthed toward Opal, who shrugged and turned the page onto a row of garter-belted waists.

Soon, another pink shopping bag disappeared out the door. A small one.

Ava walked around the store and straightened a row of peignoirs. Everything orderly, nothing sticking out. Much like how she sized up her customers, honing right in on the flaws. There was always something that needed fixing: a little cinching there, a little padding there, a little lacy something to perk up a sagging relationship. Confections, yes, little solutions coated in sugar. *Improvements.* She untangled an errant thong and breathed in the soft floral scent from the candle, let it weave a gentle aura around her, *I'm just here to help you…*

The chimes focused her attention back to the door. Bronze skin, long bangs bound in braids, scuffed boots and a worn crochet hobo bag. Broke. But then again, you never knew. Festival kids often had trust funds. Although their fingernails were not usually rimmed with gray.

"Welcome," said Ava. "Are you looking for anything in particular?"

The girl smiled and shook her head, drifting over to the negligees. They were the first rack that drew so many of the customers, long and luxuriant with decadent fabrics that invited the hands. She ran her fingertips down the tiers of a black gown, surprisingly polyester, but so, so soft. To dress in it would be to step inside a rich, silky dream, Ava knew, unable to resist a try-on herself when it had first arrived at the shop. She bit back her reservations about those dirty hands—she could come back with a steam-cleaner later—and lit into the girl with a warm smile.

"It's something special, isn't it? The voluminous cut also hides figure flaws."

The girl looked back at Ava, her eyes dipping down and back up. "I don't care about *that*," she said, with a small laugh.

Ava took a step back and blinked, not used to being the one judged, and glanced at Opal. This one was going to be a little more difficult. She put on her glasses and readjusted her pitch.

"Ah. Well, it's a little bit of indulgence for a special night. Do you have something to celebrate? An anniversary?"

"This is for *me*," the girl said, taking the nightgown down from the rack and draping it carefully over her arm.

Opal watched from behind the counter, and Ava wished she'd cut in with a remark, but she stayed as quiet and useless as Casey. Out of habit, Ava swept her gaze over the girl's body as she wandered the store, sussed out the holy trinity of problem areas. Her little potbelly protruded from the waistband of her jeans. but that was not to be solved. Nor the thighs, which could always look better squeezed into control hose. No one was ever perfect.

The girl drifted by the counter, on her way to the dressing room, when she paused to look at the candle. Her eyes stopped on the flame as she inhaled the fragrance, and Opal finally spoke up.

"You should check out the underwires while you're here. Your bra isn't offering you enough support, I can tell." The breasts, last. The most intimate correction was always saved for the end. Opal's gaze flickered down to the girl's chest, and back up to shrug knowingly. *Hey, I'm just stating a fact.*

The girl's eyes narrowed, and they all knew she'd been pushed too far. Sometimes that happened. It would just mean a one-star review somewhere online, responded to with eyelash-batting confusion over the customer's anger, and a sweet statement of treating everyone at Confections with respect and appreciation.

She turned to face Opal, whose expression remained smug, no apologies.

"You sell beauty by being so *ugly*," said the girl, her voice frosted with disgust.

The black nightgown was quickly hooked onto the nearest rack, nudging aside a couple of g-strings, spurned.

"Wheelhouse Pottery, next door?" she continued, flinging her braids out of her face, and coming up to Ava. "I just started there. We're going to be neighbors."

Ava and Opal both stared at her. Casey blew another bubble as she stared at her sisters.

"So, I'd say it's nice to meet you, but it's not." She started walking towards the door, shook her head and came back. Before anyone could stop her, she leaned down, her clay-caked fingers on the counter, and blew out the candle.

The smell of extinguished wick bled into the air, along with a little smoke, and Ava glanced at Opal. Opal looked back, and they were both momentarily speechless. The scent of passionflower dissipated as the spell broke, unveiled their forms, revealed three faces ravaged with eternal starvation. Three sets of talons that eased elastic into place, straightened bra straps, descended on goosebumped flesh with measuring tape. Three pairs of eyes that gorged on downcast lashes, reddened cheeks and nervous little sweats, pervasive modesty at the evaluations of a stranger. The dressing room behind their chairs, a soft mauve cocoon of velvet and discretion—their banquet hall of luscious, endless anguish. The soap company and the beauty magazines and the fashion billboards ensured that they would never, ever go hungry. For harpies hungered forever, and the best food was whatever could be stolen from another mouth.

Great and terrible wings rose and flexed like rotted leather behind each sister, as a noxious smell seeped into the room.

"See you," said the Wheelhouse girl, flashing a sign against evil like an occult middle finger as she strode out the door.

Casey burst out laughing.

Her older sisters both turned around to glare at her, but she looked from one to the other, and laughed some more. She'd always been the most honest of the three, never sugarcoating it with a veneer of politeness, how much they all couldn't stand each other. She got up and wound her way backwards around the racks, her wings knocking into the bustiers.

"Tightass Ava, trashy Opal. She called you out, didn't she? I like her."

A female vocalist wailed from the speakers about *love, love, loooooove* as Casey reached up and grabbed a cherub, a gilded baby about to strike with an arrow, and aimed it at the counter.

"Pow-pow, Opal! The wounds of ecstasy! Here, catch!" And she threw it across the store, Opal scrambling and breaking a talon as Casey rummaged in the pocket of her flannel.

"She's always been such a fucking *brat*," said Opal, tenderly setting down the cherub and picking up the lighter. As the passionflower once again filled their air, their wings receded, as did the awful funk, but Ava felt the pangs of her appetite. Always. The two sisters settled back onto their thrones as the third stepped onto the porch and lit a cigarette, and all three impatiently waited for their next snack to walk through the door.

L is for Lingerie

Sara Cleto

The girl had black hair and eyes like unwished upon stars—shining brightly in hopes that someone might count them. The clatter of her footsteps on the marble floor made her wince, jaw tightening and releasing with each motion. Still, she walked steadily towards me, her back straight, her hands clasped demurely in the folds of her skirt.

She stepped lightly onto the dais and perched on the stool before me, her fingers digging into the velvet cover. "I've heard of you, you know. Even where I was born, far away from here. People tell stories about you. How you break proud women and teach men to start wars. How your voice is like music and how it never goes away for long." She paused, pressing her lips together nervously. They were red where she had bitten them. "I love my husband. I love peace and a green countryside and dancing. Please. Leave me alone. Don't talk to me or dream for me. And, please, do not tell me I am beautiful."

I looked at her and saw that all she said was true. And I saw that alongside her happiness was a hollowness carved from the uncounted stars in her eyes. Her stiff spine spoke of reprimands, and her small feet arched in shoes designed to make her look taller, leaner, harder.

This girl was wrought of wishes and wanting.

I felt light gleam within me, shine off me, as I gave her face back to herself in a perfect reflection: raven hair, bitten lips, nervous fingers.

"Oh, but my Queen," I murmured, "you are *fair*."

They say that a bitter old hag made me. Her hair had been black as ebony once, but it was the color of month-old snow when she gathered sand from the beached wreckage of a ship (there were no survivors when it splintered on the rocks hidden beneath the water) and melted it in a fire fueled by rotting seaweed and carrion bones. As I burned into being, she crackled a curse of destruction. My glass cooled under an imperative to shatter lovely things—prosperous kingdoms, loving marriages, beautiful men, and strong women. They say she hung me in the castle she had hoped to make her home, in the main hall in full view of the throne. They say she spat on me to seal her will and wiped her filthy sleeve across the glass to polish me to perfection.

The girl came back. It took more than a month, but she came back. This time, she wore a high collar and gloves, concealing more skin from my gaze. Her black hair was piled high on her head underneath her golden, starry crown. She sat on the stool and looked at me. Bruised-dark smudges under her eyes gave her face a haunted cast.

"I told you to leave me alone. Not to talk to me."

"But, my Queen, I have," I told her. "I have been silent since you last were here."

"I thought you couldn't lie? You must, because you are in my dreams. You hang on all the walls and your glass stretches in all directions under my feet."

"Yes, but I have not spoken. I have not told you of your beauty, your husband's devotion, the adoration of your kingdom for its new queen."

"But you are always there, watching me."

"I am a mirror. I watch. I reflect."

She gazed at me, at herself for a long moment, her hand going to her hair. Then, abruptly, she ripped her hand away, rose from the stool, and walked out of the abandoned throne room. Her heels on the floor cracked like opening doors.

Sometimes, they tell another story: they say that a king made me. He traveled across the sea and under a mountain to meet the princess, the only heir of her father's throne. When her father died, she sat beside her husband the king on their royal dais. She would gallop through fields and trot through city streets, learning from her subjects and listening to their songs. Her husband spoke encouragingly of the nursery (still empty) and the bright, airy room filled with spindles, harps, and other instruments for silenced women. She laughed, and rode again. And so the king gathered those untouched instruments and placed them into a large stone basin. He unstoppered a black bottle and slowly poured a viscous liquid over them. The harp shivered, spindles spun widdershins, threads tangled, and an empty birdcage slammed shut. The black liquid spread and spread, coating each writhing dainty, until all was the uniform shade of India ink. The instruments stilled for a heartbeat, then shattered, black cracking to reveal a silver sheen, and melted into liquid and smoke. The king poured the mess into a frame, let it set, and then presented the newly-minted mirror to his wife, who never rode again.

The girl sent men to pull me from the wall. Ten soldiers in all, muffled in breastplates and helmets. Gloved fingers pried at the corners of my frame, and chisels chipped away at the stone wall behind my frame. When I did not budge, they poured a bubbling acid into the gap between my body and the wall. It sizzled and sang and dispersed as smoke, leaving only a sweet smell, like overripe apples, to show that it had been applied. All ten visors turned away from me throughout the rather embarrassing episode, so I could not see the wishes in their eyes. But I could still hear them rattling against that silly armor.

I told them stories to pass the time. As their hands slid helplessly against me, I crooned them the death of Elena I (drowning, by her own hand), Richard IV (sword wound, by his daughter), Blanche II (poisoning, unknown). Modestly, I refrained from sharing my involvement, at in least in full.

It never looks well to boast.

My favorite story is rarely told. A young girl, poor but beautiful as the most beloved stars, loved a boy. When he left her to marry a baronet's daughter, she cried. She cried and cried and cried, until a pond spread from her knees. Still, she cried, until a lake lapped up her thighs and across the valley. Still, she cried, until a great river poured from her eyes and rushed into the ocean. The boy and his wife's fine tall house was swept away into the sea, and when the girl heard of their misfortune, her tears ceased, and she laughed. The laugh ricocheted off the water at her knees, seasoned the salt, and hardened into a large round oval that sank to the bottom of the river, where it waited, glassy and still, drinking up the girl's sadness. It was pulled, a hundred years later, from a mound of salt, the only defining feature in a wide, lonely desert.

After the soldiers' failure, the girl came to see me. A sturdy ax with a rough, wooden handle filled her fist.

"I thought I could ignore you," she told me, hefting the ax onto her shoulder. The splinters in the wood caught on the fine lace of her dress, ripping the fabric to reveal skin smooth and pale as snow.

"Many have thought so."

"But you fill my dreams. My courtiers ask me about you." She swallowed, throat digging into her high collar. "My husband wants to know the things you whisper in my head at night. He looks at me like he thinks I might..." she gestured wildly with her free hand, "interrupt dinner to smash all the china. Or strangle him with my bridal jewels. Or slaughter village girls and bathe in their blood, like some kind of ghoul!"

"But my Queen," I said, "you are pale."

"I've always been pale," she snapped.

"Perhaps some rampion and wild greens would put color into those lovely cheeks. Or very rare meat."

The girl screamed and slammed her ax into my glass.

Before the girl came, long ago, there was another girl. A girl with raven hair, snowy skin, lips red as if she'd drunk fresh blood. She had a mother and then a stepmother. She was hunted and stalked and killed, but she survived it all. In time, she came back to the palace with a handsome prince and a deep knowledge of her own reflection in glass (a long sojourn in a coffin with nothing else to do ensures this). At her wedding, she watched her stepmother dance to death in iron shoes, and she gazed lovingly at me every day until she died with those shoes on her own feet.

It did not take long.

I laughed and gave her face back to her, a perfect reflection.

There are hundreds of stories that tell who wrought me from glass or sand or iron or tears. They tell these stories so that they do not have to tell what came after.

The next day, the girl came back. She wore a plain wool dress and sensible boots. Her wedding ring gleamed on her finger.

"I am leaving. *We* are leaving. The kitchen beneath this room is burning, and soon this entire castle will burn. Every servant, every child, every man and woman who lives here is already gone—there is no one to hear you.

"But my Queen. Your wealth. The seat of your power. This is the only place you will ever be Queen. This is the only place you will ever be courted and counted."

The lonely stars in her eyes pulsed once. "That may be. And I will miss the weight of my crown and the love of my people. But I will spend my life and my wishes far away from here."

She walked away from me, and I felt heat from the stone floor rise to caress my glass.

They say the castle here was beautiful and proud but that a rot ate at its heart until the kingdom crumbled. Only scavengers and travelers pass through this land now, and they give the charred ruins a wide berth. If they make camp and sleep too close, they hear a voice in their dreams.

"...the castle..."

"...the mirror..."

"...come to me, you are so beautiful..."

Someday, one of them will come.

M is for Mirror

Alexandra Seidel

I met him in a dark alley, a shady bar, a crowded nightclub where the light hit him from behind, fanned out around him like a shroud; I met him on a sunny afternoon, I met him when the earth still smelled of rain, I met him strolling home from church, a serene smile on his face, bright as any halo saint-makers could dream up.

I wish it mattered where I met him.

But let me give you context. I read a lot. I read oh so much. I am a librarian. No, that's a lie, I work in my uncle's book shop. Wrong again, he never had a book shop, and I never had an uncle, just strange aunts. But I do work in a coffee shop. It's close enough. For a long time I thought that I was falling in love with him and he with me and that things from there on out would be perfect.

"Good evening," he said. He had my name by then, he had my scent I'm sure. Did he smile? He must have. You never trust anyone that doesn't smile. I said it right back, good evening to you.

I was, at the time and more so now, too old to be single. Other people said that. They said, in Asia they'd call you a leftover Christmas cake or something. I smiled. It was a joke after all.

Well, my thoughts are all over the place. Forgive me. Could I please have some water?

So. I thought we were becoming a couple. But at the same time though, I don't know. I look back, and... I don't know. I can't put my finger on it. Something was off. Nothing more than that. And nothing less.

...so. He would meet me. He would say, "good evening," and I would say it back, and he would come in. Come into my apartment. It was just what we did. I don't even remember when it started.

Is... could I please have some more water? I'm really thirsty.

We were sitting on my couch, or maybe my kitchen table. I didn't really ever own a kitchen table, there was just the living room table. That's where we must have been sitting then. It's all such a blur.

I think I cooked for him. I mean, cooked for us. I would have lit candles and put on some music, I remember wondering what kind of music he liked. I do remember cooking.

I think we had dinner. We would have had dinner if he came over in the evening. It's what you do, right? So that's what we did.

What? Why do you want to know the color of his eyes? What's wrong with you to ask someone that? Can't I just... you came to me, you said being in here would be so much easier if I talked about it. Why do you want to know the color of his eyes? Please can you get me some more water? My throat feels so goddamn dry.

So. We had dinner. We had dinner every night. We'd talk, we talked so much. We probably moved to the coach at some point. You know, the dishes were always, always done in the mornings, so he would have done the dishes. He did the dishes, we continued talking while I dried, and then we moved to the couch.

Being with him was... you know, it's so weird. You talk to your friends about all of that, right? Like, when he makes a move or if he's a good kisser. Tina was my best friend, actually. She complained to me at some point that she had never met the guy, that I talked, but didn't really say anything much about him. Or something like that she said. I always woke up in bed, and... well, I guess we would have. It's just... he was always so very sweet. That one morning, there was a little bit of blood on my pillow.

I really do appreciate you getting me the extra water. These people here say I can't really be as thirsty as I am. They don't always give me as much as I feel like drinking. I'm constantly thirsty, so thank you. This is really a relief... Oh would you? Just a little more then.

That one evening, he took me out. I'm sure he took me out before, but that time I remember. It was a very strange place we went to. The whole place was almost empty, and I didn't see why it would be. They had perfectly starched white table cloths, perfectly folded white cloth napkins, and it's a Saturday evening, and there are just a handful of people there? A chic place like that? He said, "It's a relatively novel place, those of a more refined taste have yet to discover it." That's how he spoke. Always like that. He was so charming.

They had a special menu, you know, like handwritten on thick paper that feels soft and smooth in your hands, and you are worried about somehow leaving a stain on there from your sweaty fingers. There were all these meat dishes on there. I haven't eaten meat in years, stopped when I was barely a teenager. But he said, "just taste it. Open your mouth and let your tongue do some exploring, you will enjoy the sensation." I ordered the steak. Can't tell you what came over me. And then, when the waiter asked how I wanted it, I didn't know because I don't know about how you cook meat, and he just... he said: "pink and juicy for the lady."

I don't remember what he had. I frankly don't remember him eating. I do remember that he talked to me, he talked all night. I just listened to his voice, not even the words so much. When the waiter brought out the food, I had to concentrate, cutting, chewing, not spitting it back out again, but swallowing it. His voice was so very soothing throughout.

Look, I have no idea what came over me. The next day I was violently sick, and all that came out was pink and juicy. I'm sorry to put it that way, it was not a pleasant experience. I don't remember anything of the rest of the night. I called in sick the next day.

I was losing a lot of weight too. Tina got very concerned then. You look like hell, she said one day when I hadn't seen her for two weeks. What the hell is going on. And she took me by the arms and shook me. Gently I think. She meant it to be gentle.

There were strange things about him. But you can only see those in hindsight. We never went to the park with a picnic blanket and spent all of Sunday afternoon dazing in the sun. He never told me about his family. He just mentioned... what did you say your name was?

Yeah, yeah, he mentioned someone with a similar name. Very much alike. I think in the restaurant, he talked about her at length.

So after that, things do get a little hazy. Tina was... Tina wanted me to be safe, I know that now. It was another week or so from when she told me I looked like hell and shook me as if she wanted to finally shake me awake that it happened.

We must have been having dinner in my kitchen. Well, we wouldn't have, I don't have a table in my kitchen, just the living room table and the couch table. He would have had dinner.

The neighbors didn't hear anything. They asked, but no one heard a thing, and it's not the kind of neighborhood where people just say that to get out of talking to the police. I remember that we had an argument, me and Tina, when she was suddenly at the door. I remember flashes of Tina's face. I remember her forcing herself into my apartment and looking him straight in the face and saying oh my god. Like she couldn't believe what she was seeing. There was a little bit of noise too. Bubbling. Like pasta sauce. Gurgling. The food was very good that night. I really don't remember that much more. You probably know what they said they found, all the evidence. I really don't want to talk about it. I woke up in bed the next day. There was blood on the pillows.

You know, I'm sorry I snapped at you before, when you asked about his eyes. I know why you asked. I don't remember his face at all, how it looked, it was like the reflection of a face in a pool of water, always distorted by ripples.

And no, I can't tell you how I met him because I didn't meet him. He just found me. One night, the middle of the night, there was that sound outside my window, and I should have been afraid, but I wasn't, and that was that. And I know you are that girl. I think he loves you, and he hates you, and he can't decide which is greater. You realize I could be your sister, that's how much alike we look, because I realized that as soon as you walked in here. I'm really sorry. That you have to go out there again, and that I can stay in here.

What? No. No, he never gave me his name. "Oh, what would I be by any other name?" he said, mused out loud kind of. I know you know one of his names, because he told me. But please don't tell me, I don't want to know. Don't tell me.

Would you mind getting me another glass of water before you go?

N is for Names

Mary Alexandra Agner

Genevieve came to me after she'd sold so many cosmetics she'd earned the company car. She said she applied because that should have felt like a win, but it didn't. And there was this man she was seeing, felt it was getting serious, but he had children. She liked kids, she said, but she'd raised hers and didn't want to do that again.

She turned out to be one of the best pupils I had: savvy, good at a bluff, already knew how to pick out shoes to make the outfit and when to slip them off because there was dirty work to be done. She'd been on her own, making life difficult for her new step-children for almost five years when I got her emergency note: a handful of pigeon feathers dropping onto my desk accompanied by the smell of burnt pastry. I told you she was good.

Message to the contrary, I doubted she needed my help. From her holiday letters, it was clear she had her new husband under her thumb and she was *this close* from getting his kids to run off to be circus performers or something equally embarrassing for him. Picturing her success reminded me it'd been a while since I'd had a student, or a husband of my own to fleece. But it wasn't just the money I missed.

What about that small European country I destabilized? That was nearly a decade ago, wasn't it? I hadn't even cackled in a while. I tried to, but it just turned into a cough. Was I ill?

I shrugged it off. There was nothing else on my calendar; I'd go rescue her. I quickly gathered my spelling bowl, sachet case of dried poisons, a handful of candles, knife, and tossed them into my Louis Vitton. I petted the bag. Black, sleek, metal handles that could double as cuffs; it screamed *don't mess with me*. Arm through the handles, I stepped across the ring of traveling sigils scorched into the slate floor of my office and followed the burnt pastry to Genevieve's home. Poor little student, I'd just have to save her from her success.

The front door was closed and the heavy emptiness inside the foyer raised my hackles. Open floor plan. Well-stocked bar. The smell of stale cheese and room-temperature salami. Curled together in the distinct depression in the couch were a scarf and a tie loosened but not unknotted.

I waved my wand in the general direction of the tie, tracing its outline in the air, muttering under my breath. The paisleys from the necktie wiggled off the fabric and began to float toward the kitchen. Only then did I see the doorway tucked away beneath the sweeping staircase to the second floor. I raised an eyebrow. How did I miss that? But as the paisleys wafted closer, they paused, confused. The door was magicked to stay hidden but it stood wide open.

I peered inside. Large oak desk covered with glass. Pair of hardback chairs. A row of filing cabinets. A wall of windows through which fell the afternoon sun; I could feel their magick from here, static-electric like most illusion spells: no one was ever going to see through them from outside. I sniffed. Cologne.

I pulled a tea light from my bag, lit it with a moment's thought, and chanted briefly over it, dropping small bits of nightshade into the flame. Through the colored smoke, I saw thin bright lines, like lasers crisscrossing a bank vault. Traps.

I'm too old for the acrobatics of younger witches but I can do ominous levitation as well as any. I swirled up, cackling—not coughing—and grinned. Then, sighing my disappointment, I waved away the ashy, roiling fog beneath me just in case it would set off the trap magick.

I soared into the room, spotted the broken glass next to the filing cabinet and set myself down nearby. Mmm. Knees didn't like that. I bent down stiffly and sniffed the glass: an old fashioned, very likely what Genevieve would have made for her husband. She had followed him in, then. But did she drop the glass? Or did he?

I hitched myself up to sit on the filing cabinet. No alarm. Seeing the future requires a bowl of water, but a bouquet of deadly plants— dried doll's eyes, desiccated wake robin blooms, preserved blossoms from the angel's trumpet—would show me the past. I spit onto my fingers and then sprinkled the saliva over the bowl's contents.

I half-heard the sound of a cell phone ringing. A pale, glowing version of the room's door opened and a translucent outline of Genevieve's husband stepped in, talking. I can't make out his words— the past usually mumbles. He walked to the windows, looking out. Translucent Genevieve came in, glass in hand, watching her husband and smiling slightly. Such a cat-with-cream grin—that's a new look for her—what's she up to? She stopped by this filing cabinet. He turned around, yelled, threw down the phone and rushed toward her, pulling a wand from his suit pocket. She laughed and threw the drink in his eyes. He roared, grabbed for her wrists and missed. She dropped the empty glass as he waved the wand and they vanished.

I slid down from the cabinet and, fingers tight around my wand, reached for the glass. Nausea. I knew a full-body transportation spell when I felt one. When it released me, I stepped back, grateful there was a wall to catch me. Dark rock, dark rock, the smell of iron, and Genevieve. Her white pantsuit embroidered with golden ravens wasn't even smudged. How does she do it? Even after all these years I stick to black.

"Oh, Mal, you made it! I wasn't sure you'd be able to understand my note."

That stopped me mid-stride. She stood still, too, not coming forward for a crones' kiss.

Nonplussed, I looked around. The rough rock gave way to slate floors, gargoyle sconces, volcanic altar: a typical warlock's lair. Genevieve stood near her husband's body—knife handle visible in his chest—but a good meter away from the spreading pool of blood.

She was wringing her hands. "I need your help with the body, Mal."

"Genevieve—"

"You'll be so proud, Mal. I can run my husband's business better than he can, I've been cooking his books for months, but he wouldn't put me on the board." She grinned at me. "So—"

"You called me just to dispose of the body?"

Genevieve wrinkled her nose, looked side-eyed at the corpse. "It's so cold, Mal. I can't bring myself to touch it." She glanced away, swallowed. "And he's heavy."

I walked closer. Genevieve watched me, stepping back slightly as I came forward. I knelt, knees creaking, and mumbled a small spell to determine time of death. As I shaped the words, Genevieve cursed aloud, breaking my concentration and stopping me.

"No spells, Mal! What are you doing?"

I looked up at her, regretted the crick in my neck stood, and said, "Just trying to understand what's going on."

Genevieve smiled, smug. "When he wouldn't put me on the board, no matter the charms I used, sexual or magickal, I realized he had a ward. Which meant he was a warlock. But it wasn't at the house and it wasn't at his office. And, of course, if he'd been hiding his magick from me, he was probably also hiding his lair." She showed me the two cracked pieces of a white stone in her palm, some white residue. "So I needed him to bring me here. And, well—" she looked down at the body again. She shrugged. "He wasn't amenable to my ideas."

Then she cackled. Long and full-throated, just about perfect for a mature antagonist.

Up went my hackles.

"I did it as well as you could have, Mal—"

"Well, I don't know about that." I paused after I cut her off. *This* was what I had been missing. Confrontation between student and teacher, stereotypical but invigorating. I was breathing heavily with excitement and needed to disguise it, so I laughed a little, carelessly. "You've left traces of your magic in his home office, not to mention the smell of bourbon staining the carpet. His coven could probably do what I did and figure it out. Probably." I coughed haughtily. "And the teleport on the drinking glass, I'm surprised that hasn't caused you any unwelcome visitors yet." I raised my tone at the end, looked around casually as if I expected to find someone new there.

Genevieve wilted slightly with each word and I felt a surge of triumph inside. She was going to fly back to her little nest like a good student.

Then she took a deep breath and addressed a point over my head. "None of that matters. I can clean those up once the body is gone. And you're here now—"

"Because you want me to get rid of the corpse?" More fire in my question that time, more displeasure.

Her lips twisted. "Yes." Her spine stiffened to steel but her voice came out sweet and pleading, "That's what mentors are for, right?"

A touch too high-pitched but very close. Though I wasn't going to tell her that. She'd have to do better, though, to seduce me into doing her bidding. Dragging away dead bodies is for *minions*. Who did this girl think I was? And who did she think she'd become?

I felt the blood rise in my cheeks, I felt my own spine stiffen. She wanted me to do a minion's work, did she? She wanted the Queen of Darkness to stoop below her and haul off a carcass? Well—and I cackled on the inside—let her see what she would get if we went down that road. I have decades more experience at being the antagonist. Just ask anyone from that small European country—what was its name again?

But I made my voice quaver, faked being placated. "Of course, Genevieve, of course. Just let me see—" I fingered my wand as I knelt again.

Genevieve stepped away, monologuing to the broken stone. "I've smashed him to dust, just like this, and next I'll smash his coven, and I'll grow his business—*my* business—and smash my competitors—"

I rubbed my fingers through the blood, stealing its fading power. No more student, no more little bird. Time to crush her wings if she wouldn't stay in her proper place. I cackled, long and full-throated, my decades of evil lending texture to the rippling sound. When Genevieve swung around, startled, I was standing, my wand at the ready, her dead husband's blood about to fuel a wicked stepmother's duel.

O is for Opponent

Cory Cone

This is certain, that a man that studieth revenge keeps his wounds green, which otherwise would heal and do well. —Francis Bacon

I

Twenty-two years ago, Charles nearly ruined everything.

The Channings, who were Henry, his wife Mary, and their infant daughter, Joyce, were heading home from a visit to the new grandparents' house, where they'd enjoyed a weekend of family time, and where both Henry and Mary had been given some slight reprieve from fresh parenthood. They'd napped and napped, and the grandparents had loved and loved.

And Charles had watched it all from outside the house.

Henry's parents lived on a multi-acre plot of land that gave them the sort of privacy they enjoyed, but afforded the same privacy to Charles. He walked the grounds freely, and as long as no one looked outside, or glanced through any of the windows as he passed, he went easily undetected.

He'd not planned to spend the weekend spying on them, he'd simply been curious where they were all going, and intended to turn back *eventually*, but, on a whim, he never stopped tailing their car. An impulse, but one he followed freely, since by then he'd been ruminating on precisely how he'd kill Henry for six long years.

He watched them sleep, had stood right over the bed in the guest room, because in this part of the country folks didn't lock their doors. The room had been pale white, the blinds opened to the moon and starlight, and he could see infant Joyce, still with only wisps of blonde hair on her head, as she slept in her cradle.

He'd pressed a finger gently into her tiny palm, and the infant squeezed, but did not wake.

He knew it wasn't the right time.

The rain had begun by the time the family left for home. Charles waited half a mile down the road in his car for them to pass, before he, too, headed back. He was confident they didn't know his car. At that point in their lives, they really didn't even know him anymore. That made Charles angrier, the idea that his hate could be forgotten.

The morning sky clouded over, and before 10:00 AM it felt like night. The freeway was a puddle. As the furthest car ahead of them faded from view and no others appeared from behind, Charles acted without thinking and sped up, his headlights filling the cabin of their sedan. He saw infant Joyce, rear faced in her car seat, her cheeks pale white, her wide eyes like sapphires.

Charles clipped their tail light.

It happened very fast—the rear end careened left, and then right, and then they were cartwheeling off the road and down the muddy embankment off the freeway.

Charles immediately pulled over, heart racing, hands sweating, swearing at himself: "No, no, no! You imbecile! You idiot!" He threw open his door, rushed into the rain, and was instantly soaked to the skin. As he moved toward their overturned car, the storm winds threatened to throw him to the ground with each step. The sedan's wheels were spinning. Smoke rose into the air. The emergency lights blinked yellow into the wet, glistening grass.

He peered first through the cracked windshield, and saw that both mother and father were unconscious, or appeared to be, their arms dangling limply toward the car's ceiling. Despite the rain and wind, he heard the infant crying.

She's alive.

Charles pulled open the back door and looked at her. She was securely strapped into her car seat, and though shaken, appeared completely unharmed. He placed his palm against her chest and then cautiously pressed the release on the straps. She fell to his palm, and he scooped her into his arms, leaning over to block her as best he could from the rain.

There came a thud from the front of the car. Mary had woken and freed herself from her seatbelt, tumbling down. Henry, too, was coming to his senses, and working at his belt. Mary's door opened. She crawled out into the muddy grass, whimpering something that might have been a prayer, her blood streaked face washed clean in the rain. Headlights bloomed in the distance, cascading her shadow a hundred feet toward Charles's parked car.

Charles approached Mary and knelt beside her.

"Are you all right?"

"God, help us," she said. "My baby…"

Charles held the child out, and Mary held her against her breast, weeping.

"She's okay," said Charles.

She looked right at him, but it was too dark, the light of the approaching vehicle too bright, and Charles knew that she did not know who he was. He said, "Someone hit you. They drove off."

Mary hadn't heard him. She'd fallen to the ground, the child in her arms.

Henry crawled from the car, stumbled to his wife and child. He saw Charles, but also had no idea who he was, or that he was responsible for the accident. "Thank you," he shouted over the rain, then put his arm around his wife.

Charles said nothing more, and ran back to his car.

"Hey!" he heard Henry call after him, but he didn't turn back. It had been too soon. He'd acted rashly, without thought, and he was angry with himself. He had to get home, to forget that his had ever happened.

The headlights in the distance belonged to a large truck, and it pulled over. As Charles drove off, he watched in his rear-view mirror as a man wearing what looked to be a cowboy hat stepped down and approached the frightened family, an enormous black umbrella held out in his hands.

II

"You got whiskey back there?"

Charles poured generously and handed the glass to Henry. Henry took it, sipped, and made to head back to his seat, at the table directly beside bride and groom, but stopped. He turned and stared at Charles.

Charles stared back, and for the first time in a while, he felt *truly* old. Looking at Henry was like looking into a mirror. They had, after all, grown old together. Through every important event in Henry's life, Charles had been there in the shadows, and Henry had never known. But maybe, somewhere buried in a long ago memory, he recognized the man who hated him.

Henry smiled. "This is a hell of a good whiskey." He tipped his glass, and then returned to his seat.

It was time to eat. The catering company brought prepared plates to the table of the bride and groom, and to the parents, but the rest of the party would have to go to the buffet in a specified order. One of the guests, a portly man named Robert who preferred chatting with the bartender than any of the others at his table, was among the first to be called to eat, but rather than go for food, he made his way once more to the bar. Charles had a can of beer waiting for him.

"Thanks," said Robert, and though he was clearly drunk, he appeared to still have his wits about him. "Might call it quits after this one."

"Are you driving tonight?" asked Charles.

"No," said Robert, chuckling. "I have a room at the hotel. I'm not a maniac."

"I ask because I care."

Robert saluted him, strangely. "A good man, you are," he said. "A very good man." He meandered back to his seat, without even a glance at the food table, and settled back into his chair, and, if Charles was seeing this correctly, fell promptly asleep.

It took some time, but eventually everyone had their food. The catering company (of which Charles's bar services was associated) stuck around an additional forty minutes for anyone who might want seconds, and to serve an ice cream desert, before packing up and stealthily loading their supplies into the truck. When Charles had a lull in guests at his bar, he assisted them, to expedite the process, and by the time he waved off his food service companions, the space the warmers had been occupying beneath the rain tent had been converted into a dance floor.

The floor was slow to fill, but the line at his bar grew long once more, and as the drinks flowed and the music played, people loosened up and began to dance. Before long, it was time for the father-daughter dance and everyone formed a circle around Joyce and Henry. They danced to *Butterfly Kisses*.

Charles wanted to puke.

It seemed his sentiments were echoed, literally, by one of Joyce's cousins halfway through the number, when, quite suddenly, she backed away from the circle and vomited into the rain. Charles saw this from the bar, and allowed himself a smile. A group attended to the ill cousin, and it seemed that neither father nor daughter noticed. Meanwhile, the cousin, a young girl whose beautifully salon-done hair was being destroyed by the rain, now sat on her knees, hurling a second time. Some of those around her looked worried.

The dance ended, and everyone cheered. When Charles glanced back toward the vomiting cousin she was gone.

As he made change for a guest purchasing three beers for his table, someone vomited onto the dance floor. A gasp cascaded through the party, loud enough to beat out the music, and several guests rushed to this person's aid. Joyce had seen this one, but appeared committed to not allowing it to bother her. She returned to the dinner table, where her new husband was sitting. He looked pale as chalk, and was trying to tell her something, but have a hard time of it. Then he leaned forward and puked onto the table. His vomit was thick, shades of red and black speckled throughout.

Charles could smell it from the bar.

There fell upon the guests a sudden silence, almost a quiet and mournful sense of understanding, and then each and every one of them followed suit, in a grotesque display that reminded Charles, in its intensity, of a well-choreographed fireworks display—slow to start, but rolling toward a monumental crescendo, and becoming a work of art.

Even the DJ, having been served a plate—gratis—fell to his knees, clutching at his throat, and then his stomach, before coughing blood into the air and falling over. Not long after he went down, the music stopped, and the night filled instead with the cries and coughs and gags of the dying. It was a disgusting sound, not at all what Charles had imagined, and he found himself wondering where the *screaming* was. But, he saw now that when one's body is expelling so much energy just to survive, there simply isn't enough left for a good, solid scream. And the vomit, so black, so full of blood and bile, must be doing a number on the vocal chords. Where he'd expected screams, he got instead a wretched sound, like a hundred cats coughing up hairballs at once.

And it was fast, so fast he wished he'd timed it. It lasted five minutes, at most, before no one was left upright. Plenty in the party were still alive, crawling weakly toward some loved one of another, clawing at their faces, their throats, but many, so many, were already still. Charles walked out from behind the bar and waded through the dead and dying guests, toward Henry's table. Henry was on his back, his suit stained with vomit and blood, his eyes bloodshot, bulging...and moving. My God, thought Charles—*he's still alive.* His wife had collapsed onto him, her dead body contorted around his, tangling him, and he was trying with what strength remained, to free himself from her, to crawl toward...where?

Charles followed Henry's weak gaze.

He was trying to get to his daughter—*the woman of the hour!*—who, miraculously, was also still clinging to some shred of life. Barely.

Charles knelt beside her. Her make-up had smeared on her cheeks, her hair was thick with blood. The grass around her head shimmered with spent food, alcohol, and vomit. She was trying to say something, and Charles leaned in close to listen. But it was pointless. He couldn't make out a word. He smiled at the girl who, so very long ago, he had rescued from an overturned car off the freeway, and ran a finger tenderly along her cheek, over her lips. As he did, fresh tears budded along her eyes, fell crisscrossed to the grass. He let his fingers linger on her lips, then looked at her father.

Henry had freed himself from his dead wife's grasp. He was watching Charles from where he lay, unable to move any further. His body convulsed, as if touched by an exposed high voltage wire. The poison had reached his heart.

"No," said Charles, leaving the girl. "Just a little longer, Henry," he said. He grabbed Henry's jaw, getting a real good grip. Blood pooled in Henry's mouth, flowed down his cheeks and over his ears. "Hold on...just a moment longer."

Choking, Henry looked, finally *looked* at Charles. "...it's...you."

"Yes, Henry," said Charles. "It's me." He forced Henry's head to turn, so that he looked not at him, but at his daughter. He wanted him to see it happen. She had moved a little closer to her father, had even managed to reach toward him, just a little. Now, she too began to convulse, her limbs shooting out from her sides in a final, spasmodic death throw.

Charles felt Henry's muscles relax, and he looked at the man's face. "Not yet!"

Henry's daughter's movements slowed. Then stopped. When Charles looked down at her father to gloat, he saw that Henry was dead.

Charles stood up and wiped his bloody hands on his pants. The rain had stopped. Water dripped from the edges of the tent, otherwise, the night was silent. Somewhere far off, he heard a frog croak.

At a nearby table, the man who had fallen asleep before dinner was watching him. He had at some point in the evening removed his coat and white button up to reveal a Hawaiian shirt. Charles walked over and joined him at the table.

The man, Robert, lifted one of a few clean glasses of water from the table and took a timid sip. He set the glass down. "Are you going to kill me?"

Charles shook his head. "No," he said. "I don't think so."

They were silent a while.

Robert said, "I feel like I should call the police."

Charles nodded. "Go ahead."

"Would that make you angry?"

"No," said Charles. "It would not."

Robert retrieved is cell phone from his pants pocket and set it on the table. He ran a hand through his hair, then nodded in Henry's direction. "What the hell did he do to you, anyway?"

Charles thought on that a good long while. He leaned back in his chair. He inhaled a deep and earthy breath, and it tasted of blood, alcohol and rain. "I've waited a quarter-century to kill that man," he said. "I needed it to be perfect, to have the right *impact*, you know?" He sighed, looked at his warped reflection in a blood speckled glass of water. Some old man looked back at him. He began to laugh. "And can you believe it, man? Can you *believe* after all this time I can't even remember?"

P is for Patience

Jeanne Kramer-Smyth

Sunday Evening

"Charna, good news. Baila is on my roster." Evangaline tucked a stray black curl back in place and smiled at her old friend, and sometimes rival, on the monitor. "It was a near thing at the end, but I managed it."

"Thank you, Evangaline." Charna nodded. "This will mean so much to her - to have a familiar face be part of this challenging process. Our daughter is prepared. She will make us proud."

"I am sure. I look forward to her first presentation tomorrow night. I won't be able to report back after everything starts, of course, but I'm confident that she will make it through."

Monday

Baila was prompt. She looked every bit the part of a diligent applicant to The Malevolence Society. Sleek black leather pants and a blood red silk tank top. The red fabric flattered her dark skin. Elaborate braids traced across her head, ending in a neat bun at the base of her skull.

"Greetings Sponsor Evangaline." Baila tipped her head and showed no sign of a prior personal relationship with her Sponsor even though Evangeline had so often been a guest in her home growing up.

"Greetings Gremlin Baila." Evangaline remained seated on the brocade wingback chair, as was appropriate her rank.

Baila stepped to the room's eye scanner, then turned to face Evangaline as the multi-panel display screen covering one wall of the small room began to display empty public bathrooms. Baila looked from her watch to the screens to Evangaline's stoic face. She shifted her feet and clasped her hands behind her back.

Finally the screens filled with young chattering teenage girls. The video transmissions remained focused on the mirrors and provided an excellent view of all the primping and fussing the girls crammed into their brief bathroom break. The audio of the girls shrieking as the mirrors showed their hair falling out came through loud and clear.

Evangaline nodded and gave Baila a small approving evil smile but then something shifted on the screens and instead of their hair falling out, the girls' hair turned wild colors. The girls laughed and pointed. They took photos.

"This," Evangaline waved at the milling girls, "is nothing more than a schoolgirl's prank. The senior members will not be willing to accept something that would not even get one expelled from school. I know you know what you need to do. See you tomorrow."

Baila nodded and left without another word.

Tuesday

Evangaline checked her watch. Baila was late. While being late could be practiced as one of the paths to improving your evil impact, Evangaline knew better than to assign meaning to Baila's tardiness. The Malevolence Society required much more dramatic demonstrations of evildoing than being accidentally late for appointments with your sponsor. Maybe she *should* have encouraged Charna to consider one of the other societies for Baila—but even mentioning another society was risky. Evangaline twisted her hands in her lap. No matter what she might have done, it was too late. The die was cast.

"I'm here," Baila huffed as she stumbled back into to Evangaline's receiving room. She paused just inside the door to take a deep breath and then proceeded in at a more dignified pace. "Greetings Sponsor Evangaline."

"Greetings Gremlin Baila. You may begin your presentation." Evangaline looked at the screens.

Baila scanned her eye and almost immediately the panels filled with live video feeds from a dozen airborne cameras. The image stabilization was state-of-the-art, but the constant shifting in perspective was dizzying. Each screen showed a different dog, recorded from above, in some sort of outdoor pen. Barking and whining burst from the speakers.

"What am I looking at?" Evangaline covered her ears and leaned forward.

Baila fumbled at the control panel for a moment before managing to mute the sound.

"This is a wealthy sub-division outside the city that permits dogs. I have used an algorithm to map the most chaotic rearrangement of the dogs and transferred them all to different yards." Baila smiled a practiced evil smile. "When the owners return after work today they will find their own pet missing and a strange, angry animal in its place." She made a bit of a "ta da" motion with her hand toward the screens.

Evangaline began a slow nod, but before she could complete the motion, new activity appeared on the screens. The gates at the rear of each yard slid open and the dogs ran out. Each video feed stayed with an individual animal and followed them as they ran out of their yard. Baila looked stricken as all the screens shifted to show all the dogs mingling together in some sort of large shared dog park.

"You have two more chances to practice before Friday's presentation to the senior members. If you bring them something like this even the many hallowed tales of your parents' and grandparents' deeds will not be enough to convince them you belong."

Baila stared at the floor and mumbled assent before leaving the room.

Evangaline sighed. The dogs cheerfully returned to their proper yards and curled up for their afternoon naps.

Wednesday

The screens showed many angles of the same mailbox, at the edge of a suburban street. A postman, seen via three of the camera angles, walked toward them. He stopped at each of the preceding mailboxes, depositing letters and small packages that he drew from his rolling postal handcart. The audio from the cameras transmitted a combination of singing birds, passing cars, and the scrape of the postal cart's wheels on the sidewalk.

When he reached the mailbox the cameras were focused on, Evangaline held her breath. He reached out and pulled down the metal door. A loud bang followed a bright blinding flash. The postman jumped back and covered his eyes, calling out in surprise. Evangaline raised her eyebrows and kept watching.

The flash was followed by another small popping sound and something shot out of the mailbox.

"Is that confetti?" Evangaline bit out through clenched teeth as the postman was rapidly covered in small bright bits of paper.

"Yes, Sponsor."

"And why should I not interpret this as yet another prank?"

"Mailboxes are federal property and it is a crime to vandalize them? You can be sent to jail for it. Ma'am."

Evangaline avoided meeting her eyes and pointed at the door.

Thursday

"What have you brought me today?" Evangaline asked. One screen showed the front of an elementary school. The rest showed various busy locations around town, including the city zoo, a construction site, a subway station entrance, and the local amusement park.

"This," Baila pointed at the school, "is where the school buses normally drop kids off in the morning." They watched as the buses pulled up in front of all the other locations and began to disgorge confused but cheerful looking elementary school children. "I rerouted all the busses and hacked the central GPS system to take it offline. I kidnapped an entire school of children. No-one knows where they are."

"This is progress." Evangaline nodded. "Well done, Baila." As Baila smiled proudly at her sponsor, something changed on the screen behind her showing the school. Adults were stumbling out of the building clutching their chests and coughing. "What is happening now? A final stroke in your plan?"

"What?" Baila turned back to the screens and shook her head. "This isn't me. I didn't do anything to the school."

They watched in silence as adults collapsed to the ground and the EMTs arrived.

"Well," Evangaline tore her eyes away from the EMTs lifting unconscious schoolteachers onto gurneys, "that was a much better effort. For tomorrow night's presentation to the senior membership, your demonstration must have a lasting impact. Good luck."

After the door shut behind Balia, Evangaline checked the event registry. It took her less than a minute to verify that the poisoning was another Gremlin's project.

Friday

Evangaline sat front and center among the senior voting members of The Malevolence Society. Each member's seat included secret voting buttons in the armrests. As Baila's sponsor, Evangaline would see the voting tallies and announce the results immediately after her Gremlin's presentation was complete. All two dozen senior members knew of Baila's family exploits—everything from mass-transit sabotage to syphoning money from the retirement funds of government employees. It was Baila's grandmother who had managed to drug all the children of a small summer camp, making them hallucinate. The body count had been high.

Voting was done in real time. By the conclusion of Baila's presentation, Evangaline would announce the results—either admission to full membership in The Malevolence Society or rejection. If rejected, Baila would be ushered immediately into a side room to have her memory wiped. The Society needed total secrecy about the Society and all its inner workings. For someone like Baila, whose family history was so tangled with the Society's doings, the memory loss would be massive.

Baila entered, wearing the standard issue black robes of a Gremlin in their final trials. The screens in the evaluation theater were larger than those in Evangaline's private receiving room, but the system worked similarly.

"Sponsor Evangaline, senior membership, I submit for your review my final demonstration." She stepped to the eye scanner at the edge of the room and the screens filled with images of hospital rooms. The main screen showed a nursery full of newborn infants with their pink and blue knit caps. Most of them were asleep.

The demonstration began in a number of the individual hospital rooms. The sprinkler system on the ceiling began to rain down a torrential flood of water. The water rapidly covered the floor, drenched the bedclothes, and caused the electrical equipment to sputter and beep.

Evangaline sat a little straighter and gave Baila a nod of approval.

Now that they knew what was coming, all eyes went to the nursery featured on the main screen. They waited for the water to fall and to fill the infants' plastic mobile cribs. How fast might the water fall before anyone realized what was happening?

But instead of water, they first saw fire. All along the edges of the room fire began to burn, quickly racing up the curtains that were used for the small exam areas within the nursery. Evangaline looked to Baila and watched her face go still. This wasn't part of the demonstration. Back on screen the water finally began to fall, but now it was extinguishing the fire and saving all the screaming infants from a fiery death.

Evangaline used the master examiner's switch to mute the feeds. Against a backdrop of silent crying babies, Evangaline made the official pronouncement based on the voting.

"Gremlin Baila, you have not been accepted for membership. We wish you luck in your life and remind you to guard our secrets."

"Thank you Sponsor Evangaline, but I have something else to share with the senior membership before you wipe my memory and I am never permitted to return." Baila stood taller and smiled. For the first time since the process had begun, Evangaline saw the girl she remembered from her visits when Baila was a child. "Yes. I know what happens next. Or what is supposed to, anyway." She pulled a small controller from an inner pocket and gestured back to the screens. The feeds switched from showing the hospital to show people behind desks. "And yes, you do recognize these people. The Mayor. The Chief of Police. The President of the University." Baila gestured at each individual in turn. "I have arranged for documentation of the Malevolent Society activities of everyone in this room to be delivered via dead-man's switch. In the event that I don't prevent it daily, incriminating video and other evidence will be sent to each of them."

Baila scanned the room of grim faces.

"As a Malevolence Society legacy, I grew up knowing what was expected of me. My parents, my grandparents—they couldn't resist raising me to become a proud member. My sponsor, Evangaline," Baila nodded politely in her sponsor's direction, "did everything she could to coach me. She had no idea that my test runs were carefully designed to provide me everything I needed to locate and retrieve materials from your video archives. You might consider changing your request and shipping protocols. I am proof that they are quite vulnerable to subversion."

The room was quiet. Eyes alternated between Baila and the monitors.

"I have no desire to expose your activities, but I also do not want to lose my family and my life. Let me be, and I will let you be." She gave the room a little wave, then strode out.

Evangaline rushed to follow Baila out of the evaluation room into the small changing room made available for Gremlins.

"I'm impressed." Evangaline passed Baila a glossy folded brochure. "I was going to leave this in your bag if we had to do the memory wipe. Not everyone in my family is a member of The Malevolence Society. My sister belongs to another secret society here in the city."

"The Quixotic Questing Committee." Baila read off the cover before opening it, her eyes growing wide. "Do you have what it takes to complete secret quests and help people without their knowledge?"

"What can I say? Sisters talk." Evangaline patted Baila awkwardly on the back before turning to walk back to face the senior members in the evaluation room. "Good luck." The door shut behind her and a moment later, Baila found herself staring at a smooth solid wall. That door would never open for her again.

She looked back down at the brochure Evangaline gave her and smiled.

Q is for Quixotic

Beth Cato

Rita has gotten really good at avoiding me, which is annoying. Mind you, she's always been annoying in all kinds of ways. She loves to make up stupid stories about her being some hero in a fairy tale world. She's obsessed. Everything is about unicorns and magic and castles.

Back when we were younger, our moms insisted that since we were the same age and lived on the same street, we had to be BFFs, so they made us play together. Ugh. Her swimming pool didn't even make that tolerable. I didn't ever want to see her in a swimsuit. She had cellulite. At age ten.

By then, I already knew how to diet, and I was only drinking a diet soda for my dinner every night. She could have shown that kind of control, too.

Anyway. Rita has only gotten weirder over the past few years.

At the start of 8th grade, she started walking different routes to and from school which pissed me off. How *dare* she try to avoid me. I know she doesn't like it when I shout "Rita Meat-a!" at her, but I'm trying to help her. I mean, she has to be near 200 pounds by now. Doesn't she see what she's doing to herself? Every time my step-mom sees her, she clicks her teeth and talks about how Rita's skin will be permanently stretched and no boy will ever look twice at her, then she looks at me and frowns and asks what I ate today. Then I have to show her the calorie counter on my phone.

The calorie counter gives me a good excuse for her and my dad when I say I'm going to start walking different paths to school. I say I'm exercising more, but really, I want to find where Rita is going.

She doesn't say much in school these days—to me or anyone else. She just draws and reads and goes in the library over the lunch break. She frowns a lot. I mean, it's not like she has it *that* bad, even if she is a fat loser. Her parents are still together. Her dad doesn't get drunk and spend the weekend hungover or give her girlfriends weird looks when they come over to hang out.

I think that's why I hate Rita. She doesn't know how good she has it. She still wants her stupid unicorns and fairies instead. Hell, I'd take the unicorns and fairies, if I could. Anything to get out of my house and away from my bitchy step-mom and my drunk of a dad and maybe eat real food without planning out how to starve myself tomorrow.

I tried to leave at the same time as Rita for a few mornings but somehow she always gave me the slip. After school, it was harder to follow her because we end the day in different homerooms.

Then, finally, I head a different way after school and I see her down a block. She's walking fast in the opposite direction from home. I trail her down Carver Street. It dead-ends at a cotton field but she keeps going along a dry canal and I have to hang back because if she turns around, she'll see me. So I wait a few minutes, then follow.

There's a big eucalyptus grove on the other side of the field. The dry bark on the ground is crunchy so I must walk slow. I've gotten good at this from sneaking out on Friday nights to go to parties, not that I drink alcohol like the other kids. Beer has way too many calories.

The grove takes up a few acres so it takes me a few minutes to hear Rita. She's talking loud, in a language like Latin, but not. She's holding a big book in her arms and it's on fire!

Literally, on fire.

I can see the pages burning up, but somehow it's not scorching her skin. She's totally focused on saying her words and staring straight ahead.

A black hole appears, hovering at waist-level, and as it grows bigger I can see there is another world on the far side. It's dawn there, an unreal sunrise with clear-blue skies and a grassy meadow. The scene is still like a painting, then I see birds dart from the grass into the distant trees. And there's a *unicorn*. An honest-to-god unicorn standing in the woods maybe a hundred feet away. It glances toward the hole, then bounds away, deeper into the woods.

Rita keeps chanting.

The hole keeps growing.

Her book continues burning—soon only the cover will be left. I'm right behind her and she hasn't noticed me. The portal is as big as a doorway now.

She starts sobbing and says nothing for a moment. "The magic works! It works! All these years of research, and dreaming, and it works! I can go where I belong!"

I can't help it. I start laughing.

She jerks around and sees me. Her eyes go wide.

"You belong right where you are, Rita Meat-a."

Then I start running.

I've always been faster than her. My step-mom makes me run in the mornings when she thinks I'm gaining any weight. So I zoom past her, to the portal. Through the portal. Into this fantasy-land that she's somehow made real.

I stand in knee-high grass that smells like the color green. I turn. The hole is closing. Rita is running, stretching out her arm, her face awful.

The hole closes.

I'm alone on another planet. Rita isn't. Anything here could kill me. I know I should be scared, but instead, I'm excited. I pull my phone from my pocket and it won't even turn on. I throw it into the grass.

There are several small plumes of smoke rising across the meadow. Maybe it's a village. Maybe I'll see the unicorn on the way. I start walking, and I wonder how many calories I'm burning.

R is for Rita

Laura VanArendonk Baugh

Scott had dressed in yellow and black because it made him think of caution signs or even biohazard warning signs, and because black hoodies were cheap and readily available. Now, seeing himself reflected in the plate glass windows facing the sidewalk, he worried he looked like a mascot shilling for hornet killer. Still, there was no benefit to putting it off any longer. He tugged at his yellow dishwashing gloves—yellow gloves were hard to find, 'specially during the warm off-season—and went inside.

"Hello," he said to the indifferent woman at the reception desk, shielded behind bulletproof glass. "I have an appointment to see Karissa Glenn?"

The receptionist flicked her eyes at him and exhaled wearily. "Room seven." She spoke in a run-together monotone, as if the words held no individual meaning. "Please be hereby reminded you are bound by the Accords in this place of business for the duration of your time here. Inappropriate conduct such as but not limited to theft, threats, fiery destruction, smashing, or releasing toxic gas, by mechanical, supernatural, or biological means, will result in your immediate removal and termination of all agreements, contracts, and services without recourse to any fees already submitted."

He nodded. "Thank you."

She pressed a button on her desk, and the steel-reinforced door to one side buzzed. He went through it and followed the plastic wall placards to number seven.

Inside, Karissa Glenn was at a cheap laminate desk, tapping at a laptop and gnawing absently at a pencil between her teeth. Scott closed the door behind him and took a seat on the plastic chair opposite her. "Good afternoon. I'm Scott Fullin. We spoke on the phone yesterday."

"Oh, yes, hello." Without looking she returned the pockmarked pencil to a container of pens to her left. She saved the computer file and closed it, and then she made eye contact and smiled, faltering only slightly as her eyes traveled over the hoodie and rested briefly on the gloves before moving determinedly back to his face. "You're looking for a regional placement."

Scott nodded. "I've finished two internships and I'm ready to make my own way. But I thought I might have more options out of town." He liked it here, but a metropolis like this was thick with up-and-coming competition in addition to the several well-established supervillains already in place.

Karissa nodded, retrieving a manila folder from a rack on a side table. "Mm-hmm, that's not unusual. Sometimes it's easier to be taken seriously in a place where no one remembers you delivering papers or working a convenience store counter." She turned back and opened her folder. "Just give me a moment to review your *curriculum vitae*."

Scott sat back on the chair and rubbed at the fraying edge of one of the yellow duct tape stripes on his black pants. He would have to upgrade his costume, even if he got a small town placement. Maybe iron-on swatches from a fabric and hobby store?

"Oh, it says here you interned with Diabolos." Her eyebrows popped up. "That's impressive. He doesn't take many interns."

Scott smiled with mild embarrassment and shrugged. "It was a favor to my family," he admitted. When Karissa looked at him, he explained, "My mother is Lady Larcena, and my great-uncle was the Rhodium Hammer."

"That's quite a family tree," she said. "While officially we frown on nepotism, it's understandably more acceptable on the villainy side, and that will look very good on your application."

He nodded, wishing he felt more enthusiasm and less despair.

She dropped her eyes back to his file. "Diabolos included the details of your solo project...." Her voice trailed off, leaving the unspoken question loud in the air.

Scott swallowed. "That was the children's ward fire."

She looked up. "A children's hospital is an ambitious target for an internship, though not out of range for someone like Diabolos. But it doesn't seem to have gone quite as assigned?"

Scott's hands were sweating inside the heavy yellow latex gloves. "He'd given me permission to use my own judgment. I altered the target, from the children's ward to an animal shelter."

Her eyes went from his to the damning file and back to his.

"After I removed all the dogs and cats," he added. There was no point in denying it, not when she had all the details in front of her. "I burned the empty building." It needed some extra spin. "With all the scared puppies and kittens outside, it was more trouble for the shelter workers to round them up."

"There's a photograph of you holding three kittens on site."

"Well, yes. I had to be there, to take credit for the fire. I was just an intern, I didn't have a calling card or anything."

"I see." She frowned. "And did you anticipate the consequences?"

He squeezed his latex-coated fingers on the edges of his plastic seat. "That the outraged public would fundraise for a new shelter building, purpose-built instead of the converted civic offices the shelter had been using? No. That was unexpected."

A flicker of emotion flashed across Karissa's face and then vanished. Placement agents usually handed both heroes and villains and were supposed to be neutral in working with clients, but Scott wondered if inwardly she had an opinion about the displaced puppies and kittens getting an upgraded facility.

She fingered back a few more pages. "And is that when you took on some extra training with the Dark Plumber?"

He hadn't realized that report had been turned in by his mentor as well. "Oh. Yes."

She read down. "Can you tell me what happened there?"

As she had the report in her hand, this was probably a bad sign—but at least she was giving him a chance to explain. "Dark Plumber had a special bacterium to introduce to the city water supply. I substituted powdered drink mix. A lot of it. So when everyone stepped into the shower the next morning, it rained purple dye over them." He gave an apologetic smile. "I thought it would be a more effective dye, but for the most part it washed out quickly. I'd hoped it would stick."

"Powdered drink mix," she repeated, looking down at his file. "To dye people purple in their morning showers."

"A lot of very distinguished super-villains utilize a comedy theme," he said in the best indignation he could muster. "Jokes, riddles, jests. *Commedia dell'arte*. Juggling." It was a weak defense, and he knew it.

"And," she said, drawing out the word, "you are looking for a position as a local supervillain?"

"I was thinking of a small town," he said gamely. "Somewhere that doesn't need an...assertive approach."

The moment stretched between them. Scott clenched his fists on the edges of the chair, and a yellow latex glove squeaked on the plastic.

At last Karissa exhaled slowly and set the closed manila folder on her desk. "This office is private," she said, "and we are not being recorded. We have no legally protected client relationship, but I want you to feel safe to speak here, as I have only your best placement in mind." She took a breath. "Are you sure you want a villain job?"

Scott's throat closed, the familiar lump choking his words. "You said it yourself a moment ago," he answered, trying to keep the treacherous emotion from his voice. "It's quite a family tree. Mom, Great-Uncle Hammer.... I'm really tired of being the white sheep of the family. I may never make them proud, but—but I can't just throw over the family way. Not right out of my internship. Not without trying."

Karissa chewed at her lower lip for a minute. "Let me see what I can do."

She returned to her computer and began typing, then took the mouse and started clicking through database windows. Scott wanted to rub sweat from his forehead—the hoodie was warm in the closed office—but worried his hair would stick to the glove.

Karissa stopped clicking and stared at the screen for a moment, working the scroll wheel a couple of times. Then she looked over the monitor at Scott, who tried to look as if he weren't holding his breath. "You know I can't provide any names or identifying information until we reach the actual application process," she said, "but tell me what you think of this: a mid-size suburb, two supervillains already practicing, one of whom indicates in testing and interviews that he would be amenable to a mitigating influence."

Scott needed a moment to work through the demographics and get to the important final phrase. "Mitigating influence? Like, someone to—oh! A conscience?"

"A cricket, as we say," she answered, nodding. "Your role would be to assist in villainous projects but to talk your villain down, reducing overall frequency and impact. It seems like a good fit for you. The only downside is, you'd be a sidekick and not a supervillain. I don't know if you're willing to take an alternate position."

Scott's heart leapt into his tightening throat. Yes, this position sounded much more like him. Frankly, the idea of establishing himself as a supervillain was a bit overwhelming even outside of the moral concerns; being a sidekick meant someone else would be responsible for the lair, the supplies, the weapons, the grand plans, the quips. The relieving role of mitigating influence was just the icing on the cake.

But *sidekick* wasn't in the family line. Would Lady Larcena and the Rhodium Hammer be embarrassed in the supervillain community?

Karissa was looking at him, watching him as if she could read his worries.

He needed to say something. "It sounds really good," he managed. "It's just…Mom. I'm worried I would disappoint her if I'm not, you know, really villainous."

Karissa screwed up her mouth in a dismissive look and shrugged. "Deliberately disappointing your mother sounds really villainous to me."

He laughed, and he pulled off a latex glove to reach for a pen from the container. "I'd like to complete the application, please."

S is for ~~Supervillain~~ Sidekick.

Megan Engelhardt

My grandfather owned a fiddle. He bought it in Italy in 1943 but when he came home from the war it, like his canteen and uniform and memories, was hidden away and never brought out again.

Pap went to war when he was too young, but the government took him anyway—who were they to be choosy?—and sent him to North Carolina to train with guns and men and machinery. Then they shipped him to Europe and for three years he drove transports and built roads and played his fiddle and did not die.

I have a picture of him, nineteen years old, sitting on top of a loaded hay cart somewhere in Italy. There are two other men with him—I don't know their names—and all three are playing instruments. One has a guitar, one has a mandolin, and my grandfather has his fiddle. They are all smiling, but their eyes are heavy with the weight of what they have seen.

The year Pap was diagnosed with lung cancer I came home and took him to a Memorial Day service at the cemetery not too far from the hospital. The band played a medley of patriotic tunes and Pap, in his pointed brown hat and American flag tie, saluted when the mayor led the crowd in the Pledge of Allegiance. Then a young girl stood up, some contest winner for the VFW.

"These men who stand among us," the girl said, "the gone but not forgotten men who stand behind them—they knew the price of freedom, and they paid willingly."

Pap was still talking about that speech when I took him back to the hospital after the parade.

"The price of freedom," he said. "That's it exactly. We paid that price over there, in blood, and all of you who come after, you owe us a debt for that."

"I know," I said.

I owed my grandfather a big debt already. He had taken me in, raised me. He saw me through high school and college and never asked for anything in return except respect. I owed him for that—had always felt a deep obligation to him—and as I watched him take off his American flag tie and fold it reverently, I felt the weight of another obligation settle on my shoulders.

Three weeks later, he was gone.

After the funeral, after the graveyard service and the veteran's salute and the ham dinner, I went back to the red brick house where I had grown up and cried myself to sleep, the knowledge of unpaid debts clogging my throat almost more than the tears. The next day I began to sort through the house, preparing it for the estate sale and setting aside any mementos I wanted to save.

I found Pap's fiddle in the attic, behind boxes of ancient Avon jewelry and stacks of encyclopedias from the 1950s.

The leather of the case was cracked and hard, the stickers that had once proclaimed its travels faded and crumbling. A fine fuzz of light orange dust came off on my hands and pants. When I opened up the case, the fiddle was dusty but otherwise looked to be in perfect condition. Not a string was broken—the body was tightly joined, the dark wood strong and showing no cracks, no warp. Even the bow was in good condition.

I lifted the fiddle carefully and examined it. It was beautifully crafted, handmade and well taken care of, although now that I could get a closer look I saw that there was a thin layer of orange dust on the strings. I ran one finger along the bridge and the dust came off on my finger. Some flew into the air. I could see it floating in the sunbeams that filtered through the small attic window. The sun caught it and turned it to a golden shower of particles, a fairy rain dancing idly on a breeze. I sneezed.

There was a relatively clean cloth in the case. I used it to brush the dust off the fiddle and give it a good shine. It felt like the dust was invading my lungs and I sneezed three more times, but I felt better for having the fiddle clean.

I picked up the bow, tightened the strings, and settled the fiddle under my chin. I hadn't played since college, but I remembered enough. Slowly I drew the bow across the string.

One long note rang out in the attic. Another cloud of dust puffed up; I sneezed again. Still, it was good to know that the old thing made such a beautiful sound. I tried a few more notes, placing my fingers hesitantly. I thought of Pap's calloused fingers, pressed to the wood where mine were now, and I knew I could not leave this behind.

The fiddle sat untouched while I dealt with Pap's estate and settled back in to my normal life. When I pulled it out of the case two weeks later, the orange dust had crept back onto the strings and started to cover the wooden body again. I wiped it down, tuned it to my piano, and spent the evening practicing the scale, playing the simple notes over and over.

After some time my skills progressed to where I could play more complicated songs. I tried a few upbeat pieces, lilting things with the kind of fun, tricky fingerings I favored, but they never seemed to fit my mood as well as slow and mournful songs. I learned dirges, lullabies, songs of lost souls and lost loves, and the fiddle seemed to respond to the weeping willow lines of melody.

It seemed appropriate to play those songs, since all I could think about when I picked up the fiddle were the terrible things my Pap must have seen in the war. He had scratched the names of the places he'd been on the inside of his fiddle case. They made a nightmare list: Bari, Anzio, Cassino. I studied those places, learning their histories until I knew them as well as I knew my own name and trying to imagine what it had been like to be there. Pap never told me any details about his service but it was there, in every picture of him that I had—that sadness, that deepness I had never been able to fathom. I wanted to know, wanted to have that connection, so I played the sadness on his fiddle and tried to conjure up the war.

Before Pap's fiddle I knew as much about the war as anyone who paid attention in history class. Pearl Harbor and Hitler, the Holocaust and Hiroshima and a vague solemn feeling that was dispelled much quicker than it was called up. But there was so much I did not know.

I had not known that over 60 million people died in combat. I did not know that the Bari accident was a hellish series of mistakes. I did not know that the battle of Monte Cassino took all winter, a long, miserable winter of stranded beachheads and the rubble of an innocent monastery.

There was so much I did not know, and once I started learning I did not want to know. But I had to. The weight of my debts drove me on, to read and study, to look at picture after picture of soldiers, children, the starving, the dead. They seared into my soul a deep understanding that the true toll of war was that man, that woman, that baby.

And that was just Pap's war, what he called, when he spoke of it at all, "*the* war." There were others, so many others, each with their horrors, each adding millions and millions more to death's toll. There is never a war without dead, without suffering. There is never a war that did not leave behind furrows in the earth, bodies in the ground, a fog of misery and pain over history.

There is no such thing as a good war.

When I no longer felt embarrassed to play in public, I took the fiddle to graveyards, to the tall monuments recognizing that city's dead. In front of the graven names of the dead I played sad songs and thought about unpayable debts, and remembered Pap.

It was in a graveyard that I saw them for the first time. I was playing in front of a monument, taking in the lists of names while my fingers teased out "We'll Meet Again" when a chill brushed the back of my neck, like the fingers of early frost encroaching on summer's end. I shivered but kept playing. It wasn't until I saw the soldier that I faltered.

He stood to one side, just in the corner of my eye, and I would have known he was a soldier even without the uniform and round helmet. It was his eyes. They held the same sad depths I had always seen in my Pap's eyes.

Don't stop.

I heard it in my head, a hollow whisper begging into the silence that had been filled with music. The soldier looked at me, pleading in those deep eyes. The guilt, the debt, swelled up in me. I owed him.

I lifted the fiddle and played "We'll Meet Again" from the beginning. When the song was over, he nodded his head and faded with a faint smile on his face. I felt a little of the burden lifted from my shoulders. I had paid on the debt, just a bit.

He was the first. Every time I played, then, I saw them, young men and women, a great cloud of witnesses drawn to my music, given form by the dust from my strings. They came when I played and left when I was done, and I knew that I was giving them rest. I remembered and honored and paid in the only way I could.

I played at every graveyard and monument within an hour of my home. Then I went farther afield. I drove hours to play soldiers to rest at graveyards in strange little towns. I neglected my job, my friends— they didn't understand, none of them, even when I explained about the 60 million, even when I showed them the pictures, even when I played them the songs. But I knew. With each dust-covered figure that faded into rest, I was playing down a debt that could never be fully expunged.

I did not sleep. I barely ate. I quit my job, sold my house, and bought a one-way ticket to Paris. I only took a change of clothes and my Pap's fiddle. It had come into my mind that while I was doing a good thing, playing for the boys who had made it home, there were plenty more on both sides who had never left the battlefield. Their spirits would be lonely and troubled—they would have a greater need to collect on the debt.

I played my fiddle all across Europe, freeing spirits a hundred at a time or more. They flocked to my music, surrounded me with their chill faces and deep eyes, and I played concerts for them, always ending with the promise of "We'll Meet Again". On the beach at Normandy there were too many to count, a sea of gray soldiers standing shoulder to shoulder. I played there until my fingers bled and my shoulder burned from holding up the fiddle and clouds of orange mold coated my throat, and still it took a half-dozen more repetitions until the last boy faded.

I only stopped when I stepped on a forgotten land mine in Germany. The farmer who found me brought me to the hospital. The nurses said that the explosion took my legs and my left hand. My legs I believe—they are not there anymore, and isn't that a fitting tribute to the men I was playing for when it happened?—but I'm not sure why they'd lie about my hand. I can feel it, see it, still there at the end of my arm, still gripping the neck of Pap's fiddle.

They said that was destroyed, too. And it was, for a short moment—I remember, in the flash of the explosion, seeing the wood burst apart, feeling the small splinters and bits of string like whips on my hands and face. It exploded in a shower of golden sun-touched fairy dust that rained down on me amid the dirt and rocks and shrapnel, the dust filling my mouth and eyes. But as I lay dazed on the ground, through the golden haze I saw one of my soldiers approach.

He knelt down and handed me my fiddle, whole and perfect again. I took it in my left hand, and I have not let it go since.

They say it is a phantom limb, a ghost arm. They tell me I am not really playing, that there is nothing in my hand that is no longer there. I know the truth. They have no sense of the debt, and so they can't see. But I can.

I still play. There are spirits even here, in this old hospital, and I play for them when I dare. I won't stop—I can't stop—until they are gone. I know the price of freedom, and I know I have a long way to play until my debt is paid.

T is for Toll

Danielle Davis

My *Púridaia* Vadoma has never called it a curse, not exactly. But all the women in our family still make the sign of the evil eye and spit to the side with a disgusted expression whenever someone even vaguely mentions an *amriya*.

Vadoma, with her rheumy eyes and sagging, wrinkled jowels, says we're all just letting the non-Roma get to us, with their talks of gypsies and traveling circuses and curses. "*Gadje* don't understand our ways," she says. "They think everything is like what they see on TV. Our men are caravan gamblers and thieves in the night. Our women are dark-skinned whores with eyes like jewels and hips like the devil. That we entice in the innocent and take them for all they're worth before escaping to the next town under the darkness of a new moon. Or some shit like that.."

Because she is old enough to have lived through times when that was how our tribe lived, she has even more disdain for such rumors. To her, it is the duty of our tribe to show the *gadje* we meet that we are better than that. That we are people just like them.

Except for the curse, she's right.

My father owns a carpet installation company, mother handles the books and both my brothers work under my father. I do, too, in the summers for extra money, even though the rest of our tribe tease me that it's no job for a girl. I argue that it's better than working in an ice cream shop and coming home reeking of sour milk and sugar or slinging bags of groceries at a convenience store.

And in this endeavor, I feel very close to my *Púridaia* Vadoma in a way my twin sister, Lala, isn't... and not just because Lala chose the ice cream shop.

I appreciate the opportunity to use my hands to make something, to perform a task that you can see grow and blossom because of your efforts. *Púridaia* Vadoma says I should have become a gardener, but I like working alongside my family. Which is why it's such a blow to overhear my mother and my *Púridaia* a few days before my sixteenth birthday.

"You have to choose one!" Vadoma snaps. I can't see them, but I can tell they're at the far end of the kitchen, near where the stove meets the pantry.

"Don't you think I know that?" her mother hisses back. "How am I supposed to choose this? Knowing what it will do to my babies?"

"They're both old enough." I feel a sour twist in my gut, though I don't know if it's from the guilt of eavesdropping or the anxiety of getting caught.

"You've got to pick one," Vadoma intones in a grave voice. The finality of it makes my arms break out in gooseflesh. "You have until tomorrow morning. If you haven't made a choice, I'll pick for you. We don't have that much more time."

"Vadoma, don't do this to me," my mother pleads, and I realize she's the only person in the family who addresses my *Púridaia* by her first name. "Don't make me sacrifice one of my babies for this." The sourness in my stomach intensifies. My mother never begs.

"Don't speak to *me* about sacrifice, Fifi!" Vadoma shouts in a voice loud enough that I shrink back against the wall hiding me, positive she's going to step around the corner any second and see me crouched there like a troll listening to their conversation.

"I would never—" my mother begins, but Vadoma cuts her off.

"You have no idea what I live with for this family, for all of you, including your babies, to survive. Remember that you were too young to be chosen or you would be in this situation instead of me!"

"Vadoma, I—"

"You would rather I didn't pick anyone perhaps? Risk the outcome? See what happens to all of us if it's not passed along? Because we both know very well the consequences."

"I get it." My mother sounds suddenly tired, now. Defeated. The sound of it hurts my heart.

"No, I don't think you do, Fifi. Lala and Drina are the only ones in our bloodline. They are the only ones I can teach. You don't have to like it to acknowledge it. Only they can handle this... this burden. You know this, yes?"

A long pause, where I assume my mother gives some indication of assent, followed by a low murmur.

A single word.

A name.

"Really? Are you sure about this, Fifi? Because this isn't a decision you can go back on. There can be no changed minds once this begins, you know this, too." Now Vadoma's voice is gentled with compassion.

Then I hear my mother repeat it, two syllables that sounded like nails pounding into dead wood: "Drina."

My name.

The house seems to exhale around me in a subtle sigh that lifts the hair on the back on my neck in a gentle breeze.

"Drina it will be then. And for what it's worth, Fifi, I agree with you. Drina will carry this burden well. Perhaps better even than me."

A small laugh from my mother, followed by a watery sob, and then the sound of shuffling feet moving my way.

I shrink into the corner of my hiding area until the two passed the doorway and trail out into the yard.

I don't know what I've just gotten signed up for, but I have a strong feeling that it's nothing good.

There once was a girl, the daughter of a farmer, one of ten other children. Desiring more than a life as a simple farmer's wife, she left as soon as she was old enough.

She traveled across the country, eating what she could find, sleeping wherever she was able, and working for whatever coin she could entice. Her travels brought her to Hermannstadt, a tiny town at the base of a mountain range. There she discovered a school for women called Scholomance.

It wasn't a nunnery, like most all-female orders, but it taught about the metaphysical just the same.

The lessons begin the next night, in *Púridaia* Vadoma's room over the garage of our house.

I'll never admit it to her face, but I covet her room. A finished out attic, the walls turn into an A-frame shape halfway up. Instead of wallpaper, *Púridaia* has covered her walls with large scarves and blankets. The effect is a riot of color: purple dahlias here, zentangles above the bed, Hindi elephants in exotic colors. All of these things give the room an exotic feel. My *Púridaia's* room has always been a safe haven for me when I was younger, and tonight those memories are coming back in the form of a languid calm.

Cerebrally I know I should be anxious or upset, based off the way she and my mother were talking in the kitchen. However, this place is too sacred, too safe. The room smells of old incense, roses, and *Púridaia.*

I love it.

Púridaia is wearing her favorite dress tonight, the aqua-colored one with the large, belled sleeves. She makes a sweeping gesture for me to sit on the floor, which is covered with throw pillows of various sizes and colors. Some have sequins on them that change color when you smooth your hand over them the wrong way.

The pillows are all arranged on a thick braided rug woven to look like a spiral. I sit, cross-legged.

"What's this all about *Púridaia*?" I ask.

Instead of answering immediately, *Púridaia* carefully lowers herself to a pillow on the rug. She mimics my cross-legged stance.

"You're here to learn a story," she begins. "But the most important rule is this: you cannot tell anybody what you learn here."

She pauses, watching me.

"Why? Is it that much a secret?"

Púridaia hesitates. "This story? It is dangerous. This story, told to the wrong person, can kill." She laughs softly. "The most dangerous stories are the ones that really happened. They remember what was like, you see, to be alive, even for the short time it took to tell them. And like lost spirits, they crave the touch of the real world." Then her voice drops, as if she's worried someone might overhear. "The strongest ones are sometimes powerful enough to break through and touch us."

I stare. This is both the coolest start to a story and the creepiest at the same time.

She begins with the rules.

"Rule number one: You must accept this burden willingly, even if you don't understand it yet. Do you accept this responsibility, my *chav* Drina? Do you?"

I stare at her and she stares back with utmost seriousness. "Um, ok, sure." This is easily the oddest urban legend I've ever heard.

She gives me a regal nod, then continues. "Rule number two: silence is key. Under no circumstances may you tell a casual observer. The story is told only once to the next in line and only to those of the blood—no *gadje*. To tell otherwise guarantees their death.

I laugh at the absurdity but my *Púridaia* continues as if I hadn't interrupted.

"Rule number three: The story demands a price, which it will extract by itself."

"What kind of price?" I can't help myself.

"In time, you'll come to understand. Rule four: the story must be passed on. If the one who contains it dies without passing it along, it falls to the next in line."

"Would that be Lala? What would happen to her?

Instead of answering, she begins telling the story. It's haunting and my *Púridaia* is a master storyteller. As it unwinds, I become less aware of the flat feeling of my buttocks on the thin pillow or how stiff my ankles are from being folded underneath me the whole time.

There's just the story. I am hooked.

After *Púridaia* finishes tonight's section, I turn to leave. But before I can, *Púridaia* suddenly grips my chin in a firm hold and lowers her face so close I could kiss her. "*Ma Bisteren*," she says in a soft tone. "Do not forget. And tell nobody."

Later that night, I fall asleep feeling oddly light-headed. The kind of dizziness that usually accompanies wobbly limbs and a queasy stomach. Something's changing. Something's happening, and I'm a little excited to see what it will turn out to be.

At Scholomance, the girl learned great and terrible things. Things like using your own energy to heal something or someone. Potions that could turn any heart to mush or to stone. The ability to send one's spirit into an animal.

Eventually she met a boy from town and fell in love, and they were happy... for a time.

Then a caravan, ancestors of ours, rolled into town, and one of the tribe girls saw the young man and declared he would soon be hers.

Papa asks me to help him move some carpet bundles out of his truck. Only we don't even get one of the long rolls halfway clear of the van doors before my trembling arms lose their strength and my end drops to the ground with a loud thunk.

"You ok, Drina?" my father asks with his eyebrows puckered with worry. He touches the back of his hand to my forehead. "Not getting sick, I hope."

I step away in what I hope is a casual movement. I know exactly what's wrong, but I can't tell him. Rule number two and all...

I wonder if he knows about the spell. And if not, how my mother's going to explain my changes. The thought's unsettling—it feels too close to a lie and that's something we don't do to each other. *Gadje* may, but our family never would.

I excuse myself and head to the house.

In the house, I finish my History homework, an essay on whether or not Count Dracula actually existed.

It's as I'm finishing my final paragraph that the idea hits me—a way to beat the curse.

What if the story's victim wrote the story instead of telling it? The more I ponder it, the stronger the idea seems. The story has to be passed along to someone of the blood, but if I'm writing the story, being Rom myself, then nobody can get hurt—I would be both storyteller and audience.

Unless they read it.

But I could burn it. Write it and then burn it so nobody can accidentally read it. Then the story…disappears. It's the perfect solution to an unsolvable problem!

My heartbeat feels like it will crack my chest open from excitement.

No real magic was involved, though everyone assumed she must have spelled him so fast did his head turn for her.

And the shuv'hani, furious in her anger and strong in her power, cast her revenge: this story, placed on those the cursed one loves. A story that can only be told once, yet which would pass from generation to the next forever.

Púridaia Vadoma looks particularly refreshed tonight. Her skin has a golden glow in the dim light and her eyes sparkle with barely contained mischief. She's even put on lipstick, a garish red that clashes horribly with the rest of her, but which she apparently has a fondness of.

"Do you like it?" she asks as she sits down with a grandiose swoosh of her skirt. "It reminds me of when of I was your mother's age."

"I didn't realize you had that good a memory, *Púridaia*," I tease, but she just gives me a smug sideways glance before starting in on the lesson.

"Tonight we learn about the specifics of how the *shuv'hani*, the wise women, cast the spell, meaning the ingredients used, lunar phase, and the talismans utilized in the preparation…"

There are three phases to a spell: generation, transmission, and suspension. Generation works by attracting the energy needed for the spell. In transmission, you convey, or transmit, the spell's energy into the desired item or person. And in suspension, the spell's energy—

My Calculus teacher raps her hand on my desk as she passes and I realize I've been scribbling furiously on the back of my derivatives test. I've been done for the past ten minutes, but for some reason I haven't gotten up to put my finished test on the teacher's desk.

I snatch a Sharpie from my bookbag and scratch through the first half of my *Púridaia's* lesson from last night.

We didn't get to bed until one this morning and I'm suffering from it. *Púridaia* Vadoma, however, seemed just as restful as she had when we'd begun. It was like the long night hadn't phased her at all.

I turn in my test, for the first time all year worried about how I did. Calculus is a breeze for me, and I'm routinely one of the first students to turn in my tests but today, I can barely remember taking the stupid thing. Did I do well or did I just Christmas tree the whole thing while daydreaming about the properties of energy during the suspension phase of a spell?

That night, *Púridaia* asks to see my hands before we begin.

She cradles mine carefully in hers, my skin supple against the worn leather of her own as she flips my hands over. Her lips purse in and out, a kissing motion I'm not even sure she's aware of, as she examines my palms. Then she nods with a small smile, and says, "Let's begin."

When I ask what she was looking for, she stares at me with hooded eyes, silent and sphinx-like until I look away. Her eyes seem clearer, less rheumy than I remember, and knife sharp.

On my way to Advanced English, Amber Fisher and her cronies laughingly compliment me on my dye job, saying "Old is the new young, am I right?" then cackling like ninnies. Several others down the hall give me odd looks, brief sideways glances that skate away like hummingbirds as soon as they land on me, and I risk being last to dart into the bathroom to see what everyone's looking at.

It's my hair. In the time between brushing it in front of the mirror this morning and third period, my glossy, brown mane has turned dull and threaded throughout with silver, which is shocking enough. But the real horror is the fat chunk of metallic silver hair that's sprouted from my crown and falls to frame my face on either side.

It's so uniform it looks deliberate.

I stare frozen, horrified, at the mirror, only dimly aware of the final bell ringing. This has to be the price extracted by the curse. What will be next? Will I grow cataracts and become blind? Will I stoop until my spine looks like a question mark? Will I die of old age before I finish college? These questions make my skin itch with adrenaline, my body instinctively wanting to run away from this threat. For all the good it will do.

I square my shoulders and leave the bathroom. I head to the office to call my mom and request a pickup.

For an hour afterward, I wait in the front office, trying to ignore the unsubtle glances of the office staff who don't have the guts to ask me about my hair.

When my mom arrives, she takes one step into the office and stops, staring. Her face is carefully neutral, which surprises me. I expected to see shock or fear or alarm, but not this sort of surprised detachment.

But she stares at me for several long seconds, and I remain quiet too, watching her eyes as they travel down either side of my face over the chunks of steel-grey that I've tucked behind my ears.

We don't say a word on the ride home. I'm too afraid to ask, given her reaction in the office, and she doesn't seem inclined to say a single word. Doesn't even ask why I requested a pickup.

When we get home, my mother marches straight in with me following like a chastised dog.

Púridaia Vadoma and two of my brothers are in the kitchen preparing dinner.

"Great jumping Jesus, what happened to you?" my eldest brother Tobar exclaims. My other brother, Pali, just stares slackjawed.

"Leave it," my mother snaps as she brushes past them, and the two boys trade worried glances.

However, I see *Púridaia* Vadoma give her a small nod as my mother moves past her. It's a conspirator's nod, I think. Then I'm immediately ashamed at the thought, don't even know where it came from, and I step into my *Púridaia's* open-armed-embrace.

She pets my gray-streaked hair as I let the pent-up tears loose into the rough fabric of her shirt. "It's ok, *chav*. Let it loose. It will not be there long, I think. We will figure this through."

None of it makes any sense to me, but her gentle hands on my head and my hair, her soothing voice easing into my brain and down along my bones makes me believe things will get better. Hers are hands that fix, hands that heal. There is no reason for me not to trust them.

I wake the next morning to see that my hair is the white-gray of old snow.

As I stare at myself in the bathroom mirror, I notice other small changes: a fine spray of wrinkles radiating from the corners of my eyes like tiny fans. A gauntness to my face, along with dark circles beneath my eyes, as if I'm very tired.

My mother's lips purse into thin lines when she sees me at the breakfast table, but she doesn't say a word. Nobody does but their eyes speak volumes. Tobar's eyes crawl over me with worry, shown in the small V between his eyebrows. Lala keeps throwing me confused looks, then glancing at our mother before staring back down at her plate while Pali is deliberately cheerful and avoids looking at me at all. My father is the best actor of all: he swallows his coffee in several giant gulps before kissing us all on the crown of our heads, and pulling on his canvas jacket as he darts out the door.

He never said a word to me, but I felt the way his fingers spasmed on my hair, a brief clenching, that seemed to say *I see you. I still love you.*

My mother serves me an extra helping of pancakes, though, without any supporting reason. Because they're my favorite, I tuck into them without asking, but I can't shake the feeling that it's a peace offering of some kind.

There's a tension between us that's unnamed, that I can't pinpoint any reason for existing, yet which still separates us as easily as a divider. I wish I could talk to her about what's going on, because I'm certain it's got something to do with my lessons with *Púridaia*. But I remember *Púridaia's* warning, so I accept what my mother gives me, whether it's pancakes, glances or small, tight-lipped smiles.

What baffles me the most, though, is that I can tell she's unhappy about what's going on but she's permitting it. I wish I understood more of the conversation I overheard between her and *Púridaia*. Perhaps the context would've given me more insight into what's happening to me.

My hands are bony, with large, knobby joints that ache from this morning's rainstorm. And my skin has become thin and papery, so much so I can clearly see the network on blue veins on the backs of my hands. The body I see in the mirror has begun to stoop ever so slightly forward, as if my torso is too heavy for my back to support.

Today I am 16 years old.

It's late enough that no one's awake when I take a notebook, pen, and refillable Butane lighter into the garage. Huddled on a folded moving blanket, its thick wool padding a comfortable barrier against the chill of the concrete floor, I uncap my pen and let the story loose on the paper.

I write the story the way *Púridaia* Vadoma taught it to me, depicting it as a living thing of teeth and claws and me just the fragile paper box it shreds as it tries to escape. Even as my shaking fingers clench the pen, I can feel it inside me, scratching like a cat trapped in a drawer. It wants out and I want to let it out.

After I'm done, I pull the pages loose and set them on the ground in front of me. It feels like I'm staring at a snake prepared to bite. It's dangerous, those papers, and yet I feel more free for having written it all down. A quick glance at my hands shows no change, and I wonder how long until the effects start to reverse, the way I suspect they're doing with *Púridaia* Vadoma.

With a flourish of the lighter, I set them ablaze. They light immediately. As I watch, the flame turns a dark purple before fading into a beautiful lavender unlike anything I've ever seen before.

Transfixed, I watch the fire crisp the paper and send small, charred bits into the air like blackened fairies. Only after it's done do I realize how stiff my joints are from being on the hard floor, despite the blanket's padding.

When I head inside, I feel a sense of smug satisfaction settle into my core. I've figured out a way to both bear the curse and destroy it in the process.

I am like the girl in *Púridaia's* story, the one who started it all, who was determined not to let fate force her into a life she didn't want. For me, this means I can keep my family safe but also prevent another from dying.

To my mind, that makes me a hero.

Two nights of storytelling with *Púridaia* Vadoma. Two nights of writing and then burning the burden away.

Lala shuffles down the stairs as breakfast is almost over, which is a first for her; usually she beats everyone to the table.

She looks terrible. Horrible purple circles under her eyes give her the appearance of a zombie, as if she's been a week without sleep. Her dark hair is a snarl of tangles, bunched and knotted into a mane around her face.

She didn't look like that a few days ago, I'm positive.

"Oh God, what the hell happened to you?" asks Tobar.

"Tactful," I murmur to him, but I'm wondering the same.

My mother passes an affectionate hand over Lala's bushy hair and peers a her with a frown. "Feeling ok, Lala?"

Lala nods. "I was up most of the night because of *her*." She shoots a malignant glare at me.

"What did I do?" I squeak. I've had the best sleep of my life the past few nights, ever since I began the burning.

"You were talking in your sleep," Lala accuses as she slides into an empty setting at the table. "Muttering about pages and fire and some girl who cast spells."

I freeze with my food halfway to my mouth. "I did? What else did I say?"

My brain is screaming *this can't be happening* and *I was so careful!*

A huge yawn from Lala before she says, "That was pretty much it."

"I don't remember any of that." I try for a casual tone, as if the food in my belly hasn't turned to lead, a heavy ball that I want to vomit up.

"Of course you wouldn't, dummy, you were asleep." Lala snags a piece of buttered toast from the plate in the center of the table.

I can't believe it, though there's no way for Lala to make something like that up. Coincidence that I began talking in my sleep after I begin the burning? The two have to be connected.

I hastily ask to be excused and race to my *Púridaia's* room above the garage.

When her door opens to my banging, I nearly fall into her apartment.

"You've got to help me. We've got a problem." The words are almost indistinguishable from each other in my haste.

"Slow down, *chav,* and take a breath. Then tell me what is the matter." As I try to slow my breathing, I notice the healthy glow that fill my *Púridaia's* cheeks. Her skin is radiant, no longer crepey and wrinkled, her lips plump and pink, and her eyes sparkling with amusement. This *Púridaia* looks more like the pictures hung throughout our house. Almost as soon as I realize that, I realize something else, too: she looks almost exactly like my mother.

They could be sisters.

"I thought I figured out how to break the curse," I tell her, and I watch her eyes harden, the amusement turning to flinty interest.

"What have you done, Drina?" Her voice hits me like a slap.

I explain my solution to the problem, of the nights I spent writing the story and then burning the pages, of the way Lala looked when she came down today, and I see her eyes turn to chips of ice in her face.

Her shoulders square and she pulls her torso upright as if fortifying herself for battle.

"Stupid girl!" she hisses, and I reel as if struck. She's never spoken to me like that before. "Stupid, foolish girl! You think this is a game, Drina? Something written on a dry erase board that we can wipe away when it's convenient?"

"I thought I'd figured out a way to—"

"You didn't think at all and that was the problem!" *Púridaia's* voice is a thunderclap in the tiny room. She begins to pace the area between her bed and the wall, while I cringe away and wish I'd stayed downstairs.

"I had no way of knowing anything bad would happen," I mutter while I stare at my feet.

The air seems to shift as she suddenly steps very close to me, so close I have to lean back a little to look her in the eyes.

"This is no ordinary story, Drina. This is not some *once upon a time* to pass along when the time is right. This story is alive. It wants to be set free. And it will not let anybody cheat the system. Do you think you are the first to attempt such a thing?" Her voice is mocking and it goads me into a response.

"So what, I'm just supposed to let this thing eat me from the inside out? Let it turn me into a shriveled husk of the person I used to be?" My anger flares like a flash fire—as soon as the words are out of my mouth, fatigue sets in, making my limbs feel like weighted balls dragging me down toward the floor. It takes all my effort into not collapsing over on her bed.

But *Púridaia*, with the eyes of a raptor, sees and understands. "Yes. This is how it goes. How it's always gone. You think you're the first woman to regret taking this burden on?"

Now tears prick the backs of my eyes and I dash my hand across them, the hand with the thin skin and the wirey veins. "So what am I supposed to do?" I wish my voiced didn't sound as weak as I feel.

Púridaia extends one hand and gently passes it across my forehead and down one cheek, like she used to do when Lala and I were children. "You bear it, Drina, as have hundreds of women before you and hundreds will after."

"And when can I give it away?"

"Whenever you like. Whenever you feel you've carried your burden long enough."

"But why have you carried it for so long? You could've given it away anytime."

Instead of responding, *Púridaia* looks at me for several long, calculating moments. Then her lids lower and she glances down at her hands, turning them this way and that, as if examining them and truly seeing them for the first time.

"Did you know that my name is not *Púridaia?*" she asked in a soft voice. "I am nobody's grandmother. *Púridaia* is just the name your mother and I agreed to given the burden I bear."

"What do you mean?" I ask.

Now she gives me a direct look, the faded blue of her eyes the color of faded jeans. "*Beebi* is more appropriate."

I stare at her in confusion. "Aunt? But why would we call you—" And then I understand. The lipstick. *It reminds me of when I was your mother's age.* How mother never calls her *Púridaia*, only by her familiar name. How quickly my own body was aging. It's ravishing, this curse.

"Don't tell Lala or your brothers, though. We decided to wait until we absolutely had to." I don't need to ask who "we" means.

With a sob, I lean into her palm against my cheek and she draws me in for a hug. Her arms are strong, safe bands around me that make the rest of the world seem very far away. And as I sob into her shoulder, I realize I will continue to carry it for as long as I'm able. This is the real burden—carrying it until I can go no further, delaying the evil of passing it along.

This is the responsibility I agreed to.

Time marches forward and the shuv'hani of the present doesn't even remember the lineage of the shuv'hani of the past. The litany of names, the women who carried this burden before her, is lost in her hazy memories. That is the one thing she looks most forward to getting back—not her looks or a body that doesn't ache each morning with the weight of the story settling into every joint.

The memories. Who she was. Who she left behind. Who will be next in line.

"Sit down, *chav*. Listen closely." I lean forward, painfully aware of how the light in the room illuminates the crags of my face—it's not an attractive face, not anymore. But time will change that.

You will change that.

The story is a long one, and we'll get to it fully. But first, you must understand the rules that govern what you're about to hear. First you must agree to carry the story once I've told it to you.

Do you accept this burden?

Do you?

U is for Untellable

Brittany Warman

"Then Gretel gave her a push that drove her far into it, and shut the iron door, and fastened the bolt." – The Grimm Brothers' "Hansel and Gretel"

Look, I might as well tell you this, I gotta tell someone. You all already think I'm crazy anyway, so whatever. It's like you said, I'll start from the beginning.

Once upon a time.

Mrs. Morris' trailer was the end of the block, the last house before the dead end. The place was gaudy, the talk of the neighborhood right? It was painted entirely with unflattering pinks and greens and surrounded by an army of plastic garden creatures with dead, unseeing eyes and painted-on smiles. All us neighborhood kids used to dare each other to get close to it. It was a kind of game; we all knew Mrs.

Morris' house. Sometimes we'd try to steal a gnome, or sometimes the enormous rabbit with one ear by the living room window.

It began simply enough... a loss of appetite.

It was a pretty daring game, truth be told, because if you got caught, the situation was dire. Mrs. Morris would come out and you were lost. You lost and you were lost. She'd practically beam with delight, scoop you up, and take you inside her awful house to force feed you the dusty candy she kept all over the place. Some pieces were so sickeningly sweet that it felt like your teeth were going to fall out and some were sour - Jill Markison said her mouth stayed puckered for a week after eating one of those. It was awful in there. Point is, you didn't want to get caught.

Hamburgers, bananas, ice cream – once upon a once upon and they tasted of nothing. A nothing like loneliness, lioness, like a violin player lost at sea, like a mirror. I would bite my own lips to taste my blood, the only thing that ever stayed true, ever stayed me.

Plus it was just... well we didn't know how to say it at the time, but it was just sad in there. Lonely. Mrs. Morris lived alone, she didn't even have any pets, and she just kind of sat around all day and watched television until some kid wandered close enough to capture. Only she didn't see it as capturing, she just saw it as someone to talk to. Only we didn't see it that way then at all. None of us did, that's the point I'm trying to make... we were all creeped out by that woman. And Gretel wasn't.

Mrs. Morris, I've lost my ball, Mrs. Morris, you're so very small. Sing-song, in my head, sing-song, songs of the dead.

Gretel was an off kid for a long time, even you have to admit that. I'm two years older than her, you know, so she was just my kid sister most of the time, but I always knew there was something... I guess, yeah, "off" about her. She didn't like any of the things kids usually did. She was quiet. We would catch her doing things sometimes... sometimes stereotypical things you hear about "bad" kids doing, ripping legs off bugs and stuff like that, sometimes stranger things... using her own blood to brush her teeth, biting her tongue over and over to get enough to make it work. Laughing. Mumbling stuff that didn't make any sense. You know all this. But yeah, I mean, she's my kid sister. So who knows what I thought back then, I'm trying to tell you now that something's different.

Han sells seashells by the sea shore, Hansel doesn't know it's not me anymore.

Gretel started showing her weird interest in Mrs. Morris around the time of her birthday. She'd just turned eight, and our parents started letting her wander around the neighborhood more without me. I was fine with this, obviously, because who wants your little sister following you around everywhere? But even I noticed how she would go up to Mrs. Morris' door and just knock. The other kids and I would even watch her, especially when she first started doing it. Innocent little dark eyes, blonde hair in braids, she sauntered right up to that spooky house like she owned it. She went in every day for two weeks before it happened. What were they talking about in there?

Mrs. Morris, Mrs. Morris, let me in. You're so lonely, it's okay, I'm here. Wouldn't it all be better if you showed me how to make cookies in your pretty oven? Wouldn't it all be better if you just closed your eyes?

When they found Mrs. Morris' body, Gretel was still in the living room. She didn't say a word. And I know, I know, she's just a kid, she couldn't have had anything to do with it, but I swear, I look at her and I just know. I don't know what it is. That smile, the blood. She did something in that house, something to Mrs. Morris. And I'm freaked out by it, I'm trying not to be, because I know it makes me sound crazy, but I am.

Handsome Hansel, just let it be, a sweet delicious victory.

V is for Victory

BD Wilson

OFFICIAL TRANSCRIPT
CONFIDENTIAL
BEGIN

ECHO1: Tango2, respond.

TANGO2: Tango2, go ahead.

ECHO1: We need you to turn around and come back to the Institute.

TANGO2: That'll be a bitch on these roads, what's wrong?

ECHO1: Still trying to figure that out, but they're saying you're not safe to continue.

TANGO2: We're three miles from the nearest turnabout. Should be able to head back shortly.

ECHO1: Roger that, Tango2.

TANGO2: [muffled]

ECHO1: Tango2, report.

TANGO2: [gunfire]

ECHO1: Tango2, respond.

TANGO2: Mayday, send reinforcements.

ECHO1: Tango2, confirmed, reinforcements on the way. Report.
ECHO1: Tango2, respond.
ECHO1: [muffled] Get someone out there, now!
ECHO1: Tango2, respond.
END

COMMUNICATIONS RECORD
COMMANDER LOUISE SHEVCHENKO
CONFIDENTIAL
BEGIN

Director:

We located the body of target Rumsfeld. As expected, he was infected with the fungal parasite. The location of his remains (see map attached) matches a primary origin point in the simulations provided by our Institute contact.

There is little doubt he intended for this all along. All recovered buses and residents match hotspot locations in the simulations.

We've been played.

- Shevchenko

END

WEB CLIPPING
CLASSIFIED
COUNTRY OF ORIGIN: CANADA
BEGIN CLIPPING

Quarantine Facilities Open Amid Health Crisis

Today authorities opened the second of the emergency hospitals in the Toronto area, joining reports of over thirty facilities opened in cities world-wide. While details are still unavailable about the source of the contamination spreading through areas with large populations, the Public Health Agency of Canada is assuring everyone the outbreak is being contained.

However, there are reports the contaminant is being deliberately spread. Reassuring the public today, the Health Minister said there is absolutely no evidence of a campaign to infect the populace. "We need to focus on reality and not hysteria. This is not the time to fall for fake news."

END CLIPPING

ARCHIVIST'S NOTE: First use of the word "crisis" to describe the outbreak.

COMMINICATIONS RECORD

INTERCEPTED

BEGIN

THIS IS A TELE-GLOBAL COLLECT CALL FROM, Kayla Umbrage, AN INMATE AT, [CLASSIFIED] Research Facility. YOUR CALL IS BEING RECORDED.

KAYLA: Mom?

HEATHER: I'm here.

KAYLA: Thank you, for answering.

HEATHER: We don't have a lot of money. I can't afford to talk.

KAYLA: Are you even glad to hear from me?

HEATHER: Should I be?

KAYLA: Fuck.

HEATHER: Don't use that language.

KAYLA: This was a mistake.

CALL ENDED. TOTAL TIME: 2 MINUTES.

END

SYSTEM NOTICE: You have 6 files past archiving date. Leaving files on the system may result in data corruption.
ARCHIVE FILES NOW? Y/N
> Y

MEETING TRANSCRIPT
— CAPTAIN PATRICK JORDAN
— COMMANDER LOUISE SHEVCHENKO
CLASSIFIED
BEGIN

CAPTAIN JORDAN: At ease, Commander.

COMMANDER SHEVCHENKO: Thank you, sir.

JORDAN: I've read your situation report and agree with your summary. I want you to oversee the interrogation of the prisoner.

SHEVCHENKO: Prisoner?

JORDAN: Kayla Umbrage.

SHEVCHENKO: Sir, Umbrage was essential to our entry into the facility.

JORDAN: Which was, as you said, a set-up.

SHEVCHENKO: With respect, sir, Rumsfeld was behind that. Umbrage was not involved.

JORDAN: You're certain?

SHEVCHENKO: Yes, sir.

JORDAN: Then that's what the interrogation will support, won't it?

SHEVCHENKO: Sir... Yes, sir. I'll assign an interviewer.

JORDAN: Excellent. Dismissed.

END

INTERVIEW TRANSCRIPT, INMATE PATIENT 1250, Kayla Umbrage.

BEGIN

OFFICER CARTER: This is Officer Irene Carter, interviewing suspect Kayla Umbrage—

KAYLA UMBRAGE: Suspect?

CARTER: State your name for the record, please.

UMBRAGE: Kayla Umbrage.

CARTER: And your position at the Rumsfeld Institute?

UMBRAGE: Statistical Analysis Technician.

CARTER: How long were you in that position?

UMBRAGE: Two years, about.

CARTER: Can you be more precise than that?

UMBRAGE: No, I cannot.

CARTER: Very well, what did you do at the Rumsfeld Institute?

UMBRAGE: I ran simulations based on statistical models that tested data sets provided by Dr. Rumsfeld.

CARTER: And what were the models based on?

UMBRAGE: Recovered information from archaeological sites, fossil records, maybe a few guesses, I don't really know.

CARTER: What was the purpose of the model?

UMBRAGE: To try and track the movement of an ancient fungus through the world and see if we could come up with a timeline from first appearance to complete contamination.

CARTER: What did he need this information for?

UMBRAGE: He didn't say.

CARTER: You didn't ask?

UMBRAGE: Asking was not encouraged. We were told how we could assist with the Institute's purpose and we did what we were told.

CARTER: But you figured out what the model would be used for?

UMBRAGE: Eventually, yes.

CARTER: How?

UMBRAGE: I was talking to someone else, who provided information I hadn't had before. I put it together.

CARTER: Who gave you the information?

UMBRAGE: Does it matter?

CARTER: Yes.

UMBRAGE: I disagree.

CARTER: We'll come back to that. What was the information?

UMBRAGE: That the biological labs were growing fungal cultures of an ancient species.

CARTER: And what did you conclude from that?

UMBRAGE: Based on the information about the lab and the models we were running, I concluded Dr. Rumsfeld wanted to release the fungus into the wild.

CARTER: What would result from that?

UMBRAGE: Extinction.

CARTER: Of what?

UMBRAGE: The human race and any other species that fungus came in contact with. Eventually, it would just take over everything, spread everywhere. We'd all die, probably quickly, if the models were correct.

CARTER: What did you do with this information?

UMBRAGE: Called you.

CARTER: Please be more specific.

UMBRAGE: I called the Public Health Agency, which called anti-terrorism forces, which was you.

CARTER: What happened then?

UMBRAGE: We created a plan for you to infiltrate the Institute and destroy the fungus while capturing Dr. Rumsfeld.

CARTER: Is that what happened?

UMBRAGE: Not exactly. I got you into the Institute and into the lab, but they shot Dr. Rumsfeld and he died before reaching the hospital. Also, it was too late.

CARTER: Too late?

UMBRAGE: We were all infected, every single one of us. It didn't matter that we destroyed it in the lab, because we took it out the door with us. We destroyed everything for no reason.

CARTER: Did you warn Dr. Rumsfeld about the planned attack?

UMBRAGE: What? No!

CARTER: Then how did he know to infect everyone in the Institute?

UMBRAGE: What are you talk— No. That happened a long time ago. People have been carrying this thing for months without knowing it. The doctors told us it was just a rash.

CARTER: And you believed them?

UMBRAGE: Of course I did. Why wouldn't I?

CARTER: Even when it wouldn't go away?

UMBRAGE: Yes. That's just the way things were.

CARTER: The way things were?

UMBRAGE: You don't believe me, do you?

CARTER: I'd like to, Ms. Umbrage. But I need you to cooperate.

UMBRAGE: That's all I've been doing since I got here. Maybe it's your turn.

END

MEETING TRANSCRIPT
— COMMANDER LOUISE SHEVCHENKO
— OFFICER IRENE CARTER
CLASSIFIED
BEGIN

COMMANDER SHEVCHENKO: She maintained her innocence.

OFFICER CARTER: Yes sir, but that's not unusual in the first meeting.

SHEVCHENKO: And if she is innocent?

CARTER: It's far too early to tell. We need to apply more pressure.

SHEVCHENKO: This isn't enough?

CARTER: Not yet, sir.

SHEVCHENKO: Continue, then.

END

COMMUNICATIONS RECORD
INMATE PATIENT 1250
INTERCEPTED
BEGIN

Dear Victor,

Have you been watching the news? They're rioting in London.

Maybe this was all inevitable. Maybe I found out what Dr. Rumsfeld was doing too late. I keep looking at that, thinking back, and wondering if I should have made a different choice.

Three months ago, I asked you to come to my quarters to watch a movie, remember? I know I said later it wasn't, but it was a date, Victor, it was. You're so sweet and so shy and probably the nicest person I've ever met, and I wanted to get to know you better. I wanted to know what you were like when it was just the two of us. Well, the two of us and the surveillance cameras, but they don't count.

You were so nervous. That's what I remember. It was cute. I wished I had wine to offer you instead of fruit juice, but maybe it was better I didn't. We sat on my bed and you ran your hand over different spaces on my patchwork quilt and we talked the whole way through the movie. It was just about perfect.

You talk more when you're nervous, I think maybe speaking before you're really aware of what you're saying. Do you remember telling me about your day? Do you remember telling me more than you were supposed to? That was when I learned you were working on a fungus. An ancient one.

I figured out then why we weren't to talk about our work. It wasn't to preserve the experiments, it wasn't to protect them. It was so no one had enough information to put it all together. But that night, I did.

It's not your fault. Just so you know. We were talking and I told you more about what I was working on than I should have, too, but you let it pass the way you always do. It wasn't your fault. You just returned the favour.

I wish I'd been able to let it go by without hearing it.

Before the movie was even over, I knew what Dr. Rumsfeld was planning was too serious to just sit by and let happen. Before the movie was even over, I knew it would get dangerous and that things wouldn't go well if I was discovered. Before the movie was even over, I knew I couldn't call it a date anymore. You were already too close to me. If we got any closer and I got caught, then you'd go down with me. I didn't want that to happen and I was pretty sure I was going to get caught.

It was nothing you did. It was nothing you said. It was nothing about you.

I made the decision to protect you. Best laid plans, eh?

Kayla

END

SYSTEM NOTICE: You have 17 files past archiving date. Leaving files on the system may result in data corruption.
ARCHIVE FILES NOW? Y/N
> Y

INTERVIEW TRANSCRIPT, INMATE PATIENT 1250, Kayla Umbrage.

BEGIN

OFFICER CARTER: Let's talk about something else. Do you know where the buses went?

KAYLA UMBRAGE: What buses? Wait, the ones everyone left on?

CARTER: Yes, the evacuation buses that left the Institute.

UMBRAGE: Why would I know where they are? They're where ever you sent them.

CARTER: They did not arrive at their destinations.

[ARCHIVIST'S NOTE: SEE EXHIBIT 15-23, PHOTOGRAPHS, BUS AND AMBULANCE SCENE]

CARTER: This happened before they got there.

UMBRAGE: Oh my god.

CARTER: The other cultists were not recovered.

UMBRAGE: Did they kill anyone?

CARTER: The drivers of all vehicles.

UMBRAGE: Oh god. I can't believe this happened. I can't believe this is happening.

END

WEB CLIPPING

CLASSIFIED

COUNTRY OF ORIGIN: CANADA

BEGIN CLIPPING

Cult Member Investigation Begins

Yesterday the Crown Attorney announced charges are being sought against Kayla Umbrage in connection with the string of deaths attributed to the work of the Institute for Preservation of the Earth, also known as the Rumsfeld Institute after its founder Professor

Fredrick Rumsfeld. While they have not disclosed the charges against Rumsfeld, experts believe them to be related to the terrorist claims made during many of the public suicides by other Institute members.

Umbrage reportedly became a member of the Rumsfeld Institute two years ago after the professor gave a talk on preserving the environment and the need for hard data to convince others to agree with his vision. Since that time, the Institute itself has been labelled a cult, and more recently as a terrorist group, by several investigative agencies.

The recent deaths are being linked to an act of biological terrorism, though authorities have been hesitant to release specific details about the biological agent used in the suicides. We know the communicability is high and that the Public Health Agency of Canada, along with agencies in other countries, has issued warnings for areas with high populations. People are being encouraged to report any incidences of sudden rashes and to see their doctors immediately if the symptom occurs.

Umbrage's suspected connection to the terrorist attacks has not been released to the public, but her first hearing is scheduled for next week and we expect more details to be revealed there.

END

MEETING TRANSCRIPT
— CAPTAIN PATRICK JORDAN
— COMMANDER LOUISE SHEVCHENKO
CLASSIFIED
BEGIN

COMMANDER SHEVCHENKO: We still have nothing to go on, sir.

CAPTAIN JORDAN: Do we have transcripts of her original calls?

SHEVCHENKO: Yes, sir. They're pulling the records and having people go through them along with all her correspondence.

JORDAN: That will give us what we need.

SHEVCHENKO: Sir, I've listened to those calls before. She didn't say anything that would be of concern.

JORDAN: You need to change your perspective, Commander.

SHEVCHENKO: Sir?

JORDAN: We need to reassure the public they are in good hands. We need to reassure them they are protected. We cannot do that if the military responsible for that defence is the same one that raided those facilities and brought this thing out in the first place.

SHEVCHENKO: But we were.

JORDAN: No. The military that raided those facilities was one operating under false information planted by someone intent on hurting the world and its people. We are not culpable, because we were deliberately misled. That is what you said in your report, wasn't it?

SHEVCHENKO: It is what I believe. I'm just don't think this is how it happened.

JORDAN: You will find the evidence.

SHEVCHENKO: Sir, we don't know what—

JORDAN: You will find the evidence, either in the calls or somewhere else. Do you understand?

SHEVCHENKO: Yes, sir.

JORDAN: Good. Contact me again when you have it.

END

INTERVIEW TRANSCRIPT, INMATE PATIENT 1250, Kayla Umbrage.

BEGIN

OFFICER CARTER: Why did you call us?

KAYLA UMBRAGE: We've gone over this.

CARTER: Why did you call us?

UMBRAGE: I needed to stop Dr. Rumsfeld and I couldn't do it alone. I called you for help. I thought if the Institute was shut down and the fungus destroyed that would be the end of it.

CARTER: You wanted the fungus destroyed?

UMBRAGE: Yes.

CARTER: You know that would mean killing everyone in the facility?

UMBRAGE: I know that now. I didn't know it then.

CARTER: Really?

UMBRAGE: Yes, really.

CARTER: Can you prove that?

UMBRAGE: Well, killing everyone in the facility would mean killing myself, so obviously it wasn't what I wanted.

CARTER: That isn't as obvious as you seem to think.

UMBRAGE: Give me a break.

CARTER: You recognize this?

[ARCHIVIST'S NOTE: SEE EXHIBIT 12, PHOTOGRAPH, RUMSFELD RECOVERY SCENE]

UMBRAGE: Yes.

CARTER: Do you know what it is?

UMBRAGE: It's a growth of the fungus, looks like on a body that's been left for a while.

CARTER: Two days. This picture was taken two days after the ambulance carrying Dr. Rumsfeld was driven off the road.

UMBRAGE: That's him?

CARTER: Yes.

UMBRAGE: Damn.

CARTER: Can you tell us how you, and everyone in the Institute, carried that fungus for months, if this is what it can do in two days?

UMBRAGE: I don't know.

CARTER: What was that?

UMBRAGE: I don't know.

CARTER: Then don't you think it makes more sense for the infection to have been more recent?

UMBRAGE: No, I don't think that.

CARTER: Ms. Umbrag—

UMBRAGE: I know when this damn thing turned up on my thigh, okay? I didn't know what it was then, but I know how long I've been carrying it. I have no idea when it's going to turn around and kill me. I don't know how it works. You'll have to ask Vi— You'll have to ask someone else about that.

CARTER: Did you tell Dr. Rumsfeld we were coming?

UMBRAGE: No. I absolutely did not.

CARTER: Did you tell them to infect [rustling] Dr. Gerry Haan?

UMBRAGE: Fuck! No! This is messed up.

CARTER: Ms. Umbrage, calm down.

UMBRAGE: Go to hell. This is fucking ridiculous. I'm done talking to you.

END

COMMUNICATIONS RECORD
INMATE PATIENT 1250
INTERCEPTED
BEGIN

Dear Victor,

I don't know if I'm doing the right thing. I don't even know if it matters anymore.

We didn't know what Rumsfeld was planning. That's the truth, but no one is interested in it. They want to believe everyone in the Institute was in on it. They want to believe no one could deceive that many people for that long.

I feel like an idiot. I was the only one stupid enough to believe they could, or would, help.

Maybe they would have, if we'd kept the fungus from getting out. After all, if we'd won, Dr. Rumsfeld would be standing trial and they'd be looking for heroes. You, me, Shevchenko, we'd all be filling those roles. The newspapers would be running the interviews, asking Shevchenko about her infiltration of the facility, asking us about how we figured it all out. They'd be playing all the angles to show how wonderful we were, how horrible Dr. Rumsfeld was.

But reality never works out as we plan, does it?

We never talked about what we were doing there, at the Institute. I mean, other than the obvious. Save the world and all that. We never talked about why it didn't matter that we had to give up everything else in our lives to come do it. Sure, who wouldn't? If they believed they could, I mean.

I don't know that I ever really believed we would. I wanted to, I was committed to do it, but it was just such a big job. How could anyone, any group, save the world in my lifetime?

Well, I guess we have the answer now. Just kill everyone. Simple, done. Damn it, everything is messed up.

I came to the Institute because I'd lost all faith in anything. My parents, my religion, my community, it all let me down in one way or another. Not that I was entitled to anything, but there are some expectations, you know? Your parents guide you, your religion gives you faith, your community a place to belong. That's what defines those things. If they can't do that, then what are they?

Useless. So, I found someone to guide me. I found something to give me faith. I found a place to belong. It didn't matter that I had to leave everything else behind, because there was nothing to leave. It existed. I existed within it. That was all.

Seems more important now it's all falling apart. They're quarantining entire cities now, did you know? Every time I turn on the news, I hear about someone else being found. Sometimes it's people I recognize, people we lived with. Sometimes it's strangers from the other branches. Dr. Rumsfeld got what he wanted: multiple origin points.

They're still trying to contain it, but they've lost. I only know what I saw in the simulations, but I can still see that. Dr. Rumsfeld was right. It will survive, it will take over, and the Earth will move on without us.

Everything I tried went to hell. Maybe it would have been better if I'd done nothing. I think about it, sometimes, what would have happened if I'd just decided I was wrong. If I'd told myself Dr. Rumsfeld couldn't be doing what I thought and just let it go.

I think the world would have wound up in the same place, in the end. Dr. Rumsfeld would have been able to go with his actual plan, instead of this backup plan, and that would have been the only difference. No one would have been prepared, but it's not like they've handled it well even with advanced warning.

Would there be the same panic? Would there have been time? I don't think so. I think that's the problem. In trying to stop it, I just gave everyone time to worry.

I set this all in motion the moment I called for help.

Kayla

END

SYSTEM NOTICE: You have 26 files past archiving date. Leaving files on the system may result in data corruption.
ARCHIVE FILES NOW? Y/N
> Y

MEETING TRANSCRIPT

— COMMANDER LOUISE SHEVCHENKO

— OFFICER IRENE CARTER

CLASSIFIED

BEGIN

COMMANDER SHEVCHENKO: She's doing what?

OFFICER CARTER: Writing to the other prisoner.

SHEVCHENKO: [rustling] How could she not know?

CARTER: Sir, the important part is that she doesn't. We can use this.

SHEVCHENKO: For what?

CARTER: These letters demonstrate an attachment. It might be enough pressure to get her to admit her role in the attacks.

SHEVCHENKO: Her role.

CARTER: Yes, sir. It's important we do this quickly. The hearings are almost over and they must introduce all evidence before it stops.

SHEVCHENKO: The evidence we need. Damn it.

CARTER: Sir?

SHEVCHENKO: Nothing.

CARTER: I'll begin the new session immediately.

SHEVCHENKO: No.

CARTER: Commander, this is what we've been waiting for.

SHEVCHENKO: I know. I'll handle this one.

CARTER: Sir, I know it's taken longer than we expected—

SHEVCHENKO: That's not it, Carter. I can't do this to her without looking her in the eye.

END

INTERVIEW TRANSCRIPT, INMATE PATIENT 1250, Kayla Umbrage.

BEGIN

KAYLA UMBRAGE: Shevchenko!

COMMANDER SHEVCHENKO: This is Commander Louise Shevchenko, interviewing suspect Kayla Umbrage.

UMBRAGE: No, not you, too. Please.

SHEVCHENKO: Ms. Umbrage, Officer Carter has spent a lot of time talking to you, but it's time to put an end to this. Do you understand what your actions did?

UMBRAGE: Of course I understand.

SHEVCHENKO: Why did you set us up like that?

UMBRAGE: I didn't!

SHEVCHENKO: We trusted you. We went in there to help you.

UMBRAGE: I didn't set you up.

SHEVCHENKO: You brought us into a contaminated facility, a place where we were expected to take that contamination out with us. Did you know we might get infected?

UMBRAGE: Hell no. I didn't know I was infected. I didn't know Victor was.

SHEVCHENKO: Did you know what would happen to Victor, when you asked him to take us to the lab?

UMBRAGE: No, of course not.

SHEVCHENKO: You knew he could get hurt.

UMBRAGE: Yes.

SHEVCHENKO: You knew he could die.

UMBRAGE: Yes.

SHEVCHENKO: Did you feel anything, asking him to do that for you?

UMBRAGE: Of course I did. I didn't want him to get hurt. Everything I did, keeping this from him, was because I didn't want him to get hurt.

SHEVCHENKO: He got more than hurt, Kayla.

[ARCHIVIST'S NOTE: Photograph placed on table: Levine, Victor; autopsy.]

SHEVCHENKO: That's him, under all that fungus. That's him, eaten from the inside out.

UMBRAGE: Wh— no. Oh, Victor, no. How did that happen?

SHEVCHENKO: He told us the parasite is opportunistic, takes advantage when the host is weakened. He was shot, remember? In the lab, Rumsfeld shot him. He was as good as dead before we left.

UMBRAGE: Oh God, no. No, no, no.

SHEVCHENKO: He was in that room, and he's dead now, because you brought us in.

UMBRAGE: Bastard.

SHEVCHENKO: He's dead, Kayla, because of you.

UMBRAGE: I know that.

SHEVCHENKO: Don't you think you owe us, and owe him, the truth?

UMBRAGE: I told you the truth. I had no idea what he was planning.

SHEVCHENKO: Look at what you did, Kayla. Not just to us, look at what you did to Victor. Don't you think it's time you stopped lying, stopped pretending this was all a mistake?

UMBRAGE: I'm not...

SHEVCHENKO: He can't have done all of this by chance, Kayla. Every single step of it was planned. There is no way Rumsfeld would have left out the most important part. Rumsfeld needed someone to come to us. He needed someone to bring us in. He needed you.

UMBRAGE: I'm telling you—

SHEVCHENKO: Every single step, Kayla. Look at them, from the fight in the lab, to leaving in the ambulance, the attack on the buses, taking the members all over the world, putting Rumsfeld up on that cliff. Each and every step carefully planned, and all of them, all of them, relying on someone in the organization figuring out what he was up to and deciding not to go along with it. All of it needed Victor to make an off-handed remark, to you of all people. Do you really think it was a coincidence?

UMBRAGE: It was.

SHEVCHENKO: It wasn't, Kayla. We know it wasn't, it couldn't be. Which means someone was in on it, and if it wasn't you, it was Victor.

UMBRAGE: Victor would never have done anything like that.

SHEVCHENKO: Really? You said it yourself, he always followed the rules, so why break one? Why tell you the fungus he was working on was ancient?

UMBRAGE: He was nervous.

SHEVCHENKO: Come on, Kayla. We both know no one gets that nervous. Maybe it wasn't an accident. Maybe he didn't slip up. Maybe he did exactly what he was supposed to do and gave you the information you needed to put the pieces together.

UMBRAGE: That's ridiculous.

SHEVCHENKO: Maybe he's a murderer and a martyr to the cause, just like Rumsfeld.

UMBRAGE: No.

SHEVCHENKO: It's one or the other, Kayla. It has to be. And since Victor isn't here to tell us, we have to rely on you. So, which of you was it?

UMBRAGE: ... Me.

SHEVCHENKO: What was that?

UMBRAGE: It was me. I set you up. I knew what Rumsfeld was planning and I brought you in to make sure it would work.

SHEVCHENKO: Are you willing to sign a statement to that effect?

UMBRAGE: Yes.

SHEVCHENKO: Thank you, for telling the truth. I'll be back with the stenographer.

END

SYSTEM MESSAGE

ARCHIVE REQUIRED

You have 36 files past archiving date. Leaving files on the system
may result in data corruption.

ENCRYPT AND ARCHIVE FILES NOW? Y/N

> Y

WEB CLIPPING

CLASSIFIED

COUNTRY OF ORIGIN: UNITED STATES OF AMERICA

BEGIN CLIPPING

Doomsday Cult Hearing Concludes

Today marks the end of the hearing to determine the responsibility
of Kayla Umbrage, a member of the cult the Institute for Preservation
of the Earth, in the global outbreak of a fatal, parasitic, fungal
infection. Umbrage has maintained that she had no knowledge of the
plan to release the fungus. This despite being a member of the team
that created models and projections for the spread over the world,
identifying the most effective means to carry the spores from the
Institute to as many population centres as possible.

Umbrage has no approved council, as this is a hearing not a trial
and a lawyer is not required, but the prosecutor for the state has issued
a press release stating she believes this final day of the hearing will
resolve all issues regarding culpability for the event.

END

COMMUNICATIONS RECORD

INMATE PATIENT 1250

INTERCEPTED

BEGIN

Dear Victor,

There were so many of us. All of those people. There is no way every single one people decided Rumsfeld was right, died for the cause after all. I didn't. You didn't. You didn't decide to, I mean. You still died, though. You still died.

What was the point of all this?

I look down at the rash on my thigh, I see that damn fungus embedded in my skin and I see the end. There's no cure, no way to remove it. Maybe if they amputate my leg, but I can't guarantee there isn't another bit of it somewhere else. I know how I'll die, even if I don't know when.

Maybe that's what they've realized that I haven't. All the Institute members, the ones killing themselves in the middle of cities, maybe that's the real reason they chose to die. Even if they didn't want the human race wiped out, even if they thought Rumsfeld was wrong about that, they're committed now, aren't they?

No one heard Rumsfeld, not until he did this. They thought he was a quack, that the world could just keep on running without humans having to change a thing. If nothing else, humans will have to change everything now, won't they? It's a damn high price to pay for it.

I'm just not sure it's too high. Not anymore.

I'm sorry. I'm so sorry.

Love,

Kayla

END

MEETING TRANSCRIPT
— CAPTAIN PATRICK JORDAN
— COMMANDER LOUISE SHEVCHENKO
CLASSIFIED
BEGIN

COMMANDER SHEVCHENKO: Can we block the media from the hearing?

CAPTAIN JORDAN: Unlikely to do much good.

SHEVCHENKO: It will stop details from getting out.

JORDAN: It will increase distrust and lose us control of the message. Is Umbrage under control?

SHEVCHENKO: She won't be testifying and won't be speaking at the hearing.

JORDAN: See that she doesn't. And make sure someone acts as her lawyer. If the press is there, we don't want any appearance of impropriety.

SHEVCHENKO: Understood.

END

COMMUNICATIONS RECORD
INMATE PATIENT 1250
INTERCEPTED
BEGIN
    MAILER-DAEMON
    MESSAGE DELIVERY FAILURE
    MAILBOX [Victor.Levine@IPESentinels.com] EXCEEDED STORAGE CAPACITY
    REDELIVERY ATTEMPTS EXCEEDED TIMEOUT
    MESSAGE UNDELIVERED
END

WEB CLIPPING
CLASSIFIED
COUNTRY OF ORIGIN: GREAT BRITAIN

BEGIN CLIPPING

Riot at Cult Hearing

The hearing for Canadian Kayla Umbrage, one of the few members of the Rumsfeld Institute captured by authorities, took place early this morning, with rioters attacking the accused on her way into the court house. Protestors threw bottles, stones, and other objects at Umbrage and her security detail as they attempted to enter the building. The group was forced return to their vehicle and leave scene for their own safety.

Judge Cochran held the hearing with the accused in absentia. Umbrage submitted a statement admitting to participation in the terrorist attack and was remanded without bail awaiting trial.

Umbrage was reportedly injured in the attack when one of the thrown bottles struck her head causing a severe laceration. She was taken to an unspecified medical facility for treatment. While the wound required eight stitches, she was able to return to her holding facility and is expected to stand trial in three months' time.

END

MEETING TRANSCRIPT
— CAPTAIN PATRICK JORDAN
— COMMANDER LOUISE SHEVCHENKO
CLASSIFIED
BEGIN

CAPTAIN JORDAN: Congratulations on a job well done, Commander.

COMMANDER SHEVCHENKO: Well done, sir? Umbrage died.

JORDAN: That was inevitable. She was infected. It was only a matter of time.

SHEVCHENKO: She could have been protected.

JORDAN: After causing the outbreak, she didn't deserve it.

SHEVCHENKO: She didn't deserve it.

JORDAN: Glad you see reason. We'll be able to move on from this now.

SHEVCHENKO: Move on?

JORDAN: Of course. They've found and punished the ones to blame. That means people can let go of their anger and focus on solving the problem, on doing what needs to be done.

SHEVCHENKO: Do you really think that's what they'll do, sir?

JORDAN: It's what we'll make happen. There is no other choice.

END

SYSTEM MESSAGE

ARCHIVE REQUIRED

You have 56 files past archiving date. Leaving files on the system may result in data corruption.

ENCRYPT AND ARCHIVE FILES NOW? Y/N

> Y

SYSTEM MESSAGE

ARCHIVE REQUIRED

You have 78 files past archiving date. Leaving files on the system may result in data corruption.

ENCRYPT AND ARCHIVE FILES NOW? Y/N

>

SYSTEM MESSAGE

ARCHIVE REQUIRED

You have 109 files past archiving date. Leaving files on the system may result in data corruption.
ENCRYPT AND ARCHIVE FILES NOW? Y/N
>

SYSTEM MESSAGE
WARNING: MEMORY EXCEEDED
SYSTEM SHUT DOWN EMINENT
ARCHIVE REQUIRED
ENCRYPT AND ARCHIVE FILES NOW? Y/N
>

SYSTEM MESSAGE
SYSTEM SHUT DOWN

W is for Witness

L.S. Johnson

Paris, 1750

1.

He had been told to go to a tavern far in the suburbs. At first he had gone to the riverfront where, he fancied, such business was usually discussed, but his carefully worded inquiries had elicited only a fearful amusement. At last a man had explained: *Monsieur, for what you ask you need the devil himself*—and provided Linard with a whispered address.

The devil, it seemed, did his drinking outside of Paris, out of reach of both police and priest.

That had been the previous evening. Now Linard rode past the remains of the old city walls, past the decrepit inns crowding the road just past the city gates, past the windmills turning long into the night. He turned away from this unpleasant vista and instead peered through the back of the carriage at the receding silhouette of Paris. Somewhere in that shadowy mass was his clean, soft featherbed, his warm fire, his nightly glass of wine, all ensconced in his stylish yet modest house, precisely the domicile one would expect of a respectable merchant.

In Paris, appearances were everything.

God tested Man, that was His way. Linard knew, instinctively, that this was his test, and with every turn of the carriage wheels he was drawing closer to failure. *The devil himself.* A better man would forgive, even if it meant losing everything—his business, his house, his growing reputation as not only an importer of fabrics but a fashion-maker. Oh, God was giving him a test worthy of Job, for was it not on the very same night he had seen Madame Royale in his blue silk that his wife had told him she was with child? He had sold half his goods the next day, every young woman had been in a frenzy to match the princess, so much money he had hired two men to walk home with him while he clutched the box to his chest and begged God to keep him safe, for he was going to be a father, a success, a father, a success...

The carriage halted.

Linard stepped out and promptly sank into mud nearly to the tops of his shoes. Thankfully he was dressed in the oldest clothes he could find to keep from being recognized. The driver held out his hand silently, and silently Linard pressed more money into it, hoping it would be enough to keep the fellow waiting.

It was a long walk back to Paris.

As he squared his shoulders and made for the low door and its raucous noise, it began to rain. Yes, Linard said silently, looking up at the heavens. Yes, I know, but I am not that strong, and hell is a small price to pay.

And with that, he entered the tavern.

Job, Linard thought, had it easy.

As if he heard Linard's thoughts, the man sitting across from him sighed, a sigh that abruptly ended in a sour belch. He was younger than Linard and more handsome by any standard, but his suit was worn to a shine and his face bore the signs of a rapidly approaching dissolution. He had introduced himself as François and Linard had nearly laughed aloud, for these men were always François or Louis or Charles, no family name to be held against them like another chit. How many François did he see every day, dawdling in the streets to no purpose, drunk before dinner? Sometimes he thought Paris was filled with them and the coarse company they kept. A whole generation of Frenchmen given over to drink, cards, and whoring. That he had to confess the full story of his humiliation to this man—it was yet another injury he could lay at his wife's feet.

This particular François was looking at him with what might have been a thoughtful expression, save that his eyes were unfocused and his mouth open. For a moment Linard thought he had fallen asleep.

Finally François shook his head bullishly and lurched forward, and Linard primly leaned a little ways across the table.

"Monsieur Linard, I must tell you something," François said. He smiled, baring a mouthful of uneven, yellowed teeth. "Every man thinks his wife is a slut. *Every* man. All these fellows?" He flicked a dirty hand at the room. "Married to a whore, every one of them—or so they will tell you. Even if your wife has indeed put horns on you? Women are fickle, they are like children, they only think of their own pleasure. You should not take it to heart." His voice dropped lower, a sickening purr. "If you want my advice, you will keep those pretty louis d'or you carry, go back to Paris, and amuse yourself." His grin broadened as Linard clapped a protective hand over his coat pocket. "As well for the bull as the cow, eh? I can give you an address if you need one. The ladies there are remarkably talented."

Linard made himself take a breath before fixing François with his sternest gaze. Just another merchant trying to fleece him, he told himself. Another nobleman's brat who thought he could outwit Linard because Linard had married into his trade. Nothing but a lowborn hustler lolling in rag trade velvet and a filthy wig, stinking of brandy; oh, he had met the likes of François before, and he always came out the better in the end.

"*Monsieur* François," he said coolly, "I think this has been a mistake. I asked for someone who could solve a very particular problem, in a manner requiring both boldness and discretion. You lack both qualities, and others as well." He smiled, the barest curling of his lips. "Pimps like you can be found on every street in Paris, and some of them will even pretend to respect you. You are nothing but a waste of my time."

He started to rise, but François' hand shot out, seizing Linard by the slight bulge in his coat pocket. His eyes were suddenly clear. "You misunderstand, Monsieur," he said. "We can solve your, ah, *problem*. Only I have had others cry foul after the fact." He had not let go of Linard's coat. "This thing will be on your head, no matter who commits the deed. Are you *certain*, Monsieur?"

"Yes," Linard said at once, though his throat was dry.

Slowly François released him and sat back. "How do you know?"

"Pardon?" Linard shoved his hand in his coat pocket, feeling the coins. They suddenly felt heavy, impossibly heavy, he thought he might fall over from the weight of them.

"How do you know the child isn't yours?"

Linard hesitated. He knew no one would hear over the din of the tavern; still he found it difficult to form the words.

His featherbed. His wine. The crackle of his fireplace. Waking to chocolate and fresh bread and the soothing glory of his account books.

He whispered the words, but they were lost in a roar of outrage from the bar.

François cupped his ear. "The boy is what?"

Linard swallowed. "He is *dark*," he repeated.

For a moment François looked surprised, then he began to grin. "The child is dark? That is your complaint?" He snorted. "So, what, she's had it off with a—"

Before Linard knew what he was doing he was halfway across the table, his hand stinging and François' cheek flaring red. But the younger man only chuckled. "And now I understand you, Monsieur."

"I—I apologize," Linard gasped, sitting back down and dabbing his face with his handkerchief. The tavern, drafty when he first entered, now felt unbearably close; he was sweltering beneath his coat. "Only—you can see how deeply I am wounded. We spoke our vows before *God*. And then she presents me with—with *that*—"

He could not speak further; he pressed the handkerchief to his mouth.

François was biting his lip, though whether in sympathy or stifled mirth Linard could not tell. "And what was her explanation?"

"She had no explanation," he rasped. "She swore her fidelity, she said the coloring comes from her family. She is a brunette, to be sure, but nothing like... and I am as you see." He gestured to his own pale skin and watery blue eyes. "She cannot even be bothered to lie, she mocks me to my face. Her father's portrait hangs in our hall! And I am to believe that child is a product of our union? I know her family has never approved of me; they think me some sport of nature, because I am an educated man born of peasants. But I always thought that she..." He took a shuddering breath, why was he even telling this whelp such things? "As God is my witness, there is *nothing* of me in that child."

François, however, merely shrugged at this outpouring. "So just put her away. Stick her in a convent, or in the hospital."

"I cannot," Linard said in a low voice. Oh, he was a fool, a fool! Tomorrow all of Paris would be awash in gossip, yet he could not stop his mouth from moving. "Her father gave me the money to start my business," he continued. "If I put her away, her family will exercise their share to my detriment, despite the distance—"

"The distance?"

"Her family owns a plantation," Linard explained. "Her brother was at university, but he has since returned to the islands. She has no family in France. But that is not to say she is without friends, if they start to talk, my reputation... and I have so many competitors, they will use any advantage. I cannot in *any way* be implicated..."

"And what of the boy?"

Lost in his fearful reverie, it took Linard a moment to grasp the import of François' words—

and in that moment, high above the roar of the tavern, a baby squalled. Linard's whole body jerked in instinctive response; he looked around wildly, half-expecting his wife to appear. The heat, these questions, and now this? What fool would bring an infant to such a place?

"Well?" François prompted. "To be clear, Monsieur, I myself do not give a fig. But I will be asked in turn."

Linard felt a strange laughter rising in his throat, something between a giggle and a scream. "The boy? What does it matter? I... I thought to send him to the country to nurse, and when the time was right I would bring him to an orphanage. What does it matter?" He swallowed down a cackle. "They told me you work for the devil himself, Monsieur; now you tell me such a man has scruples? Unless he has a use for the brat?"

François did not respond; he simply looked at Linard for a long moment, his expression unreadable. The baby had settled into fitful crying, a staccato within the hum of raised voices and clinking metal and glass. Linard's shirt was sticking to himself. He had a sudden urge to weep.

"Very well, Monsieur," François said abruptly. "We can provide you with what you want—for a price." He leaned forward again, his breath rank. "I will take what you carry now, as a deposit. You will bring twenty more on the day, and nothing will happen if you arrive with less."

Linard swallowed. He could not tell if he was relieved or disturbed that the price was so low. "I can manage that, though I will need a little time, to gather such a sum."

"You deal in textiles, yes?"

For a moment Linard just blinked, then, "pardon?"

"You deal in fabrics? Silks, wools, that sort of thing?" François cocked an eyebrow at him.

"Yes, but I do not see—"

"Twenty louis d'or, then, plus a bolt—a full bolt—of silk. With matching trim. We will send the color to you beforehand."

"Pardon?" he repeated, astonished.

"You heard me." François' smile hadn't wavered. "That pocketful now, twenty more, plus one bolt of silk with trim to match, enough to finish a dress. Color to be determined." He held up his hand. "We will arrange for the carriage and the location, but you must accompany your wife and use our carriage back. Is that understood?"

Slowly Linard nodded.

"Then we have a deal, Monsieur." He held out his hand.

"You cannot leave any trace," Linard said to the outstretched palm. "Not so much as a hair. She *must* vanish utterly, I *must* be able to claim ignorance—"

"I give you my word, Monsieur," François said, his hand still extended. "Your wife will cease to exist, and you will in no way be implicated in her disappearance."

Taking a breath, Linard placed his hand in François', clasping it tightly. The young man's palm was hot against his own; suddenly the little alcove was cold, someone must have opened a door and let the chill autumn air in. He shivered, and only then did François release him. At that moment the baby ceased crying, as if smothered.

The robust fire seemed to bake the very guilt off Linard, let him shed the night's excursion like the blackened crusts of fat his mother used to wrap their meat in. Her strong fingers diving in, cracking and prising open the flaking crust, flecks of burnt grease painting her hands as she revealed the simmering roast within. He could smell it even now, half-asleep in his armchair, and he wondered if the cook could concoct it with some instruction.

The wineglass in his fingertips was slipping—

and then he heard it, or more precisely *felt* it: a weight against his bedroom door. No knock, just a faint rustling and the sense of a presence.

"Jacques," his wife whispered. "Jacques, husband, please—are you awake?"

He sat still and stiff in the chair, as if she had caught him in some shameful act, keeping his gaze on the fire though the door hid her from view. Still the undulating flames made him think of her in the canopied bower of her bed, and what other body had joined her there?

"I saw you return, before. Could we not speak?" She paused, then said more loudly, "only I have been studying his face tonight, and he has your eyes, Jacques. Truly he does. If you would only look at him, really look at him..."

Linard jerked to his feet, the wineglass falling to the carpet. Three brisk steps and he was at the door. He hit it with the flat of his hand, a resounding thwack that was answered with a cry of fright.

"Go back to your room, Madame," he said. "You have shamed me enough, would you humiliate me before my household now? Go back to your room or I will find you a more suitable accommodation."

As he spoke his hands trembled as if palsied. He pressed them under his arms to steady himself, taking deep breaths; only then did he see the splash of wine on the pale satin of his waistcoat. Ruined, now. Everything ruined.

From behind the door came a low, shuddering breath. "He is your *son*, Jacques." Her voice thick in her throat. "He is yours, you must acknowledge him! If you do not I will write to my father, I swear it." She slumped against the door. "For God's sake, Jacques, open the door..."

The knob turned one way and another, but the door did not so much as shudder. He had tested every door when he first examined the house, tested every hinge and bolt, felt every inch of the paneling and looked up every chimney, ran every tassel between his fingers: was it worth it? Or would he be mocked for paying such an amount? He had lain awake at night imagining her stepping into the house and laughing and laughing, *Jacques you idiot, this isn't worth a sou!* His knee-buckling relief at her restrained praise when she arrived: *a nice house, well apportioned. It will make a good start for us, until we can afford Saint Germain.*

Now he saw, as clearly as if the door were glass, how she had slid to her knees before it, how her round, lovely face was swollen from crying. No more laughing at him, ever.

At last came the slithering sound of her retreat. Linard reached for the fallen wineglass but he seemed to keep reaching for its shadow, not the thing itself. Finally he drank straight from the bottle, closing his eyes and waiting for the thick, berried heat to carry him off.

Yet still he was seeing, even with his eyes closed he was seeing: the simmering fire, the plump undulations of her featherbed, her sweet round face. Today was Thursday, his night to go to her as stipulated in their contract. She should be waiting for him now, in that negligee of thin silk he had imported expressly for her, so fine and smooth he had blushed to touch the bolt. Always trying to win her with such gifts: fine silks and satins, thickly piled velvets for her manteaus, buttery furs with which to line her muffs.

Only now she opened her arms to another, a shadowy figured that blotted the cream of the silk, and she laughed as she embraced him, a low, sultry laugh Linard had never heard before. *Husband*, she sniggered. *Good, good husband.* Laughing together now, and she was eagerly pulling up her negligee, almost wrenching it off...

And when the bottle slipped from Linard's hand, when his mouth fell open, weighted with drink and sleep, still he was seeing. Not a stranger atop her but François, his skinny body bucking against hers, his nakedness revealing what Linard had only glimpsed in the tavern: a bruise on the side of his neck, fresh and purpled, with two red scabs like holes punched in his skin.

2.

It was with difficulty that Linard extracted himself from the armchair the following morning, nearly stumbling as he staggered to his feet. His head pounded unmercifully and his back ached; his waistcoat smelled of sweat and wine, and there was a wet patch on his shirt where he had drooled through the night.

For all this, he felt refreshed and resolved. He opened the shutters to a grey autumn morning and his own yard, where already his servants were busy running to and fro. Their visible purpose thrilled him as it had not done for some time. He had grown inured to the sight over the years, the awareness of so many lives depending on his acumen and generosity. Now, however, it returned to him as sharp as the first days of his business, and his chest swelled. Beyond the walls the street was already noisy and he sensed his own people among the traffic, doing *his* bidding.

Serving *him*.

When the knock came, and his servant entered with his chocolate and letters, he kept the mail but sent the chocolate downstairs. Today Monsieur Linard would break fast at his own table, in his own house.

He dressed and washed briskly, tossing the soiled waistcoat in a corner. There would be others, there were already others, and the color was no longer fashionable. Today was a work day so he put on a suit of dark linen, a plain cloth but of so fine a weave it looked as rich as velvet from afar. Up close, however, there were visible marks on the cuffs, ink drops and wax spatters. A working suit. In the office he had a fine wool justacorps should he need to make an impromptu appearance in the shop.

He chose a small, light wig and powdered himself. As he dabbed on rouge he felt as if a door was closing inside him, a kind of finality. Despite his lack of sleep, the face in the mirror seemed younger: a strong, intelligent visage, perhaps even handsome.

Oh, Jacques Linard may have failed his test, his dance with the devil may have stricken him from God's rolls, but damn it all, he was going to enjoy whatever life he had left.

He just needed to take care of his wife first.

With a purposeful gait he strode to the dining room, his footsteps echoing. As he walked he heard an odd sound, and he realized it was himself, humming an aria from an opera he had seen when he first arrived in Paris. How green he had been, how hungry! He had nearly lost that part of himself, had nearly let her humiliate and ruin him.

He opened the dining room door and found himself confronted with his wife's exquisite, astonished face. And for a moment, just a moment, he was no longer Jacques Linard, draper to royalty; he was Jacques Linard, bumpkin, astonished in turn that a woman like her would so much as glance in his direction...

And then a wailing filled the room, so high and piercing it made his teeth hurt, and they both looked at the bassinet in the corner. Linard's hands became fists.

"Why isn't it in the nursery?" he demanded, his voice raised above the squalling.

She averted her face; her lips moved but he did not hear her words. "Well?" he repeated, bringing his fist down on the table.

At that she turned back to him, her eyes welling and bloodshot. "Because *you* insisted I dismiss the nursemaid!" she cried. "Because *you* don't want anyone else to see him!"

Linard tasted bile again. He swallowed, then flicked out the tails of his coat and sat down. Grimly he set to opening his mail, slicing through the paper with his knife, glancing and tossing aside bills, orders, updates from his agents overseas. In his fury he nearly did the same to a plain, creamy envelope, only to find himself arrested by the elegant flourish within, and beside it a tiny nest of yellow threads pasted to the paper:

Match Yellow Provided
Tonight

Somewhere inside him the door slammed completely shut.

"Take it to the nursery," he said, pouring himself a cup of chocolate.

"And do what?" His wife asked, her voice quavering. "He needs a nurse, Jacques, we must send for someone."

"You can nurse it yourself." He took a long swallow of the chocolate, savoring its bitter richness, and leaned back in his chair. Her mingled fear and outrage were as pleasant as the drink. "It is perfectly natural."

"Don't be disgusting," she spat, placing a hand over her powdered décolletage. Once he had laid his own hand there...

"After all," he continued, raising his voice, "you *are* its mother, are you not? Or did you just find it in a gutter somewhere?"

"Jacques!" Her cheeks were mottled red; she glanced at the maid who stood silent and impassive by the door. "For God's sake, not *here*."

"You would tell me what I can say in my own house?"

The crying, which had settled into fitful yelps, suddenly began again, as loud as a scream.

"Madame is finished," Linard barked at the maid, making her jump with visible fright. "Help her back to the nursery."

At once the maid rushed to gather up the bassinet. His wife rose, her hands shaking, but when her eyes met Linard's she raised her chin. A pride that he had admired, once; now, he reminded himself, it was synonymous with his humiliation.

"Very well, Monsieur," she said in a low voice. Slowly, deliberately, she curtsied at him, her red-rimmed eyes never leaving his face.

Linard met her gaze equably, waiting until she was at the door; as she made to step into the hall he barked once more, "Madame."

She stopped, her delicate throat working.

"This," he waved the note at her, "is a new client. A most important person, perhaps the most important of our lives." A small part of himself was astonished at how easily the words came. "We have been asked to come, with some samples, tonight. You will be ready and presentable, and you will be pleasant. Do you understand?"

"If I do this," she replied huskily, "can I send for a nurse?"

He hesitated, but what did it matter? In light of what was planned, lying to his unfaithful wife was a small, pardonable sin. Still his tongue would not move; instead he nodded once. Only when she had left did he let himself glance once more at the note.

Match Yellow Provided
Tonight

Somewhere in the house the baby continued crying, a thin, nasally sound, like a trapped insect.

Linard sent word to the tavern and went to work. He waved away the offers of a chair, passed the fiacres without a look; he wanted to walk.

In his mind he still saw his wife, her red eyes and her fearful loathing. It raised his chin, it straightened his spine, so that he strode through Paris like a conquering hero. How she must hate herself for what she did. Though the streets were filthy, not a drop touched his clean white stockings; though the streets were crowded with laborers and workers, horses and sedans and carriages, not a one grazed the cloth of his coat or jostled the brushed felt tricorn upon his head. The very city, it seemed, was stepping aside for him, allowing him an untouched passage to his building near the Pont au Change.

How she must hate herself for betraying him.

Around to the back and his delivery boys grinned and saluted him, like little soldiers; through the doors and his clerks rose and bowed, bidding him good morning. Linard flushed with a kind of triumph. How she would learn, too late, the horror of what she had done. The smell of the fabrics, carefully stored from floor to ceiling, was as sweet as perfume. The whisper of their textures as the clerks took them down and replaced them, passed them up to the shop and brought lesser ones back, was a chorus singing his praises. How she would know, too late, just what her selfishness had cost them both. When he trotted up the wooden stairs to his office overlooking the backroom and his inventory, able to glimpse the storefront where the door was already opening to the first customers, he found himself bowing before he could help himself, a feted artist receiving his ovation.

How Linard would make her pay.

And then he was behind his desk, surrounded by the soothing stacks of ledgers and order forms, goods out and monies in, the numerical reckoning of his worth. Job had his wealth restored to him greater than before, but Linard would settle for what was rightfully his. Already he could see it: ennoblement, a house in an up-and-coming faubourg, regular visits to Versailles. Ten years more, perhaps. And with the right choice of wife—

Somewhere, far in the distance, a baby screamed.

Linard's whole body spasmed as if physically struck. He leapt to his feet but the sound vanished the moment he stood.

Slowly he sat back down, ears straining, but there was nothing save the hum of commerce outside his door. Still he waited, listening, his powdered brow creased, until at last he took a breath and bellowed for a clerk. Moments later three bolts of silk were before him, each more yellow than the last. He laid the scrap of paper beside each one, his eyes darting from thread to fabric and back again. At last he chose the dearest and ordered the clerk to coordinate ribbons and lace.

Never let it be said that Jacques Linard did not know the value of a service. Never let it be said that he could be rooked by anyone. Even his own wife.

The carriage was dark and without ornament, but the inside was clean and there was fresh matting on the floor. It was a damp night, with a promise of icy rain in the air. Across from Linard his wife burrowed deeper into her pelisse, shivering. She had worn her dark blue damask, his favorite of her dresses; yet another attempt to placate him. The light from the lanterns flashed across her face, and for the first time he saw faint lines in the corners of her mouth and eyes. When was the last time he had seen her unpowdered? The day after the birth, he realized, and how old she had looked then, as if all the life had been wrung from her; he had wondered if he could bring himself to desire her again.

And then, of course, they had presented him with *that*.

Did her lover still want her? For a moment he envisioned a compromise: she would go to this man and they would leave France for good... but was he to spend his days alone, or in the company of some tawdry mistress? What would be said about him in turn? The entirety of his reputation was built upon his elevated sensibility and taste. Take a whore to bed and he would be just another jumped-up shopkeeper with ambitions beyond his breeding. Another François.

But if she vanished utterly, he could say what he pleased about her. A few weeks of increasing worry, followed by a seemly mourning period... every one of his clients would come to comfort and gawp in equal measure. And then the gossip, the gossip, until all of Paris knew of his tragedy, until all of Paris would come to his doorstep to watch his refined soul struggle with grief.

The muff on his wife's lap rippled and twisted like a living animal. He knew she was picking at her cuticles inside, a nervous habit.

The wheels suddenly fell silent: straw in the streets, some great house seeking peace from the traffic. A recent death? His wife's face went a shade paler. Then the clattering came again in a rush, the bumps bone-shaking as the uneven paving gave way to rutted earth. They were at the far end of the city now, the narrow, grimy homes of laborers crowded between the smooth walls and closed gates of new townhouses. Soon the old structures would be gone, Linard knew; such was the way of things. The trick was to be the one building, not the one forced to move.

He closed his eyes, going over the day's business in his mind. The green damask that had arrived was decidedly not the shade of green he had ordered. There was an order that had come in from a tailor, for a substantial amount of good grey wool; Linard suspected a new livery being created. Some discreet questions and he might be able to gain an introduction to the client...

The carriage stopped.

For a moment his eyes met hers, each as startled as the other, and then his wife flushed and looked away. "You did not say it was so far," she murmured.

Linard leaned out of the window. He looked at the open gate before them, then up at the driver. "We have arrived?"

The shadowed figure nodded without turning around and guided the horses forward. The opening was so narrow Linard had to duck back inside. He glimpsed stone walls, unusually high, and a heavy lock and chain hanging from the gate. An imposing, grand house rose out of the clinging mist, its windows tightly shuttered, and Linard shivered in trepidation. From the sticky jackass in the tavern to this? He had expected a cottage leased for the night, the better to make all evidence vanish by daybreak. Not even the additional coins in his pocket could cover the expense of such a residence.

Unless, of course, they had murdered the owners as well.

"Jacques," his wife whispered, "have you made a mistake?"

At her words his hackles rose, and the now-familiar disgust stung the back of his throat. He gave her a withering look before stepping out of the carriage, setting the cool mist to swirling as he lunged across the courtyard with the paper-wrapped bolt under his arm. Leaving her to make her own way he strode to the front door where two lanterns burned, the only light other than the visible glow behind the doors. The brass knob was wet with condensation. Behind him he heard the coachman mutter something and his wife's lighter response; Linard looked over his shoulder to see the ruffian helping her across the cobblestones. The lanterns picked up her simpering expression. Was this truly her nature, then? To throw herself at any man, regardless of station?

Did Linard mean so little to her, had he been so callously used?

When she reached his side he rapped briskly at the door, then suddenly turned to her, his anger boiling over. "Can you not control yourself for a moment?" he snapped.

"What?" She gaped at him. "Jacques, he was helping me…"

He could not bear her wide eyes, or the visible heat in her cheeks. "Every other woman knows her place," he continued, spitting the words out. "Every one save *you*. You wear that dress ill, Madame. You would do better in nightclothes, or nothing at all."

She clapped a hand over her mouth at the last, smothering her cry, and quickly turned away to dab at her eyes with a handkerchief. "Does it please you to humiliate me?" she asked in a shuddering whisper.

"You would know about such things," he retorted, then leaned in close, his lips nearly touching her ear. "Whore," he breathed.

The word tasted delicious, as delicious as the tremors that wracked her frame. Sated, Linard straightened once more, smoothing cravat and lapels. As if it had been waiting for them to finish, the door finally opened, and he bowed without so much as a glance in her direction.

When he stood, it was to find himself face-to-face with François. Only this François was no dissolute young man; this François wore a suit finer than Linard's, with a face that beamed health beneath fine white powder. He bowed to Linard, then took his wife's hand and kissed it. Linard saw her reddened face soften and loudly cleared his throat.

"Monsieur," he said to François' raised eyebrow. "We are here, as directed."

"Indeed," said François. The whelp's lip actually curled. "Enter, please. Madame is waiting for you in the salon."

Linard bit back his exclamation—Madame?—and followed his wife into a hall so dimly lit as to appear uninhabited. The door shut behind them, cutting off the draft and swallowing every sound. Above them a handful of candles steamed in a chandelier, casting into shadowy relief a pair of portraits and a richly brocaded chair. Linard looked twice at the latter: he knew that brocade, it had been au fait just a few months ago, its price rising to such absurdities that he had delivered every bolt himself lest it become soiled in transit. What villain could afford such luxury? Suddenly his payment seemed a sorry thing.

Ahead of him François led his wife by the elbow, his head close to hers, and her laughter rang out, nervous and echoing. A sound not unlike the baby's cries; Linard fought the urge to clap his hands over his ears even as he glared at François' grinning face. Oh, he had grinned like that once, he had felt that flush of triumph at amusing her, until he understood that she was laughing at him, not his wit.

Nearly over, now. Just a few more minutes and his dignity would be restored like the wealth of Job. All he had possessed and more, once he was rid of her.

They entered the salon and the light momentarily overwhelmed him, leaving him blinking on the threshold while his eyes adjusted. A hundred candles gleaming from every corner; he blinked and blinked and at last saw the woman turning from the fire.

She was very tall and very beautiful. Her skin was heavily powdered and her rich black hair dusted with hazy grey; her lips and cheeks were brilliantly rouged. There was not a single spot on her face, none of the little silks that peppered the faces of young Parisian girls...

His wife, the night he met her, and the little scarlet heart that had hidden a pox scar...

The woman walked slowly towards him, stately in her carriage; despite her youthful face she carried herself like a dowager. As she reached Linard he straightened in turn, trying to match her height, but she towered over him by at least a hand's breadth.

"Monsieur Linard," she said. "I am Madame Gagnon."

He bowed and took her hand, only to nearly exclaim again: her skin was cold, as cold as a winter's day. Still he mastered himself and let his lips just brush her knuckles; out of the corner of his eye he saw his wife drop into a neat curtsey. As he rose his mind began to fit the pieces together. Clearly this woman was the villain's mistress. They were hiding out here, or leasing it for some greater scheme. Linard's money would be a last payment and then they would flee, perhaps using the silk to make the woman a distraction, so no one would remember the murderer at her side—

At that moment Madame Gagnon's brown eyes grew wide. She clapped her hands together like a little girl and squealed. The noise made him grit his teeth, so like the infant's squalling, but he followed her gaze and looked down at the bolt. The paper wrapping had torn slightly, providing a glimpse of the yellow silk within.

At that he smiled. Here at last was something familiar. He held the bolt out with another bow. "As Monsieur François specified," he said. "May I commend you on your taste, Madame. Yellow is most becoming on a woman of your coloring."

She snatched the bolt from him, tore the paper off, and unwound a length. The noise she made as she stroked the fabric was catlike. She smoothed it over her skirts, turning one way and another in the firelight. "Magnificent," she said. "Perfectly magnificent." Her voice dropped, as if she had forgotten they were there. "To think this was once the color of a Jew, the color of Judas himself…"

"I have heard," his wife put in brightly, "that Madame Pompadour has ordered all yellow roses for her garden this spring. Madame might have anticipated the spring's most fashionable color. We also have a lovely green damask, just arrived today, which would bring out Madame's eyes wonderfully. Perhaps she might come tomorrow?"

Madame Gagnon did not look at her; her eyes still followed the yellow ripples cascading around her. "Unfortunately the sun makes me quite ill, I am unusually sensitive to its effects. That is why I asked Monsieur Linard to come; that, and I am always intrigued to see how far a man will go for me." She glanced slyly at Linard, who felt his cheeks flush.

His wife only nodded. "Either Jacques or I would be happy to come again. Madame must also see the new cotton fabrics from England, they are most unusual and wonderfully light for summertime."

Linard watched his wife, watched and listened to the easy cadence of her voice. When she turned to him, her expression so proud and pleased, he felt a terrible, clenching pang. How many times had they done this? Visiting his most prestigious clients together, gently selling them on more, more, would not Madame like a rich red to contrast, might Monsieur like a second layer of lace at the cuff, a little silk corsage was becoming quite fashionable… theirs had been an instinctive partnership, he had never taught her what to say. She simply *knew*, with some kind of feminine intuition, just the right phrases to close a deal.

Inside his coat the coins were as heavy as lead. He found himself envisioning a scale, with his wife's smile weighed against the shrieking creature she had presented him with...

"She is the woman, I take it?" Madame Gagnon said, still smoothing the silk down over her skirts.

At once his wife's smile vanished, and Linard's stomach vanished in turn. "Yes," he said, his voice coming out as a croak.

"Jacques?" Her tone was light, but he could detect the note of unease beneath it. "Jacques, what does she mean?"

"I hear you are a new mother," Madame Gagnon continued in the same tone. "A most robust little boy."

"That is true," his wife replied, her voice still tinged with unease. "We are both quite pleased."

Madame Gagnon again looked slyly at Linard. "I hear he is quite handsome, a little man already. It must be such a relief knowing you have someone to care for you in your dotage. What is his name?"

The taste of bile. He looked from Madame Gagnon to his wife, marveling at how only her eyes betrayed her uncertainty; her face stayed in its mask of pleasantry. "His name is Xavier," she said. "A family name."

"Za-vee-ay." Madame Gagnon sounded out the name, smiling, smiling at Linard. "A fine name for a son and heir."

"Does Madame have any children?" his wife asked.

Madame Gagnon's smile vanished. "Not any more," she snapped. Her arms curled around the bolt, cradling it against her chest; and then she abruptly tossed it on the sofa as if it was nothing more than rags. "François said you also had ribbons, and money."

Linard began fumbling in his pocket, his fingers tangling and unwinding the neat bundles of looped satin and lace. Suddenly Madame Gagnon stepped before him. Her icy fingers wrapped around his wrist, and oh! she was cold, cold, she seemed to radiate cold.

"Jacques?" His wife's voice was querulous now. "Jacques, perhaps I should..." but she trailed off uncertainly.

Madame Gagnon's hand slid into his pocket, groping and digging, and Linard was suddenly, utterly terrified. Her expressionless face studied him as if he were nothing more than an insect, something to be crushed on a whim. From his outer pocket she produced the ribbons and lace, grunting with approval. When her hand slid beneath his lapel, finding the inner pocket swollen with coins, it seemed a grotesque inversion of a seduction; he felt himself contract as if bathed in icy water.

"Madame," he said, wincing at the high, nervous tone of his own voice, "should we not wait for the gentleman to arrive?"

She paused, looking at him curiously: a speaking insect, now. "Gentleman?" She giggled as she worked the pouch of money free. "I have never heard François described as such. You two must have had quite a night."

"Perhaps if we could have a drink..." His wife's voice grew distant, as if she were backing away.

"I mean your, your husband." He desperately wanted to see what his wife was doing; he desperately wanted to be the one backing away. "Your master?" he added, in a nervous squeak.

At that she laughed, a loud, masculine guffawing. In another woman he would have found the boldness appealing, but in her it seemed a terrifying prelude. Her hand was still fondling the coin pouch beneath his coat, the coins rubbing against his chest in turn like dozens of small fingers. When her head dropped to his he thought she would kiss him, but instead her mouth nestled against his ear.

"Monsieur Linard," she whispered. Her breath was so very cold. "I have no master."

She drew the pouch free and shoved him to one side, so hard he stumbled and fell to his knees. Gasping, he turned and looked, but all he saw was Madame Gagnon's shadow—

and then his wife darted to the far end of the room and cowered behind a chair, her expression one of terror.

"Jacques! Jacques, do something!" Her eyes darted frantically between him and Madame Gagnon. "For God's sake, do something!"

His stomach lurched at her words, but then Madame Gagnon turned to look at him and all sensation left his body.

Between her red, red lips were two long, pointed teeth, like a serpent's fangs.

For what you ask, you need the devil himself.

"Jacques," she said, slurring his name, "has done enough, Madame Linard."

At her words his wife's expression transformed: first a horrified comprehension—and oh, wasn't that what he had craved, all this time? Why, then, did it make him want to weep atop his terror?—and then something far uglier.

"Damn you," she yelled, her voice echoing in the room. "Damn you, Jacques." Her eyes were as wild as an animal's. "You think me a slut, you think me unfaithful? I fucked them *all*." Madame Gagnon moved closer to her, but she seemed not to notice. "I fucked your clients and your friends, I fucked your clerks and your delivery boys—"

Slowly Madame Gagnon reached out, stroking her head.

"—I fucked the footmen and the maids too, I parted my legs for *everyone* who came to the door, I hung my bare cunt out the window because anything, *anything*, was better than *you*."

Her large hands wrapped around his wife's neck and she screamed, a blood-curdling cry that seemed to come from her very soul.

It was the scream that made Linard move. He ran for the door, only to trip over his own feet and fall headfirst on the parquet, landing in a pile of what he realized were his own ribbons. Ribbons everywhere, they were drifting through the air like snowflakes and his wife was screaming and screaming, a thin, high-pitched sound of terrified desperation.

At last he reached the door and seized the knob, his sweaty palms sliding over the polished metal. For a moment he thought it locked and nearly fainted from sheer terror, but he finally managed to wrench it open, and the cooler air of the hallway was like the hand of God Himself.

"Jacques!"

The cry was earsplitting, louder than anything he had ever heard, and Jacques Linard looked back.

He had one fleeting glimpse of Charlotte's bloodless face, wide-eyed with terror and pain, more pain than he had ever seen before.

And then Madame Gagnon turned, blocking his view, and he realized he was staring at the devil made flesh. Her fangs were stained red, her mouth was a glistening smear of red, and when she grinned at him it was to bare a mouthful of stained teeth with small pink shreds between them like so much gristle.

She flung her arm in his direction. Hot, wet drops struck his face, and he fell backwards into the hall as if dealt a mortal blow, his head striking hard and rendering him senseless.

Linard awoke to the faint gleam of dawn through the open doorway of the house. His head was pounding; as he propped himself up on one elbow the world lurched before his eyes. For a moment he thought he had been to a party and drank too much.

And then he remembered everything.

At once he was on his feet, seizing the wall to steady himself. The stairwell, the hall, it all swung one way and another, as violently as a ship in a storm. His neck throbbed with pain, and it was with mounting fear that he reached up and felt the sticky wounds under his loose cravat. When he drew his hand free his fingertips were smeared with drying blood.

He did not look in the salon; he could not look. Instead, Linard ran, faster than he ever had in all his life. He ran out into the cold grey dawn, stumbling through the muddy ruts of the courtyard; he ran into the road and back towards Paris, pausing only to remove his shoes. Not once did he look back.

3.

Linard sipped his wine with care, relishing the spreading warmth in his belly. He could not keep warm, not since that night. It was an unusually mild autumn evening, yet he was wearing a wool shirt and thick stockings, and had called for a lap blanket when he sat down to dinner. His fingertips were numb. He had barely made it through the day, demanding fires and cordials, powders for his head that still ached intermittently, three days after.

The two holes on his neck had scabbed over, then became small pink dots that he found himself touching repeatedly. They were the only proof of what had happened, the only evidence that he had not dreamed the whole encounter. The only proof that he was now utterly damned.

Around his neck he wore his mother's rosary, wore it day and night.

Yet the wine was soothing, the table setting impeccable. The last rays of sunlight filtered through the curtains; here in the back of the house the hue and cry of Paris was muted. On a whim, he had asked for mutton, but as rare as possible. Hadn't his mother sworn by rare meat for strengthening the blood? The springy flesh pleasant in his mouth, gushing red juices that tasted unusually satisfying. He took the gazette from where it lay folded neatly before him, smoothed it open, and began to read—

And then, long and loud, came the sustained wailing of a child.

He rang for the maid, pressing a hand over the renewed ache in his head. The door opened at once; they all seemed on edge lately, it only infuriated him the more. "What is that racket?" he demanded, turning to her—

Only to gape at the expanse of blue damask before him.

The maid curtsied, making the rich fabric shimmer. "Xavier is teething, Monsieur. I am going out, but I have left…" she trailed off as she rose to standing, then said nervously, "Monsieur?"

He abruptly closed his mouth, so hard his teeth audibly clicked. "Where did you get that dress," he said hoarsely.

"Madame gave it to me. She often gives me her dresses when they are out of fashion—" she broke off again as he lunged out of the chair and seized her arm. "Monsieur! Please!"

"When were they here?" he demanded, shaking her. "What do they want? Is it blackmail, is that it?"

"Monsieur!" the maid shrieked. "Monsieur, please! You're hurting me!"

"Take me to them!" he roared, her body jerking loose-limbed in his grasp. "I won't be toyed with, do you hear me? I won't be mocked! Take me to them!"

The door opened again and a footman rushed in, breaking Linard's grip and drawing the maid away. On his heels was the cook, smelling of baby-sick, who helped the trembling girl into a corner. "What is wrong?" she asked.

"He thinks I stole it," the maid gasped.

"I think she was given it by a man we both know," Linard snarled, "and I won't be played for a fool."

"But the dress was in her room days ago, Monsieur," the cook said. Her eyes never left Linard's face. "Madame told me herself that she was only going to wear it one last time, to meet your client. She must have hung it there right after she returned that night. Before she went to the country," she added pointedly.

At the last Linard flinched. He eyed the cook warily, but the woman's face seemed guileless.

In the silence, the baby began crying again.

"For God's sake, make it stop," he muttered, then gestured to the door. "Get out, all of you. And make that noise stop, I cannot bear it..."

They filed out, closing the door. Linard heard them talking in the hallway, how was it that he could hear them?

"Kid needs a nurse," the footman muttered.

The cook hissed sharply, then added in a low voice, "he needs a mother. Not that the one he has is worth a sou." Then, after a pause, "you best give that dress back. No use giving him more to rage about."

"Thought he was going to kill her," the footman put in. "Thought he was going to break—"

Again the cook hissed, and their footsteps moved swiftly down the hall. Linard slumped back in his chair, rubbing his neck. *Thought he was going to kill her*. If they believed that of him and *her* body was found, what might they say in gossip, or to the police? And yet he could not but play innocent for some weeks, and what if François was indeed out to blackmail him? Only now did Linard see how the low price could have been a lure, the better to ensure his complicity and extort him over time.

And if he balked at paying, and found Madame Gagnon on his doorstep?

He stumbled out of the dining room and hurried to the safety of his bedroom, locking the door and shutters alike. He needed to think; he had to think. Too soon to start making any claims about his wife's fate, but at this rate he would go mad long before the opportunity came, or François appeared with his next set of demands.

Again his fingers drifted up to his neck, stroking, soothing. The closed door muffled the sounds from the nursery, until he could not tell if the child was still crying or he was just listening to its echo in his mind, an endless sustained wail that had etched itself inside his skull. He would go mad if he did not act. He would go mad.

Thus he set himself to plotting once more.

He sat, Jacques Linard, at the desk of his wife, carefully assembling samples of her handwriting for whoever he might find to forge it. The rosary clinked against the edge of the desk as he worked. He had spent much of the evening planning matters out, step by careful step. A confession of an affair, hinting at incipient madness; he could take it to the police and stop François' schemes before they began. The servants would understand, they already believed her a poor mother, he could hear their gossip *I knew there was something not right in her.* It wasn't foolproof, this scheme of his, but it was plausible, and in Paris plausibility was more than enough.

As he reviewed her letters, her lists, her scraps of poetry, he found himself eyeing a pretty little vase that stood beside the inkwell. White china decorated with scattered yellow flowers; it reminded him of a floral cotton he had just ordered. Only yesterday he had word that one of the most fashionable salonnieres wanted to see it.

Like Job, all would be restored to him, for like Job he had been little more than a pawn. He suspected a whole conspiracy, from the riverfront informant to François to Madame Gagnon herself. They had known of him and his rising fortunes. Now they would try and take everything from him.

In the nursery, the baby started its relentless keening again, and in a sudden fit of anger he smacked the vase aside. It shattered on the parquet, revealing a little trove of baubles: worn ribbons, a string of dark blue beads, a rouge pot with a cracked enamel lid, a gold locket. All jumbled together, all tarnished and grimy. Linard found himself reaching for the unfamiliar locket: proof of her inconstancy? Though it was clearly old, the surface scratched and the latch difficult to work open—

but then it did open, and he found himself staring at the two portraits within.

On one side was his wife's father as a younger man. On the other was a woman's profile, equally as elegant, but her skin was brown, her head crowned in ebony curls threaded with ribbons.

He had never seen her mother. She had died in childbirth, the whole marriage had been frowned upon...

The locket tumbled from his shaking hands. It could not be his child. Yet his mind was racing now, filling with a host of random memories, so overwhelming he clutched at his temples. His wife after a country sojourn, fretting about her sun-darkened skin that had turned a smooth, pale brown. His wife at the riverside, when they found themselves surrounded by a crush of disembarking sailors, their visages hailing from every corner of the world: *I'm not frightened, Jacques, it feels like home*, and he had thought that by *home* she meant *Paris*...

The rich brown hue of her eyes, that had looked black as night in her bedroom, when she opened her arms to him...

It could not be his child. *I never knew my mother,* she had told him that the first night they met and he had told her in turn that he had never known his father. The man had been a sailor breezing through their village, a single irreparable night creating Jacques Linard and only the kindness of an older farmer saving his mother from infamy.

What color was his father's skin?

A single irreparable night.

Grief crashed through him, making him shove his knuckles in his mouth to keep from wailing aloud. Not Job, not Job at all. What story was this? How would he be saved?

In the house, the baby's wail ratcheted up, becoming a rattling keening that seemed the cry of an older soul. On Linard's neck the scars flared into a burning itch that he found himself frantically clawing at. His mark of Cain. He crossed himself and brought the rosary to his lips. What should he do, he cried silently to the ceiling, what story was this, how would he be saved?

As if in answer a gust of cool air raced through the house, stirring the neat stacks of papers on the desk. Everything fell silent. His ears rang with the echoes of the baby's cries, and then that too faded, until the only sound was that of his nails scraping at his own skin.

Before him the locket sat open, the two faces smiling at each other, wise to a secret he was only now beginning to glimpse.

Just then a cool breath grazed his ear, and an arm clad in yellow reached over his shoulder. Smooth, slender fingers turned one of the letters over.

"Not exactly a wit, was she?" Madame Gagnon remarked. "Thankfully she had other qualities."

Her voice, her proximity, it turned Linard's body to ice, save for the heat of the marks on his neck. "What do you want?" he whispered. "I have paid you…"

"Whoever said I was here for you?" She ran a finger beneath his cravat, teasing the itch, then slid her fingers around the string of beads, drawing them up and out; when the cross emerged she laughed, making it dance before him. "Monsieur, Monsieur. Do you honestly think *He* will forgive you?"

Linard could not speak, watching the holy object pressed between her fingers, fingers that had crushed his wife's throat. The itch maddening. A shadow moved in the corner of his eye and the floor creaked.

As if on cue, the baby began crying again, high and thin.

"You can hear that child all the way down the street," Madame Gagnon said, her tone one of gentle admonishment. She wiggled the cross at him, as if shaking a finger. "The poor thing will die before you can pawn it off."

"I am doing what I can for it," he whispered.

"For *him*," she corrected, withdrawing in a rustle of silk. "You have a remarkable eye for textiles, Monsieur Linard," she said behind him. "It is a pity you are otherwise blind."

At that he regained some of his composure. "State your business, Madame," he said. "And then leave at once."

Madame Gagnon laughed at that, the same bold, pealing laugh at that night. It made a hideous counterpoint to the baby's wails. "I told you, Monsieur. We have no business, you and I," she said. "Only I thought you might want to see your handiwork? And to bring Xavier home, of course."

For a moment he could not comprehend what she had just said; it was as if she had spoken in another language. "Xavier?" he repeated.

"You told François you had no use for him. I do."

It was as if everything had slowed, or perhaps it was Linard, perhaps it was his body that had suddenly turned to mud, thick and unable to respond. Before him the cross sat on the desk, nothing more than polished wood and string; foolish to think it would make any difference. Yet when at last he opened his mouth his own small response surprised him.

"No," he said.

"Yes," Madame Gagnon replied in the same easy tone.

"No," he repeated, stronger now. He pushed the chair back and rose to face her, his hands in fists. The mild amusement on her face only spurred his defiance. "He is not yours. He will never be yours."

Madame Gagnon raised a hand, setting the cascades of yellow silk shimmering, and he tensed for the blow; but she only gestured to the hallway. "It is not your decision to make, Monsieur."

Now Linard heard it: a slow, wheezing breath. His heartbeat sounded loud and frenetic in contrast.

"I think we can all agree," she continued, "that mothers know what's best for their children."

Slowly, inexorably, Linard turned.

His wife stood in the doorway, staring glassy-eyed at him—glassy-eyed but alive, moving, her lips damp with spittle. For a moment he thought her some kind of joke, a poor doppelgänger, but then he realized she wasn't wearing makeup, and when was the last time he had seen her without rouge and powder? Her dress too, it was some filthy linen rag, not the blue dress he had left her in. Of course, he realized stupidly, she gave the dress to the maid.

"Charlotte," he said hoarsely. Something was trickling out of the burning scars on his neck; he felt feverish. Was this it, then? The moment when his suffering was finally over, his family restored to him, all doubts taken from him by the mighty hand of God? "Charlotte," he whispered, "forgive me..."

She opened her mouth as if to speak, but instead two long, pointed teeth pushed forward from her gums.

"I promised your wife would cease to exist," Madame Gagnon drawled, stepping behind Charlotte and laying a hand on her shoulder. "She is not your Charlotte, not anymore; but I don't think she was ever *your* Charlotte, do you?" She stepped back into the hallway. "The heart is a mysterious animal, Monsieur Linard. Of your usurper I could learn nothing, but there was once a kind young man who paid your wife three separate visits." She held up three long fingers over Charlotte's shoulder. "Years ago, and he was as pale as snow, and she made penance for it after. But you were so driven in your work that she despaired of ever being loved..."

The memory came back to Linard, all at once: a night long ago, when he had come home late, he had walked back just to shake off the strain of the day. Impatient clients and delayed orders, their income threatened, so many things swirling in his mind, so that he had nearly missed the man climbing over the wall of his house. He had called and given chase but the ruffian had fled... save he had been no ruffian at all, Linard had glimpsed velvet just as the young man vanished down an alleyway...

That, and his wife had been awake when he entered, though she was usually asleep by that hour.

She despaired of ever being loved. But it had all been for her, everything for her. Her face that first night after the birth, eyes wide and earnest: *Xavier is yours, he is yours, I swear it to you on my own life!*

"No," he said.

Charlotte made a hissing noise, something deep and animal; her eyes narrowed in a way Linard knew quite well, from the few times she had dared to challenge him outright. He could not think. *She despaired. He is yours, I swear it.* The baby was crying, crying; from behind Charlotte Madame Gagnon gave him a last, unreadable look and then disappeared down the hall in a swirl of yellow.

Down the hall to the nursery.

"No!" he cried, reaching for her, but Charlotte was upon him then, clawing and grabbing at him as she forced him back. Her eyes black and bottomless and her skin like ice. Linard struggled against her, trying to wrench free of her arms but she was so strong, when had she become so strong? Never had she been able to so much as push away his hand.

His legs tangled with hers and they tumbled to the floor, rolling one way and another as each tried to gain leverage. At last he managed to get a leg over her and bring his forearm down across her neck, his ears straining for sounds from the now-silent nursery, listening for the baby, listening for *Xavier*—

Beneath his arm something cracked, a muted, fleshy sound, but Charlotte only grinned at him, baring those strange teeth.

And then she twisted her head forward and drove them into his forearm.

Linard howled and tried to yank himself free; she worried his skin like an animal until a piece of his arm tore loose. Blood poured over his sleeve as she seized his head and bit into his mouth, teeth cutting into cheek and tongue as he screamed into her. They fell backwards onto the hearth and all was bright and hot, everything was burning...

Past Charlotte's crazed, reddening face he glimpsed Madame Gagnon in the doorway, cradling his son against her chest, kissing his son with those red, red lips.

"Poor little thing," she said, rubbing his back. "All he wanted was to be held."

And then she turned away, and all was heat, and pain.

X is for Xavier

Pete Aldin

And with that, she stormed out of my life forever, slamming the door behind her hard enough to topple glasses from the kitchen shelf. I sat for hours, picking broken shards from the fruit bowl on the counter, picking cutting words from my memory.

We always hurt the ones we love. That's what the cliché tells us. It's bullshit. We nurture and soothe and tickle and caress and reassure the ones we love. It's the ones we *used to love*—they're the ones we hurt. And, God, but if she hadn't hurt me.

And me? I had sat there, letting it happen, allowing her to deconstruct me, bathing in the shame of it. A putz.

Why didn't I fight back? She had her own flaws, so many flaws, and I brought up none of them. She had insecurities—and I did not use them against her. I took it in a stunned silence and let her go without so much as firing a parting shot.

Hurt.

Discarded.

Humiliated.

Once upon a time, when I was very young, I thought I might be damaged. So did my teachers apparently. I heard one telling another that I'd grow up to be a "serial killer". He noticed me listening, turned his back and continued the conversation in whispers. I had no idea what the words meant, but I distinctly recall wanting to kill *him*. It was the first time, the very first time I had that thought, that desire. That sweet desire.

And whenever I thought of ways to hurt people, I'd push the ideas away, out of sight—but not *too* far, as if to the back of a cupboard where no one could else see them but I'd know where they'd be if ever I wanted them.

I never had a reason. Until she left me, deconstructed my dignity and left me as a pile of personality-shit on a kitchen chair.

People like her had been doing things like that to me all my life. But no one I had loved, not since my parents.

She taught me a lesson, The Lesson. The world is full of dirt. And I am the broom.

And that is why you're here. Tied to a lawn chair, my sock in your mouth. You look like her, talk like her, and when I watched you treating that bus driver the way Yvonne treated me, I knew.

You're dirt.

Dirt, meet Broom.

Y is for Yvonne

Michael M. Jones

"Fucking terrorist."

I winced as the awful words hit me, but tried not to let it show how much they hurt. It was Rachel Ferguson, the bane of my existence, who had spat them in my direction. She was just ahead of me, perched on top of the small stone wall which ran around Goodwin Square Park, flanked by two of her friends—Jenn and Joan? I could never keep them straight, they were twins and equally awful in their vapid ways—with a lit cigarette dangling from her fingers. She saw me look, and raised one hand to give me the finger.

I couldn't help it; I hunched down, as if I could find refuge in my hijab—the same thing which marked me as a target in Rachel's eyes—and picked up my pace. I'd really hoped that by staying late to help paint the set for the spring musical I'd avoid Rachel since she and her friends usually went to hang out in her dad's garage after school, but I also knew I couldn't rely on her being predictable.

Well, except when it came to making my life miserable. We were both sixteen, but sometimes it felt like she'd been terrorizing me forever.

"I can't wait until they finally come for you," she called, harsh laughter in her voice. "Think you'll get sent to a secret prison, or will they just dump your ass in the desert with the rest of the towelheads?" Her friends joined in with shrill giggles. Jenn—or Joan—passed a bag of chips to her sister. They always let Rachel take the lead, but followed her example like good little minions. Cowards.

I kept walking. I knew better than to give Rachel the response she craved. She was always spoiling for a fight, and made no secret of wanting me to react, to fight back. To stay strong, I called my father's advice to mind. "Do not give them the opening they desire, Masuma. Don't raise a muss or make trouble. Because that's what they want. They want to be the victim, you the aggressor. And who would the police believe? Not you, my daughter. They will blame you for everything, no matter how it looks." He'd spoken from hard experience, with the physical and emotional scars to prove it, and a younger, wide-eyed me had taken it to heart. You didn't even have to follow the news to know that it wasn't a great time to be a Muslim in America. Even in Puxhill, a city celebrated for its diversity and tolerance, hate found a way to flourish.

And so I absorbed Rachel's words, praying extra-hard every day and night for the strength to withstand them, to reject them, to be the better person. I honestly didn't get why she was so obsessed with me. Up until a year ago, she'd been intimidating, not to be messed with, like a guard dog... but then she turned cruel, more like a rabid beast, and started picking on me. I wasn't even the only Muslim girl in school... just the easiest target, I suppose. As I passed them, I held my breath, hoping they'd be content with the usual verbal abuse. and watching me scurry away.

Nope. Rachel tossed aside her cigarette, hopped to the ground, and seized my arm in a rough grip, forcing me to stop and turn to face her. A static shock jumped between us, so strong I felt it through my sleeve. I yelped, trying to pull free, but her fingers dug in even harder. "Where the fuck are you going in such a hurry?" Rachel demanded, her breath stale with smoke and bitterness. "Got somewhere better to be? You maybe planning to blow up a church or something?"

She was several inches taller than me, and considerably thicker, and I knew it was mostly muscle. She had a raw physicality which made her constant threats of violence all the more frightening; right now, it sent a shiver throughout me. I'd never seen such unbridled anger in her eyes before. She was wearing her usual steel-toed boots, much-abused blue jeans, and a heavy metal t-shirt that looked older than she was. A thin silver chain hung around her neck, vanishing under the neck of the shirt.

She yanked my arm. "I asked you a question. You got somewhere better to be?"

I pulled again, this time managing to free myself though I felt something in my sleeve rip, and winced. I liked this shirt. "Leave me alone!" I said. "Just stop it already!"

Too late, I saw the feverish glee in her eyes. "Or what?" she demanded. The hand that had just held me now balled into a fist, pulling back in preparation for a punch. "You gonna fight back? Go on, take a swing. You can even have the first shot." When I didn't immediately respond, she bared her teeth in a feral grin. "Or will you just crash a plane into my apartment building? That's what your sort does, right?"

Behind her, Joan and Jenn stood up. "C'mon, Rache," one whined. "Let's just get out of here."

"Yeah, let's head to your dad's garage and see if he's got any beer in the fridge," the other added. "It's one thing to give the Muzzie shit, but this is going too far."

Rachel turned briefly to glare at them. "Too far? My brother's dead because of scum like her!" she snarled. "Maybe you two bitches are too weak to handle this, but me and the fucking camel jockey are having it out, here and now!"

That's what she thought. The second she took her eyes off me, I dropped my backpack and bolted.

304 · MICHAEL M. JONES

I didn't get far. Behind me I heard a snarl of rage, pounding footsteps, and then something heavy slammed into me as Rachel tackled me to the ground. We hit the sidewalk in a painful heap of limbs. At least dressing modestly meant my arms and legs had some protection, though my palms burned from where they took part of the impact. I struggled under her weight, attempting to scramble free, pushing at her, but she was on me and not letting go.

I tried yelling for help, but she muffled me with a hand over my mouth, and my screams died unheard. But where *was* everyone? Of course Jenn and Joan were long-gone, unwilling to act either way and we were in a residential area bordered by a park, not a major street, but you'd think someone would be out walking their dog, or parking their car, or sitting on a bench, so where were they? How could she do this in public without anyone noticing? And when had it become so overcast?

I kicked and slammed my hands against her to no avail. So I bit her hand—eugh, it tasted awful, like dirt and grease and smoke and anger—and when she pulled it away in surprise, I found the opening to shove her away. I scrambled back to my feet. "You *bit* me!" Rachel exclaimed in a mixture of anger and disgust. "Like a fucking animal!"

"You're the one acting like an animal!" I shot back, trying to catch my breath. "What is *wrong* with you?"

"You killed my brother!" she all but shrieked, something inhuman flickering across her face as she stood again. "He went to Afghanistan to fight raghead terrorists like you, and all we got back was a coffin, a flag, and a we're so sorry, he was a good soldier, and it's all! Your! Fault!" She lunged at me while I was processing her words, fingers splayed like claws, aimed at my face—no, not my face, my hijab—and I just barely ducked backwards, feeling the breeze against my skin.

"I didn't do it!" I shot back. "It wasn't me, it wasn't my family—my folks came from Egypt! I was born here in America!"

But she was beyond reason. She lunged at me again, and this time, as I put up my hands to protect myself, I accidentally grabbed the chain around her neck. And instinctively, I yanked at it. The chain broke, and spilled into my fingers, along with what it had held.

We both froze, though for different reasons. I was startled, sure, but her surprise was born of an outrage which seemed to briefly overload her. Like I'd committed an unforgivable violation. I could feel the mixed emotions coming off her like a cloud. I opened my fingers to see just what I'd accidentally seized.

It wasn't a cross, or her brother's dog tags—things I could have imagined her wearing now that I had a little more insight into her nature—but instead a tiny, ugly little clay thing no bigger than my little finger. It was vaguely female, and it felt so very, very wrong in my hand. Hate and anger spilled from it, oozing into my exposed skin, and suddenly, I was furious. At Rachel, for making my life a living hell for months. At the adults who didn't listen, at the society which made my father distrust the authorities, my mother afraid to speak up in public, me afraid to fight back—I just wanted to lash out and *hurt* someone.

Starting with Rachel, who stood before me, eyes glassy with confusion and anger, who represented everything stupid and awful and hateful in my life. She threw herself at me, I met her midway, and a darkness came upon us both, a sharp cutting wind pulling us together as we kicked and scratched and struggled. We slammed into the waist-high wall of the park, somehow toppled over it onto the slightly more forgiving grass on the other side, continued our mindless, irrational battle, and a voice inside my head whispered encouragement.

Fight her.

Hurt her.

Kill her.

And I tried. For a moment, I tried, and I hated myself for doing so. I wanted nothing more than to destroy Rachel, just as she blamed me for everything wrong in her life, and—

—this wasn't me. These weren't my thoughts. Oh sure, it was my frustration, my anger, my desperation, but it wasn't *me*. The burning in my left hand was a constant reminder that I'd never let go of that tiny figurine even as it bit into my skin.

I tried to let go, but I had a death grip around that figurine stronger than my own will. *No*, said the voice inside me, *you are mine now. You will fight for me. You will hate for me. You will wreak chaos in my name, and I will live again.*

"No!" I screamed, trying to reject this ancient being's claim on me. For just as I heard its voice, now I understood its nature. Its name came to me. Zaltu. A so-called goddess of strife from the dawn of history. I didn't know if Zaltu was jinn or devil or something else cast down from Allah's grace, but a tiny shred of its power resided in this trinket—where had Rachel gotten it? —and it had infected us, turned our dark impulses against us.

For that moment, Rachel and I both paused, pulling apart as some measure of sense returned. "What the fuck is a Zaltu?" she mumbled, eying me warily. Had I spoken out loud, or had we shared the same moment of comprehension as Zaltu tried to possess us both? It didn't matter.

"Something awful and wrong," I replied. "Something that should have died thousands of years ago."

I cannot die. I am immortal. Mankind will never be free of strife. I am everywhere, cackled the voice. *And you two will bring me such glory.* And it conjured up visions of fire, and explosions, and riots, of a city tearing itself apart through hatred and misunderstanding. It didn't matter which of us won this fight. Zaltu had such plans for either or both of us.

"No!" I said again. I tried to pry my hand open, but it wouldn't budge. "Rachel, *help* me!"

"Help *you*?" she spat. "After all this, you expect me to help you? My brother is dead because of you!"

"Rachel, *please!*" I begged. "I'm sorry about your brother. He was a good person. He was brave, and he served our country well, and he didn't deserve to die, and I know how much it sucks and how much it hurts, but I didn't do it, and taking it out on me won't change a thing!" I met her eyes, pleading. I saw something in her expression, a hint of pain and sorrow behind the anger. Was there a shred of understanding? Please, I begged Allah, please help her understand.

"You don't get it, do you? Nick was the best person I knew! The rest of my family—" Rachel shook her head, blonde hair flying. "He protected me. He loved me. And then he left and... all I have of him are his t-shirts and that thing he brought back on his last leave. He said he found it in the desert, and he gave it to me and... and it's *mine!*" Just like that, the moment had passed and I'd lost her. She went for my hand, but not to help me, instead to steal back Zaltu's figurine. And she was none too gentle as she pried my fingers open; I feared she'd break them in the process. I yelped in pain. She didn't seem to care.

Fight her for it, hissed Zaltu. *You stole me fair and square, the power is yours now.*

As Zaltu's madness again closed over me, I found myself engaged in a terrible tug-of-war with Rachel but in that last moment of clarity, I surrendered myself to a power much higher than Zaltu. The words came from deep within my heart, and I meant them with every fiber of my being.

O Allah, unite our hearts
and set aright our mutual affairs,
guide us in the path of peace

Liberate us from darkness by Your light,
save us from enormities whether open or hidden.

I stopped fighting. I stopped resisting. I gave all of myself up to this prayer for peace, and trusted in Allah to make everything right, to give me the strength I needed. I prayed for myself... and for poor Rachel. Please, please help her also.

And as I prayed, the darkness lifted from me. Zaltu's words grew quieter, quieter, quieter, until they were but formless whispers and then not even that. Her figurine fell from my hand onto the ground, and Rachel lunged desperately for it... only to pause inches away.

I didn't know what sort of battle was going on inside her head, and I was afraid to interfere and risk screwing it up so I just kept praying silently. I hoped that Rachel could find her own strength in whatever she believed in, strength to resist Zaltu's influence. But she'd been listening to those whispers for a long longer than I had so was there hope for her?

She looked me in the eyes and stomped on Zaltu's figurine, crushing it into dust. A tiny scream echoed in my head, quickly fading into nothingness. A pressure lifted, one I hadn't even realized was weighing me down. The overcast sky returned to normal—sunny heading towards twilight and that meant sunset prayers weren't too far off for me—and the noise of the city surrounded us both once more.

We stared at each other. Bruised, scratched, in disarray, we both looked awful. She had a long cut running along one arm, and the beginnings of a black eye. I suspected I hadn't fared much better. As I scrambled to my feet, my palms throbbed with dull pain; Zaltu's figurine had left a deep imprint in my left hand. I hoped that faded quickly. My hijab had come loose, and I fixed it. Rachel watched me with a dull fascination as I adjusted first the bonnet underscarf, then the outer layer, until everything was back to normal. I'd heard her speculating, all too loudly in the past, about what I was hiding under the headscarf. "See," I said dryly, "it's just hair under here. No swarms of bees or snakes or anything else weird."

It was strangely refreshing to take even a tiny jab back at long last. Rachel snorted with tired derision and asked, "So… everything inside me? The horrible shit I said and thought? It was that goddess, Volvo?"

"Zaltu," I replied automatically. I thought about sparing her conscience with a lie. No, she deserved the truth. I shook my head. "No, she merely brought out what was already there." We'd both have to live with things we'd said, or thought, or did. I cringed to think what Zaltu could have done with me if *I'd* already had that sort of grief and anger in my heart.

"Well shit." Rachel considered this for a moment, and then shrugged. "I'm… y'know." She met my eyes for a moment.

I did know. That was as close to an apology as I'd ever get from her. I nodded in acknowledgement. "Me too."

Rachel turned away. She hopped over the wall, back into the sidewalk and off she went, down the street, leaving me to retrieve my backpack and head home as well.

I knew we'd never be friends. We'd probably never find common ground or understanding. We might never even speak to one another again. But that was okay. We could co-exist in peace. We'd overcome a tiny piece of evil today, simply by choosing not to fight anymore.

I'd accept that as a win.

Z is for Zaltu

Thank you for reading

E is for Evil

We would appreciate it a great deal if you
would leave an honest review on Goodreads and
wherever you purchased this book.

Your stars and a couple sentences mean the
world to us!

Truly.

The importance of reviews cannot be
overstated—they often make the difference
between a book's success or its utter failure.

Always Be The First To Know!

Whether it's a new release, a call for submissions, cover reveal, super sale or I just want to share a new story I've written, you will always be among the first to know if you sign up for my newsletter.

I promise to respect your privacy and your inbox. I will only email you when I have something exciting to share, probably about twice a month.

Subscribe now and you'll receive a free download of my award-winning post-apocalyptic short story, "Starry Night" as a welcome-to-the-newsletter present!

Subscribe to Rhonda's Mailing List!

http://bit.ly/StarryStory

www.ingramcontent.com/pod-product-compliance
Lightning Source LLC
Chambersburg PA
CBHW030640020726
47493CB00006B/1801